Playing the Player

by

Lea Santos

2010

PLAYING THE PLAYER

ISBN 10: 1-60282-185-2
ISBN 13: 978-1-60282-185-9

This Trade Paperback Original Is Published By
Bold Strokes Books, Inc.
P.O. Box 249
Valley Falls, NY 12185

First Edition: October 2010

Credits
Editor: Stacia Seaman
Production Design: Stacia Seaman
Cover Design by Sheri (graphicartist2020@hotmail.com)

Acknowledgments

Thanks to the following brave souls, most of whom, surprisingly, still take my calls, texts, and e-mails:

—St. Louis medics Karen Fischer and Emily Rice, for the bouncy ride in the rig, but mostly for tolerating my no doubt idiotic litany of questions. (I'm smarter now, promise).

—Paramedic Peter Canning, for penning the fabulously insightful books *Paramedic* and *Rescue 471*.

—Elena Sandoval-Lucero, for schooling me in the basics of teaching those critters called…oh yeah, KIDS.

—Stacia Seaman, for totally ruling in every possible way.

—The ninth-century civilization known as the Mufti people of Aden, who first acted on the brilliant notion of brewing coffee—need I say more?

—Last but not least, thanks to my best plotting pals and willing readers, LaRita, Terri, Heather, and Harold the Chicken, for helping me get it right and believing in my belief about the concept and trajectory of this book. Squawk on, peeps. Squawk freakin' on.

Dedication

This one's for Niner, my über-rockin' Ninja adventure pal.
So glad we reconnected. What's…THAT?

When fate throws a dagger at you, there are only two ways to catch it:
by the handle or by the blade.

CHAPTER ONE

Some people wore their hearts on their sleeves. Graciela Obregon wore hers on her left inner thigh. Corvette-red with the words UNBREAKABLE angling through it, the racy tattoo had been half of a sweet two-for-one offer she hadn't had the willpower to pass up. Tat number two? A yellow caution sign, outlined in black, that read EASY VIXEN—right on her chest.

What was I thinking?

She didn't oppose tattoos in general. Many of them were hot.

But *Easy Vixen*? *Unbreakable?*

She couldn't even blame alcohol or peer pressure for the damn things. The tattoo artist, a behemoth biker nicknamed "Burn," was famous for her slick salesmanship, and Grace was a sucker for a screaming deal. The truth was simple—Burn's bargain had reeled her in. She shook her head. More proof that making wise choices had never been, and would never be, her forté. Thinking things through? Looking at outcomes? *Pros and cons?* Ha! To her, "pro" referred to football, and "con" described about sixty percent of her lackwit ex-girlfriends. When it came to weighing consequences, Grace had to admit she generally acted first and regretted it later.

The old Grace.

That's right, the *old* Grace. Her hands tightened on the steering wheel. She had to remember that. As soon as the *new and improved* Grace could psych herself up to face the pain and fear, those damn tattoos—and all reminders of her former player persona—would be history. No more chasing the fast life to outrun her demons, no more having that one last nightcap or finding false security in the arms of women who were nothing but good times and bad news.

No more *easy vixen*.

A morose sigh escaped her lips.

Too bad little Stevie Santiago had accidentally exposed her "inner vixen" to a roomful of parents during her very first Back to School Night. One misplaced tug on the hem of her sweater, and the gig was up. A shudder moved through her at the memory. She wanted her students' parents to view her as a competent teacher, not the reformed wild child she truly was inside.

Damn that tattoo.

With one eye on the highway traffic, she adjusted her rearview mirror until it reflected her chest, then glared at the offensive yellow diamond. Unfortunately, it glared back. Almost every neckline exposed the ugly thing. This one hadn't…until little Stevie had tugged.

Mental note: buy more turtlenecks.

Ugh. She hated turtlenecks. Yet how was she supposed to convince the world she'd turned over a new leaf when she wore a self-imposed value judgment just above her heart? Annoyed, she jerked up the zipper of her sweatshirt jacket until it caught a bit of skin at her throat.

"Ay!" She loosened the zipper and rubbed at the pinched spot, irritated that she'd let the old feelings get to her.

Maybe it was a sign.

Her *abuela*, DoDo, believed strongly in signs of all kinds, and Grace had to admit, DoDo's superstitious ways were contagious. Maybe little Stevie's accidental exposure of her *Easy Vixen* tattoo was a sign that she belonged back behind a bar, swabbing spills and pouring poison, rather than behind a teacher's desk influencing future generations.

"It's *not* a sign," she muttered. "It's not." For good measure, she hastily crossed herself. Her life had changed so much over the past four years. For God's sake, she had a brand-new teaching degree. It wasn't like someone rolled up that diploma and slipped it into her G-string as a reward for a particularly energetic lap dance. She'd earned it, one grade at a time. So why did that familiar self-doubt still flare up at unexpected moments, threatening to incinerate her newfound pride until nothing was left but a charred landscape of past mistakes and bad choices?

Let it go, Gracie. People can change.

"Even me," she whispered, with stiff-chinned determination. She'd show everyone. Didn't she owe it to Mama to be the best person she could possibly be? Didn't she owe it to herself?

With a sigh, Grace made a conscious effort to change the maudlin direction of her thoughts. She whipped through the moderate traffic on I-25, releasing her tension to the feel of the cool September wind tousling her hair through the open window. Denver's familiar skyline glittered against the backdrop of sunset's colorful streaks, reassuring her like a much-needed hug from an old friend. She had always found comfort in familiarity.

In fact, earlier, as she'd prepared to meet the parents of her first class of students, she'd caved to the urge to bring along her very oldest friend. Totally lame, she knew, but no one had to know. She cast an affectionate glance at the threadbare stuffed animal safely belted in the passenger seat next to her. Lumpy, faded to gray, and nearly furless, her best teddy buddy, Ms. Right, slumped obediently against the upholstery.

She'd been so much more dependable than all the Ms. Wrongs strung along the time line of Grace's jaded dating history. Unlike them, Ms. Right had stuck by her through every bad decision she'd ever made and the repercussions that followed. The little bear had scars, stains, a missing ear, and a mismatched button eye to prove it, and still, she'd never let Grace down. That kind of loyalty didn't come easy.

Grace chuckled. Silly, she knew. A twenty-seven-year-old rookie teacher gathering courage from a synthetic stuffed bear? Eh, well, maybe it was childish, but truth? She didn't care. She set her jaw. Loyalty went two ways, and Grace wouldn't abandon Ms. Right just because she was respectfully employed and…almost thirty.

Sheesh! When had that happened?

No matter. Chronological age meant squat if you were living a good life. And she was, because—finally—nothing stood between her and the future she'd worked so hard for.

Un-freakin-believable.

Grace Obregon.

Teacher.

Head of her own class of bright-eyed third graders. She was… *respectable.* The very thought made her laugh out loud in the empty car. But it wasn't empty, was it? She glanced again at her battered bear.

"I'm sorry. You're someone, aren't you, baby?" She patted the bear's head. "You'll always be my best girl."

Focusing back on the road, Grace flinched at something she didn't even really see. Not at first. Slowly, horribly, the phrase *car accident* registered in her mind, but by then, the semi had glanced off the cement barrier, tossing a cascade of sparks and leaving snakes of black rubber on the concrete. It jackknifed and swerved in front of her, like a huge, gray beast, wildly out of control. Everything ground to slow motion, while somehow at the same time racing through her brain faster than she could react. The world became a series of flashpoint images.

The rear of the semi rushing at her face.

Her hands jerking the wheel, but not quickly enough.

The Explorer skidding, leaning, slamming.

A power burst of adrenaline shot to her extremities with the first impact, and she realized, sickly, there was no avoiding this. The screeching brakes made an eerie background track as everything around her began to spin and smash, sky and earth flip-flopping in her vision. Her teeth slammed together, cutting into her lip. She tasted blood, saw stars, all on a tidal wave of unbelievable pain.

Something plowed into the side of her head at the same time her leg twisted like it was stuck in a meat grinder. She tried to scream, but the airbag exploded against her chest, knocking the wind from her lungs. The last thing she saw before losing consciousness was Ms. Right, glass-covered and blood-splattered, whirling out of the shattered windshield.

Madeira Pacias reread the address she'd scrawled on the back of a crumpled deposit slip. Concert traffic from the Pepsi Center clogged the highway from Alameda all the way through downtown. The jam was moving, but switching lanes in time to exit would be sketchy if she waited to merge until the last possible moment, like usual.

She double-checked the directions against the green sign ahead, then tossed the paper aside and eased into the center lane. Plenty of time. Cranking up the stereo, she tapped her hands on the wheel in time with sexy Shakira singing "Ojos así." Excitement for the night ahead welled inside her. If luck was on her side, she might even arrive at Karma, the brand-new lesbian dance club in LoDo, early enough to snag the best woman-watching table. The prospect of something fresh drew her out of the restless funk she'd been battling lately, a low-grade sense of discontent, the origin of which she hadn't yet pinpointed.

But new women always cured what ailed her, and since she'd pretty much harvested her usual spots for *chicas*, the opportunity to plow through a ripe crop of lovelies sounded delightfully distracting.

Lately every time she walked into one of her regular haunts, she found herself surrounded by ex-dates and former lovers, which could prove a little uncomfortable. But, hell. She never pretended to be anything except exactly what she was: a lover, sure...but a *leaver*, too. She knew it. The women she bedded knew it.

No promises and no disappointments.

Women looking for the U-Haul and commitment-ceremony type gave Madeira a wide berth, which she mirrored. The others? Well, she enjoyed the others, but she made damn certain they enjoyed *themselves* even more. She left them, yes, but at least she left them smiling. That kept her slate full and her bed warm, which worked for her. As far as relationships went, *all's well that ends—*

Enough said.

Now if only the rest of her life were half as satisfying as her sex life, Madeira would be in good shape. She expelled a breath of frustration. Maybe it was work. Who knew? She'd been in the States six years, always working alongside her *hermana*, Torien. Initially, the arrangement suited Madeira—she and Toro did what was best for the family. Always. But the family was thriving. Mamá and their twin sisters, Raquel and Reina, had chosen to stay in Mexico, but they no longer struggled financially, and they visited often.

As for Toro and her gorgeous wife, Iris—since they'd cut the ribbon on their nonprofit foundation, OUR WORLD: Building Communities One Garden at a Time—Madeira had never seen two people happier. Working alongside them for the past three years had been an honor, and Madeira was good at her job. But facts were facts: OUR WORLD belonged to *them*. Madeira was growing a little bored. It wasn't the job, it was her.

She engaged the blinker and accelerated into the fast lane of I-25. Enough of this brooding. The sooner she slipped into her regular groove—*cervezas y chicas*—the better. Life wasn't all about work,

work, work. Hadn't she struggled to convince her *hermana* of that, years back?

"Gotta walk your own talk, sister, or you're nothing but a good-lookin' player talkin' shit." Madeira glanced up and gave herself a self-mocking wink in the visor mirror.

A high-pitched screech yanked her attention back to the road, then everything happened at once. A semi slammed into the jersey barrier, jackknifed, and careened out of control across the congested northbound lanes. Cars and trucks knocked against one another like billiard balls, a destructive chain reaction. Flying glass, crunching metal, and billowing smoke cast the entire highway into pandemonium. Amidst it all, the semi burst open and lost its load—hundreds of flapping, squawking chickens.

Madeira hit the brakes, swerving into the center emergency lane. She cringed against an impending rear-end collision, but luckily, the car behind her skidded to a stop inches before kissing her bumper. Cars ahead continued to crunch, crumple, and roll. Madeira's heart lurched as a red Ford Explorer clipped the back of the semi and flipped end over end, twirling and casting a cone of debris like a tornado. She'd never seen anything like it.

"Hijole madre." She crossed herself, then kissed the rosary that hung from her rearview mirror as the Explorer came to rest on its demolished top.

Madeira glanced through the settling dust at the other cars fortunate enough to have avoided the worst of it. People gaped, wide-eyed and frozen, as though the chaos were just another high-budget Hollywood spectacle.

It's real. Do something.

Scrambling from her truck, Madeira ran into the center of the carnage, dazed and blinking. Jesus, there had to be thirty crumpled vehicles besides the semi. *Where to start?*

She took a step, but a traumatized chicken ran headlong into her leg, spun, then bolted the other direction. Disembodied moans and loose feathers floated in the smoky air around Madeira. Chickens squawked and flapped. An injured but mostly frightened Rottweiler limped beside a totaled Chevy pickup truck, fear showing in the whites of its eyes, yelps frantic and high-pitched.

Madeira swallowed past the lump of nausea in her throat. Some bystanders hung back, their ashen faces pinched in expressions of shock, cell phones pressed to their ears. A stout old man wearing work pants and a long-sleeved white shirt was the first to take action. He darted from vehicle to vehicle, peering inside each one. Squatting awkwardly beside the overturned Explorer, he banged what was left of the driver's side and called out, then tilted his head to listen. After a moment, his face lifted toward no one in particular, but his eyes met Madeira's. He beckoned her with a frantic wave. "Someone's stuck in here!"

Madeira scanned the scene even as her feet propelled her toward the old man. Where were the ambulances? What did she or any of these bystanders know about such a catastrophe? Sirens wailed in the distance, but no telltale flashing lights approached. No comforting police-band radios punctured the air with their unintelligible garble. In fact, cars stood in a motionless gridlock as far back as the eye could see. Madeira couldn't bear to think about how difficult it would be for the emergency vehicles to get through.

Despite an overwhelming feeling of ineptitude, Madeira kept moving. She jerked her chin toward the Explorer, chest heaving more from adrenaline than exertion. "Did you see anybody?"

"Naw, but I heard someone groaning." The man patted his sizeable paunch with a paint-stained hand. "No way I can squeeze in there. We can't flip it over. Might hurt 'em worse."

Madeira heard the call to action beneath the man's words. She shot one worried glance at the unknown fluid dripping from the mangled engine, realizing she was completely out of her depth. "Keep a watch for…flames, I guess. I'll go in."

The old man clapped a gnarled palm on Madeira's back. "Take care, now, hon. Don't need no more victims than we already got."

Madeira gave him a grim nod. Unconcerned about the glass and fluids ruining her clothing, Madeira dropped to her stomach and shimmied through the narrow opening between the crushed roof and the doorjamb. It was so dark and jumbled beneath what was left of the SUV, she struggled for her bearings at first. Sounds faded to a muffled drone, distancing her from the inconceivable horror of the pile-up. She bumped her head on something and sought the shadows for clues until she recognized it as the backseat. Above her.

Reality socked her in the gut.

The cramped space smelled of exhaust, gasoline, night air, and something both metallic and oddly…warm.

Blood.

It took a moment for Madeira's eyes to adjust, but when she spotted the female driver, her throat squeezed. Congealing blood striped the driver's face in a macabre crisscross pattern. She hung precariously from the seat belt, her long, glass-speckled dark hair pooled on the crumpled car roof below her.

Definitely unconscious.

Please don't let her be dead.

Madeira felt for a pulse, her hands shaking. After a moment, she blew out a tense breath and replaced it with a rush of cool relief. A strong and steady beat thrummed in the woman's neck. Good sign. Better than the alternative, at least.

As Madeira lifted her fingers from the driver's neck, she stirred, and one swollen eye blinked open. She studied Madeira, disoriented, then let out a groan that sounded suspiciously disappointed. The eye closed. "You're not Ms. Right."

Struck by a wholly inappropriate urge to chuckle, one corner of Madeira's mouth quirked up. The woman would be surprised to realize how uncanny her assessment had been. "You're good," Madeira said, her tone equal parts wryness and nerves. "It usually takes women at least one date before they realize that."

The eyes wavered open again. "What?" The woman swallowed, and Madeira followed the movement of the muscles in her throat.

"Never mind." Her position couldn't possibly be comfortable, but Madeira didn't dare move her. Still, it agonized Madeira to leave the poor woman hanging—literally. Her amusement faded. "You doing okay?" Dumb question, she realized. Epic dumb.

If the woman heard her, she gave no indication. "Am I dead?" she asked, her words raspy. "Are you…an angel?"

Madeira shook her head. "You're not dead. And, ah, I'm no angel." *Trust me on that one, sugar.*

"You look like one."

Madeira's brows raised. "Yeah?"

"Well, not really. No wings…" the woman murmured, so quietly Madeira barely heard her. "Maybe a devil instead. I probably died and went to hell for Stevie Santiago and the tattoo fiasco." She grimaced with a pain Madeira couldn't even imagine but empathized with nonetheless.

"Tattoo fiasco?"

"Don' wanna talk about it."

"O-okay." Madeira's heart thudded. The driver had seemed mentally together initially, but all this crazy talk had Madeira rethinking that assessment. Was she hallucinating? Madeira leaned closer, speaking in clear, gentle tones. "Listen, I don't know about anyone named Stevie Santiago or…or any of that. But you aren't in hell." She recalled the scene outside the car in grisly detail and felt like a liar. "Well, not exactly. You crashed your car. Remember that?"

A long moment passed. "Yeah." The woman cleared her throat with effort. Her brow furrowed. "Did I hurt anyone?"

Something unfamiliar constricted Madeira's chest. "Not a soul. Not even a chicken."

"Thank God." The woman's body seemed to relax in degrees. "I don't think I could live with that."

A ripple of surprise moved through Madeira. The woman had a pretty selfless attitude, considering her current physical state. If anyone was an angel in this mashed car, it was she. It showed in her immediate concern for other people's welfare over her own. That kind of beauty came from within, and even blood, broken glass, and bruises couldn't hide it. With a flutter of guilt, Madeira wondered if *she'd* be so magnanimous in the other woman's place. *Not damn likely.*

"Is Mama here?" the woman asked, her voice thin, like a scared little girl.

Madeira glanced around, rocked by an unexpected surge of protectiveness. "I don't know, *rayito de luz*. Was she with you?"

"She always is." A pause ensued. "Did you just call me 'sunshine'?"

"I…I guess I did." Something in Madeira's gut uncoiled. She reached out and brushed some strands of thick, wavy hair out of the blood drying sticky on the woman's face. Who was she? What circumstances led her to this unfortunate place and time? Who would worry for her? Who would cry? "Just relax and stay still. Rescue's on the way."

"C-can you get me down?"

"No, babe. I don't want to move you."

"Okay." Silent tears carved wet paths through the blood, and the woman reached back clumsily and gripped a fold of Madeira's pants leg between her glass-slashed fingers. "Just don't leave me. Please."

Madeira didn't speak immediately. She couldn't seem to pull enough air into her lungs to emit the words. Finally, with effort, she managed to say, "I'm not getting out from under this car without you, okay? That's a promise."

The vow seemed to soothe the injured woman, but only for a moment. She stirred again. "Where's Ms. Right?"

Madeira shook her head. Maybe this little bit of *rayito de luz* was trashed. Didn't drunks tend to repeat themselves? Madeira sniffed, but smelled nothing. Unsure what to say, she tried for a light tone. "I'm afraid that's not my area of expertise."

Zero acknowledgment of Madeira's playfulness. Instead, the woman's eyes filled again, and she blinked rapidly. "But she was…in the car."

Tears thickened her words, and it suddenly struck Madeira that perhaps *Wright* was the woman's last name. Maybe *Ms. Wright* was—

Dread plunged to the bottom of Madeira's gut. She'd been glib without fully assessing the situation. What the hell was the matter with her? "Wait. Who is Ms. Wright?" Surely this stranger wouldn't address her mother in such a formal way. Madeira had immediately noted the rainbow freedom rings that must've been hanging from the rearview mirror, but now lay pooled in the rubble. She went for the assumption. "Your…partner? Or—"

A weak laugh bubbled out. "No, of course not."

Madeira didn't trust the laughter. Even with her appalling lack of medical knowledge, she understood shock could affect a person's emotional reactions. She needed to know if they should be looking for a body outside the ruined vehicle. "Listen to me. Was there another person in the car with you?" It occurred to Madeira that she still hadn't asked. "What's your name?"

"Grace. No. I was alone." She squirmed, and before Madeira could reply, Grace's breath hitched. "I can't feel my leg." A blade of hysteria edged her voice.

"Okay, don't panic. Let me take a look." *As if that would matter.* Allowing herself a split second of relief knowing Ms. Wright wasn't a passenger who'd been thrown from the wreckage, Madeira ventured a glance at Grace's legs. They looked trapped and a little…twisted. Madeira would bet at least one of them was broken. She could only hope the shock wouldn't wear off enough for the pain signals to reach Grace's brain. They'd both be in trouble then.

Madeira mustered an encouraging smile. "Don't worry. Your legs look fine, Gracie."

Liar, liar.

"Really?"

"Yeah."

"You have a nice accent." Grace sounded calmer, but slurred and sleepy. Sweet. Guileless.

Keep her talking. Sí. Madeira couldn't help Grace in any of the ways that really counted, but she could occupy Grace's mind with small talk, keep her focused on something other than her injuries. "I come from Mexico. I thought my accent was gone already, no?" Madeira teased, knowing full well her accent would likely remain forever.

"No. I like it. It's like…whiskey."

"Hmm." Madeira swept some bits of glass from Grace's hair, careful not to tug on the rich, auburn strands. "Intoxicating, I guess you mean."

"No. Rough."

"Rough?" Madeira protested.

"But warm, too."

"Ah, that's better." Madeira felt more pleased than she probably should, considering the situation and Grace's obvious lack of coherence. But injured or not, Grace carried her half of the conversation. Good sign. "Yours is"—she rubbed her chin—"like Kahlúa. Smooth. A little bit sweet, but with a kick."

Grace rolled her unfocused eyes. "Oh, please. Sounded like…a cheesy pick-up line."

Madeira laughed softly, snared in her own net. "Definitely a cheesy line, *rayito de luz*, but you were supposed to swoon."

The playfulness dissipated as quickly as it had appeared. Grace's skin paled, and she seemed to weaken before Madeira's eyes. "Swooning is a distinct possibility, but not…because of any lame pick-up line, I'm afraid." Grace moaned, reached ineffectually up toward her legs. "It hurts, Jesus fucking Christ. I'm so tired." Her eyelids drooped, and then she lay still.

Utterly.

Still.

Madeira's lungs emptied in a whoosh as panic set in. What now? She went with her first instinct, gingerly shaking Grace's shoulder and touching her cheeks. "Stay with me. Gracie?"

Grace's eyelids fluttered. "Okay. I'm t-trying."

Try harder. Don't die.

Madeira's worry spiked. "I know. I know you are." She spied a plastic water bottle and grabbed it, elbows banging against the twisted metal window frame as she yanked off her formerly favorite shirt. She wore a thin tank top under it; what did it matter? Madeira removed the bottle cap and slopped water onto one sleeve, then used it to wipe Grace's face. "You're doing great, babe. Really great."

"But I still need…to find…Ms. Right."

Again? Holy hell. Madeira paused in her ministrations and furrowed spread fingers through her shag of hair. "Listen, Gracie," Madeira said, with feigned seriousness. "I gotta say, you aren't looking so hot. It's probably not the best time to be thinking about a woman hunt."

"No, she's a *teddy bear*," Grace said. "Ms. Right is my bear from… when I was little. I know it's stupid…"

"It's not stupid."

"She was a present from Mama—"

Grace's voice broke, and that unfamiliar protective tidal wave choked Madeira. The ferocity of it knocked the wind out of her. A teddy bear, not a woman. A goddamn teddy bear, of all preposterous things in this surreal situation. "I'll find her for you." Madeira danced her fingers along Grace's hairline. "Don't worry."

"P-promise?" Grace's pain-dulled eyes locked with Madeira's. "She went…flying out."

"I promise, babe. *Sí.* I promise," Madeira whispered.

"My…grandmother. She'll worry."

Madeira straightened. At last, something concrete she could do for Grace. "I'll call her. What's her number?"

Grace's teeth began to chatter. Beneath the blood streaks Madeira hadn't completely cleaned off, Grace's face looked ashy gray. "I c-can't remember."

"That's okay," Madeira soothed, dabbing cool water on Grace's forehead. "Shh. Don't worry. How about her name?"

"Dolores. We call her...DoDo. Like the...bird."

"Dolores what? What's her last name?" Madeira waited, but Grace didn't reply.

Just like that, all the fight had drained from her.

"Grace? Gracie!"

Nothing. *Nada.*

Seized with dread, Madeira felt again for Grace's pulse. The familiar beat thumped against Madeira's fingers, and relief loosened her shoulders. Still steady and strong. She sat back on her haunches as best she could in the cramped space, and studied Grace, knowing there wasn't much else she could do.

After a few minutes that dragged like hours, warbling sirens cut into the unreality of the upturned car. Madeira sagged with relief. Thank God. Gracie would be with the paramedics soon, and then Madeira's job, such as it was, would be finished.

Well, *almost.* Madeira shook her head.

What had possessed her to make promises to a woman she didn't even know?

I won't leave without you.

I'll find your bear.

I'll call your grandmother.

Clearly she'd left her brain back in the truck, because she didn't *make* promises to women.

Loud banging reverberated along the destroyed body of the vehicle, alerting Madeira to the rescuers' arrival. Madeira kissed her fingertips and pressed them gently to Gracie's forehead, then scrambled from beneath the vehicle and gave her welfare over to them. Madeira had expected them to speak with her at length, but once they learned Madeira was just a bystander, she dropped into last priority. No problem. The less time they spent with her, the more they could devote to Gracie and the other victims.

The fall wind gusted, but the chill hardly registered on Madeira's nearly bare chest. For a few minutes, she stood aside and watched cops, firefighters, and paramedics take calm but urgent and oddly chaotic control of the crash site, feeling simultaneously relieved and clammy with regret. If only Madeira had been able to do more for Gracie. She'd been conscious when Madeira crawled under the car but unconscious when she'd left.

That couldn't be good, no?

The cold eventually touched Madeira's nerve endings, hardening her nipples beneath the thin tank. She shivered. Rubbing her palms up and down her arms, Madeira reluctantly backed away from the Explorer, somehow missing a woman she'd spoken to for no more than ten minutes. Insanity. How had that happened?

When her heel bumped something soft, Madeira leapt away, remembering the chickens. But luckily, they'd already been corralled by bystanders. Instead, Madeira peered down upon the ugliest, most battered one-eared teddy bear she'd ever seen.

She smiled ruefully.

Sí.

Madeira hadn't known Gracie long, didn't know her at all, really. But this was exactly the kind of bear she could imagine Gracie loving. The poor little thing wasn't brown or gray or blue or green, but some hybrid non-color Madeira couldn't even identify. Glass stuck to what remained of her sparse fur, to say nothing of the blood, gasoline, and motor oil staining that worn-out little body. One stuffed arm hung by a thread, and bits of foam had leaked from the hole in the bear's shoulder, leaving her flat and wobbly.

Teddy bear roadkill.

Squatting, Madeira gathered all the dry stuffing she could find and crammed it back into the body, then held Ms. Right up at eye level. "And I thought I had problems. *Hijole.*"

Relieved that she could fulfill one of her promises, Madeira started toward the crushed Explorer, but the firefighters had just begun to cut open the vehicle with the Jaws of Life. She stopped short. Much as Gracie had fretted for the little bear, she needed medical attention more than she needed Ms. Right.

Ms. Right. Madeira scoffed. What kind of woman would give her childhood toy a name like that? Not *Madeira's* kind of woman, that's for goddamn sure. Just the opposite, as a matter of fact. Sweet and captivating as Gracie had been, she was the polar opposite of Madeira's type. A shiver shook Madeira, followed quickly by a prick of surprising disappointment. Ridiculous.

If she'd met Gracie under normal conditions, Madeira's honed female radar would have alerted her immediately that Gracie fell smack-dab into the off-limits category. Those extra-strength commitment vibes women like Gracie emitted would've tripped alarms all over her brain. Gracie wouldn't have had the chance to catch Madeira unawares and implant that intoxicating sweetness in her mind, emblazon herself on her senses.

Bad circumstances. Nothing more.

Madeira ignored the uncomfortable ache in her gut as the low, gray night clouds began to launch arrows of cold rain into her eyes and onto her way-too-bare flesh. The firefighters bent to lift Gracie from the wreckage, and Madeira, realizing she couldn't bear to watch, turned toward the warmth and familiarity of her truck.

Half dressed, chilled, and emotionally spent, she steered into the slow trickle of traffic easing past the chaos. She would keep her promise and return Gracie's beat-up, sad-sack Ms. Right.

Soon.

First she would fix the bear's arm and spruce her up a little… maybe even buy a ribbon for the little thing's neck. Anything that might coax a smile onto Gracie's lovely face.

Against all reason, Madeira's heart lifted at the prospect.

CHAPTER TWO

Chisme averiguado jamás es acabado.
Gossip once begun will never be done.

Exactly one year later…

Grace crumpled the newspaper in her lap and shot a look of slack-jawed dismay toward her despicable ass of a little sister.

She couldn't speak.

She couldn't breathe.

She couldn't even tamp down her own horror long enough to close her mouth.

For lack of a better response, Grace snapped the newspaper open again, praying what she'd read had been one big, hideous hallucination. Alas, no. It was repulsively real.

Next to the vampy mall glamour photo that she'd been pressured to take—and despised—loomed the headline:

Anniversary of the Accident:
Survivor Searches for Her Samaritan Soul Mate

"Lola! Jesus, what have you done?"

Starry-eyed and oblivious, Lola clasped her palms together, the half-moons of her impeccable French manicure resting against the backs of her paraffin-waxed hands. "I know, I know! Isn't it the best?"

Grace shook her head, baffled by Lola's cheeriness. And

cluelessness. "The best what? The best way to kill me? The best revenge for every evil thing I've ever done to you? Are you out of your fucking mind?"

Laughing, Lola stood and retrieved the coffee carafe, topping their mugs. She moved about casually, as though they were merely sipping morning java while sharing the Dear Abby column. Situation normal—not!

"Oh, come on. You said yourself you were dreading the media follow-up for the anniversary of the crash. I just gave them something a little more uplifting to focus on. Would you rather they dwell on all the pain and loss, or on this?"

"I would rather not be involved at all. And this is called a *lie*." Grace shoved the paper aside and lurched to her feet. Holy Hell. She'd have to flee the state. So much for her goal of restarting her teaching career with an impeccable reputation. A new identity might be in order. Was there a witness protection–type program for people who'd experienced public humiliation at the hands of their well-meaning but riotously deluded siblings? Surely Grace would qualify.

Hell, she could be the poster girl.

She jammed spread fingers into her hair and paced the length of the kitchen, her focus, for once, off her pronounced limp. Every time she passed the newsprint-covered table, she glanced down on the article, feeling sicker with each glimpse.

One year ago today, her life had been ripped apart by an out-of-control semi. Today, her nearly repieced life had been shredded again by an out-of-control, matchmaking sister. She didn't know which was worse.

"Whatever possessed you to do such an idiotic thing? I mean, do we even dangle toes in the same gene pool?" Grace understood that her twenty-four-year-old sister saw everything through a romantic filter, but still. Lola was allegedly a grown-up, half owner of a thriving salon and day spa. She couldn't possibly have believed Grace would be happy about this.

In direct opposition to Grace's inner turmoil, Lola looked positively thrilled. Her sappy smile never faded. Clearly, selling this fabricated tale of unrequited love to the newshounds had seemed like a good thing in the rose-colored world of Lola. And as if the "seeking soul mate" rubbish wasn't horrid enough, Lo had shared tales of Grace's bartending past and fed the reporter some copy-worthy shit about how Grace had paid her way through college hoping to escape "the racy night life."

It made her sound like a reformed hooker, for God's sake.

She was no angel, but—

"I was doing you a favor. This is for *you*."

Grace spun, a murderous gaze trained on her sister.

Lola's smile dimmed from 200 to 75 watts. She flicked a glance at the door, as though weighing her odds of escape should flight become necessary. "Why are you staring at me like that?"

"I honestly think I'm going to have to kill you," Grace said, in a matter-of-fact tone. "I'm racking my brain for alternatives, but none are coming to mind."

"Cut it out." Lola rolled her eyes. "It's not the end of the world. Besides, this is a good thing."

Grace barked a short, humorless laugh. "In what possible way is this good?"

"You've been moping around like a lovesick puppy since the accident," Lola said, as if it cleared up everything. "I thought you'd be thrilled to reunite with this woman."

Was Lola high? Delusional? Psychotic? "I haven't been moping *or* lovesick, dumbass. I've been recuperating." Grace gestured toward her scarred leg. She'd been damn lucky to escape the twenty-seven-vehicle accident with nothing more than a totaled car, a comminuted fracture of her right femur, a crushed patella, and a disrupted life. Five people had actually died on the highway that evening, including a seventeen-year-old girl also named Grace, a coincidence that never failed to shake her. She'd been mending, not moping. Sheesh! "But that's not even the point. What does my emotional state have to do with you selling my ass out to the media? And why now?"

Lola began to tick off reasons on her fingers. "Well, physically, you've gotten so much better, but you still seem depressed—that's one. Right now is perfect timing, with the anniversary coming up—number two."

"I just started back at school!"

"I know. But I think you need closure on this, Grace. We'll call that reason number three."

"Thank you Dr. F-ing Laura," Grace snapped.

"Look, you tried to find out who the woman was earlier in the year. What's the difference this time?"

"The difference is, I merely wanted to thank her for what she did that night. For her kindness. You've turned it into some kind of dating game. And, incidentally, if I've been down—which I still deny—it is because my life has been on hold for a year," Grace interjected, her tone grudging. She hated being forced into the position of defending her hermit lifestyle of late. "I suppose you think I should be gleeful about that?"

"Well, no—"

"My so-called mopey attitude has nothing to do with *some woman*." Grace's mind began to catalog all the hurdles she needed to jump now that she'd ticked "walking" off her To-Be-Relearned list. "I'm worried about my career. I have a lot to prove to the school now that I've got my job back. I'd like to be tenured some day, and—"

"Yadda yadda. *You* are the one who gave me the impression you were into this Samaritan woman." Lola twirled her gold pinky ring, the tiny scissors and blow dryer charms that dangled from it tinkling.

"When?" Grace demanded. She didn't recall giving any such impression.

"That first night in the hospital, the night of the accident."

Grace barely remembered that night. "You're kidding, right?"

"Why would I be kidding? You gushed about her. Ask DoDo if you don't believe me. You said her voice sounded like whiskey, and that one look at her made a woman fantasize about hot, urgent hands and red satin sheets."

The sexy image washed over Grace like a tidal wave of wet pheromones, but she shoved it away. "Dude! I was whacked on morphine! Besides—"

"So you don't want to find her? You no longer want to thank her for helping you? The statute of limitations on gratitude has expired?" Lola asked, leveling Grace with a stare.

Grace sputtered, feeling flustered and trapped. "No! I mean, sure, I'd like to thank her, b-but that's not what you set up with your stupid little newspaper ploy. Wanting to thank her has nothing whatsoever to do with her being my"—Grace leaned over the paper and read—"'Samaritan Soul Mate,' God for-fucking-bid. That very phrase makes me barf in my mouth. Or because of some drug-induced comments about hot, urgent hands and red—" Grace's tummy tightened. She flailed an arm at Lola and strode toward the cupboard for a water glass. Her parched throat shook with panic. She jammed the glass beneath the faucet. "For God's sake, I barely remember what the woman looks like."

A skeptical sort of silence yawned in the room.

"Reeeally?" Lola drawled.

Okay, so not *reeeeally*. Scarcely a day had gone by when Grace hadn't flashed on an image of the unbelievably gorgeous woman who'd helped her that night.

But big deal.

The stranger had comforted her during a traumatic crisis. That didn't mean Grace wanted to spend the rest of her life with the chick. Why couldn't Lola grasp that?

Grace guzzled her water, then set the glass on the counter with a clunk and nailed her sister with a glare. "Here is the bottom line. I don't know her. I don't even know her *name*. Thanks to what you've cooked up, I don't *want* to know her. I will show my gratitude by praying for her health and happiness every night for the rest of my natural born life, okay? *You* can deal with the newspaper fiasco. Tell them you made a mistake and I'm not interested."

"That might be a little hard." Lola blurted a nervous *heh-heh-heh* chuckle.

"Why?"

"Because I sort of...pretended to be you when I gave them the story." She bit her lip and crinkled her nose.

Grace sank into a chair and pressed the heels of her hands into her eyes until she saw stars. The whole thing was a nightmare, but try as she might, she couldn't wake herself up. "I can't believe you've ruined my life like this."

"It's not as bad as you think. Look at it as an opportunity to put the past behind you."

Without lifting her face, Grace mumbled, "Yeah, with a woman *you* just convinced that I'm a woman hunter."

"Don't be so...annoyingly youish." Lola tapped out a slow, smug rhythm on the table top with her nails. "Aren't you even curious?"

Okay.

Fine.

She was curious.

She didn't dare admit *that* to her meddling sister, who'd take it completely out of context and start planning the goddamn commitment ceremony in Ptown. Besides, the point was moot. Grace could never face her mysterious savior now, not after that contemptible article made her look like a woman-crazy, daytime-talk-show-guest-wannabe. Hell, Grace had read the articles. Whoever the woman was, she'd think Grace was in some sort of misguided love with her.

Ugh! She slumped lower, until the back of her chair supported the bottom of her skull. It was all too tiring. "Lo, you are a whore. And if I had the energy, I'd definitely kill you. You get a reprieve because I'm just too damn exhausted by it all."

Lola's voice took on a breathy quality. She tossed her perfectly coiffed hair like an Aveda model, then reached across the table and covered Grace's hand with her own. "Don't be mad." Exasperation wrinkled her brow. "You crossed paths with that hot woman for a reason. Don't you want to find out why?"

"I can tell you why." Grace snapped her fingers in Lola's face twice. "And pay attention, because I'm not going to repeat it. I crashed my damn car, in epic form, and she stopped to help. Period. Simple freaking concept!"

"Don't be so pragmatic."

"Don't be so unrealistic!" Grace released a long groan of disgust. "You should lay off the *telenovelas* for a while, sis. They're poisoning your brain."

"So *you* say."

Grace stood up and leaned across the table until her face was level with Lola's, then gripped her sister's chin. "Read my lips. The last thing I want or need in my life right now is a woman. Especially *that* woman."

The phone rang. Grace indulged in one final tweak of her little sister's annoyingly perfect chin before crossing to the counter and snapping the receiver up off the charger. "Hello?"

"Grace Obregon?" the scratchy, older male voice inquired. His words sounded as if they'd been spoken as an afterthought, around a cigarette clamped between his molars.

Grace tucked the phone between ear and shoulder and crossed her arms, feeling surly. "Who's asking?"

A pause. "It's Harold LePoulet with the *Denver Post*. We, uh, have a little problem with your search for this Samaritan Soul Mate woman, doll."

Doll. Grace bit back a giant *fuck off.* The last thing she needed this morning was some sexist wordmonger plying her with kissy-kiss names. "A little problem, eh? So take a number and get in line, *sweet cheeks*. I have a 'little problem' with it myself."

For another shock-riddled moment, he didn't speak. When he did, his clipped, clear tone told Grace he'd plucked the omnipresent cigarette from his mouth and leaned toward the telephone for emphasis. "Well, your little problem just morphed into a big one, *muffin*, which is why I'm taking the time out of my busy day to call you. You wanna not bite my head off for doin' you a favor?"

"A favor?" Grace scoffed.

"You're the one who dumped this fluff story in my lap, if you'll recall," he said, his tone incredulous. "And you were a lot more enthusiastic during *that* phone call, if I can just point that out."

"But I—" Grace bit her lip, wanting to deny it, but not relishing the thought of explaining Lola's rash impersonation. Wasn't it against the law to lie to the newspaper or something? She listened to the clacking of this Harold's computer keys and ringing phones in the background and started to feel guilty for taking her hostilities out on the man. He was just doing his contemptible job, after all. This fiasco was Lola's fault, not his.

"Sorry," she offered grudgingly. "I'm having a bad day."

"Which brings us back to the matter at hand."

Grace gulped, and a sense of foreboding washed over her skin in the form of some pretty radical goose bumps. Had her life been an *actual* horror flick, instead of merely *horrific*, right now would be the perfect time for the scary music to commence. She hugged her free arm around her middle and took a slow, deep breath. "The matter at hand, meaning what?"

"Meaning it's only ten a.m., and we've already had a hundred and forty-three alleged Samaritans call up claiming to be your girl, *honeybunch*. You're gonna have to provide me with some kind of clue to narrow it down."

❖

"Hey, Ms. Pac-Man," came the voice of Madeira's new partner, paramedic Simon Fletcher, from behind the newspaper. Simon had kicked back to read while Madeira scrubbed out their ambulance—a rookie's lot—after a shooting pick-up they'd handled earlier in the shift. Madeira didn't mind doing the grunt work. She wanted to earn her way in this career field.

"Yeah?" Madeira called back, without getting out of the rig. She'd barely finished her last EMT clinical last week, and every run felt brand new. She didn't want to be out of service any longer than necessary or they'd risk missing a good trauma. The more exposure Madeira had, the sooner she could apply for P-school—paramedic training—her ultimate goal. Paramedicine wasn't a lucrative profession by any means, but at least it helped her feel like she was making a difference.

Madeira slopped hydrogen peroxide liberally onto the floor, wiping up the blood with disposable towels. Simon still hadn't replied. Thinking he hadn't heard her, Madeira raised her voice. "What do you need, Fletch?"

"Didn't you say you stopped to assist on that huge pile-up that happened a year ago on I-25?"

Madeira's motions stilled, and that familiar grip of sorrow seized her. She hadn't expected that question. She fought to shake the lancing regret, as she'd done so many times over the past year, then took a seat on the side bench and peeled the rubber gloves from her hands slowly, one finger at a time. After discarding them and the soiled towels in a red plastic box marked "DANGER: BIOHAZARD," she smoothed shaky fingers through her hair and concentrated on keeping cool.

No sense worrying about a past she couldn't change. Taking one deep breath, she moved to the back of the rig and glanced around the open door. All she could see of the lanky, redheaded man was the bottom of his size-thirteen Rocky boots, propped one atop the other on the table, and his fingertips curled around the edges of the open newspaper. "Yeah. Why?"

"What happened with that?" Simon asked.

"Happened? Nothing. What do you mean?" Madeira rolled her stiff shoulders. Their shooting victim had been a good 280 pounds. Add to that the weight of the stretcher, longboard, portable EKG, other equipment, and the fact that people *always* seemed to have medical emergencies on the top floors of buildings—Murphy's Law—and it added up to one heck of a strength workout. She hadn't noticed the muscle tension until now.

"I mean you told me one of the reasons you decided to become a medic was because of some accident victim you helped. Was this the accident?" Simon flicked down one corner of the paper and pierced Madeira with his gaze, then snapped it open again, veiling his far too perceptive face.

Helped? Not quite. Madeira wished she'd had the foresight to keep her mouth shut about her reasons for pursuing emergency medicine. No one knew all the reasons behind her career change decision, but back when she'd discussed it with Simon, it had been small talk—nothing more.

These questions threw that conversation into a whole new light.

Now Madeira had to work her way around a truth she didn't relish sharing.

She cleared her throat. "Well…I *failed* to help her, if that's what you mean. She ended up dying."

The paper flattened on Simon's lap with a swift crumpling sound. His thin face slimmed even further as his jaw dropped. "She died? While you were there?"

Madeira forced what she hoped was a mild *it's all good* smile past her clenched jaw. The whole situation made her feel worthless and swamped with *if onlys*.

"No," she said, a bit hesitantly. "She…the woman…had asked me to look for…something that she'd lost when her vehicle rolled. But then she lost consciousness." Madeira flicked her hand dismissively. "Look, I should really finish cleaning the rig. This is a long story." A story that tore her up inside.

"That can wait. I'm all ears," Simon said.

Reluctantly, Madeira quickly explained how she'd gone to return the item—which remained unnamed—but had been prevented from doing so because the firefighters were busy with extrication. "When I called the PD a few days later," Madeira explained, "hoping to find her and return her…property, they told me she'd died en route to the hospital. End of story." Madeira turned and took refuge inside the ambulance, knowing she couldn't school the emotion off her face and not wanting Simon to catch it.

Her stomach churned.

Her hands shook.

Ah, God, Gracie.

Simon remained silent for a minute, and Madeira began replenishing the in-house bag with airway supplies and trauma dressings, hoping the man had exhausted his list of questions. Madeira had opened the drug box and checked its contents before Simon spoke again.

"So you never got to return whatever it was she sent you looking for?"

Salt in the wound. "Nope. Too late."

Too little, too late. She'd held on to that bedraggled teddy bear ever since, a poignant reminder. Every time she looked at the sad, homeless thing, it strengthened her resolve to become a paramedic, to give back to the world what she hadn't been able to give to Gracie. If Madeira had known how to help that night, Gracie might have lived. Madeira would have been able to return the bear and go on with her life. Instead, that bear, and a woman Madeira had known for one blip of a moment, had changed…everything.

"Jesus, man. I didn't know. That's rough."

"Yup. Bad deal," Madeira said lightly. *Understatement of the century.*

"So…what was this woman's name?"

What the hell was with the interrogation? "Grace," Madeira said, her voice emotionless. Inside, she churned. Gracie had been so full of life. Injured, yes. But alive. Madeira didn't want to talk about her.

"Graciela, maybe?"

Madeira snapped the drug box closed and frowned, her patience on its knife edge over the barrage of intrusive questions. "Don't think so. Grace Mannerly, the police department told me. All I knew was her first name. Grace."

"Mannerly," Fletch mused. More silence ensued, after which Madeira heard Simon mutter, "It has to be a different person."

Madeira eased out a slow breath. She truly didn't want to think about this. Not anymore. She wanted the past to remain exactly where it belonged. Unfortunately, curiosity got the better of her. She leaned out of the ambulance, arms braced on the edge of the roof. "When are you going to tell me what these annoying cryptic questions are all about?"

"I'm going to assume you haven't read the paper today," Simon said.

Madeira snorted. "I'm going to assume you don't remember being a brand new EMT on your first rig? All I've been reading is the policy and procedures manual, EKG strips, and obituaries."

"In that case"—Simon folded the newspaper with measured movements, turning it until the article he'd been reading faced Madeira. His expression was half smirk, half bald interest—"You might want to take a little look-see at this."

Madeira jumped off the back of the rig and walked closer, wary. Hands on her hips, she leaned forward and read the headline.

And then again.

She blinked. Twice.

What the hell?

She quickly scanned the first paragraph of the story, then, nauseated, she glanced at the picture. Her breath whooshed out as though Simon's boot had connected with her solar plexus.

Holy Mother of God.

It's Gracie.

Alive.

Part of Madeira bubbled with profound relief, inexplicable, leg-weakening excitement. Another part reread the opening paragraph of the article and balked. Granted, thank God Gracie had survived the accident after all. However, through some convoluted sense of the U-Haul brand of female reasoning Madeira couldn't even fathom, the very much alive Graciela Obregon seemed to believe *she*—Madeira Pacias—was her soul mate. "*Dios mío.*"

"That her?"

Madeira nodded.

"Looks like she's alive and well after all. Not to mention…she wants you, partner."

"Uh…so it seems," Madeira said, a strong sense of fight or flight kicking adrenaline through her system. Heavily weighted toward the flight option, of course.

A forever sort of woman. Wanting *Madeira.*

Definitely a fate worse than death.

❖

That sexy little soul mate seeker was seriously cramping Madeira's style. She swiped at her beer bottle and, peering over the bottom of it as she drank, made a conscious effort to search the noisy, smoke-filled club crowd for a no-strings woman to ease her mind. There were blondes, brunettes, and redheads galore. Tall, willowy sirens and petite cuddle bunnies. Slim wisps and several sexy, curvy, substantial types that would make Madeira feel as if she were getting her woman's worth. Many of them offered sly smiles and the unspoken promise of a good time as they walked past…or over the shoulders of other women as they danced.

But none of them were Gracie Obregon.

Madeira snorted. Had she completely lost her mind?

She didn't even know this Grace woman. Not really. Just this morning, she believed in her heart that Gracie was dead, and she'd made peace with it. Madeira was paying restitution for Gracie's supposed death the only way she knew how—with her life's work. But as fate would have it, there had actually been two Graces in the pile-up: Grace Mannerly, a seventeen-year-old from Littleton, and Madeira's Grace. Graciela Obregon, all-woman and very much alive. Now that Madeira knew Gracie was alive and *looking for her*, she couldn't seem to evict the no-longer-dead Gracie from her weak-ass mind. To make things worse, Fletch had been adamant that Madeira should make herself known.

But out of fairness to herself and Gracie, Madeira couldn't do that. She'd read those articles. Clearly, Gracie wanted something Madeira could not give. Ever. Not in her nature. So, meeting Grace for the second time, for real this time, was completely out of the question. Why put either of them through the ugliness of it?

The pounding bass ceased briefly while the DJ addressed the energetic crowd. Taking advantage of the relative quiet, Madeira's sister-in-law, Iris Lujan, leaned forward. "If you want my opinion, I think you should contact the paper and identify yourself." Iris and Madeira's big sister, Torien, had been reading the articles for the past several minutes. "Just to meet her, see how she is. What could it hurt?"

"Are you kidding?" Madeira gestured toward the squares of newsprint spread out on the table before her sister. Toro continued to study them, her stoic face arranged in a thoughtful expression. "I'll come out looking like a jackass if I tell her 'thanks, but no thanks,' especially with the whole world watching."

Iris rolled one shoulder. "Why make that determination already? You might like this girl. She might be *the one*."

Madeira should've known better than to ask romantic Iris how to handle this problem. "I have no interest in finding *the one*. Remember?" Madeira swept an arm in front of her, indicating the crowd. "When the garden is so full of different blossoms, who but a fool would restrict herself to daisies?"

Iris's eyebrow arched, and her lips twitched with barely stifled amusement. "Ah, but maybe this Graciela's a rare orchid."

"Maybe." Madeira shrugged. "But even so, variety makes a better bouquet."

Iris stuck a finger into her mouth and feigned gagging.

Madeira grinned around her tension, glad she could joke her way out of this pressure-cooker conversation. "I'm serious. I couldn't deprive all these lovely ladies of the prospect of my company." She winked, trying to relieve the tightness in her chest. "It would be cruel."

"Oh, please! You have to grow out of this crap sometime." Iris sputtered with laughter, and soon Madeira found herself chuckling, too.

Madeira reached across the four-top and patted Iris's hand. "I appreciate your input, sis, but your solution doesn't work for me. I'll leave the monogamy to you old folks who are no longer interested in having any fun."

Iris and Torien shared an amused, smoldering look that made Madeira feel uncomfortable and vaguely defensive, then Iris tossed her lovely long hair over one shoulder. "I just think you should meet her, Mad. No one's going to force you at gunpoint to move in with the woman just because she's entertaining romantic fantasies you don't share."

Madeira expelled a rough sigh. *Fuck.* Maybe she *was* overreacting. She glanced at her big sister. "What do you think, Toro?" Madeira had razzed Torien regularly for years about being too serious and pragmatic, as the little sister/big sister credo dictated, but the truth was she valued Toro's opinion more than anyone's.

Toro stroked her chin thoughtfully. "You sure you want to hear my perspective? Old, boring, monogamous woman that I am?"

Madeira twirled her hand impatiently. She needed some insight. If there was one thing Madeira could say about her *hermana*, it was that Toro was no romantic. She wouldn't be swayed by the sap factor of the situation like her partner had been. "Tell me," Madeira said tightly.

"Iris's right. Make yourself known now, before the media attention grows."

Dread sank like a corpse with cement boots to the bottom of Madeira's gut. "Grows? You think it's going to get worse?"

"Absolutely. The more elusive you are, the better the story, the more papers it sells, and the harder they'll try to find you. Save them the trouble." A beat passed while the sisters stared at each other. "Meet the lady."

Madeira froze, unable to grasp the advice. Was Toro actually telling Madeira to hurl herself—an unwilling sacrifice—upon the altar of romanticism? What the hell had happened to the older sister Madeira knew and loved? "What makes you think they'll ever find me either way? If I never come forward…"

Torien signaled the waitress and twirled her hand in a circle over the nearly empty bottles on their table, then met Madeira's eyes. "They will. Someone will remember you and then you'll look bad for not having stood up. Mamá would be disappointed if you showed such a lack of honor."

Madeira groaned, rubbing her palms over her face.

Toro's expression turned playfully smug, her tone a knowing rumble. "What are you afraid of, Mosquito? A *woman*?"

Madeira's jaw clenched. She recalled asking the same pointed question when Toro had met Iris and struggled to resist *her* charms. Turnabout might be fair play, but it stung like a snake bite.

Besides, Madeira couldn't answer. Not honestly.

Frankly, she *did* fear reuniting with Gracie, because Madeira wanted to see her far too much. Talk about setting herself up for trouble. The thought of doing something so clearly against her nature filled Madeira with roiling anxiety.

"What *are* you afraid of, Madeira?" Iris asked softly.

"I don't know. Nothing," she lied, averting her gaze to the crowd as Lady Gaga began singing about bad romance. The dance floor flooded with people anxious to get their grooves on. "I have no interest in finding a soul mate. Now or ever. This Grace woman wants a soul mate and has her crosshairs trained on me. That's a pretty damn big problem."

Iris and Torien exchanged another one of those annoying cryptic glances.

Madeira spread her arms. "What?"

Toro quirked her mouth and tipped her head to the side. "I've just never seen my little sister trying quite so vehemently to avoid a woman, that's all. I find it interesting."

"Ver-r-ry interesting," Iris added, tapping a slender finger against her chin, her green eyes sparkling.

Enough. Madeira drained her beer with more bravado than she felt, then clonked the bottle on the table. She reached down to adjust the already perfectly adjusted waistband of her low-slung jeans. "Well, you two just sit here and wallow in your mutual interest, then. I'm going to find myself a hot little distraction while I'm still young and free." Madeira tipped off the bar stool and started to swagger into the sea of possibilities.

"Go for it, Mosquito," Toro drawled. "But trust me when I tell you, you aren't going to dance, drink, or date this one out of your system. I can see it on your face."

Madeira faltered, but managed to avoid turning around by stiffening her spine and curling her fists. She set her sights on a petite, curvy brunette she'd taken home before and stalked in her direction. Familiar territory. Not usually Madeira's style, but right then, touching base with something comfortable seemed like the smartest thing to do.

Go away, Gracie. I'm not your Ms. Right.

❖

But Madeira realized a few days later, after working the problem to utter distraction, she *had* Gracie's Ms. Right. Soul mate considerations aside, *that* was the core issue. *That damn bear*, Madeira told herself, was the sole reason she now hovered in a deserted corridor inside Front Range Trauma Med Center, cell phone clutched to her ear.

Three days had passed since Iris and Torien had foisted their bad advice upon Madeira. She'd brooded, stewed, and waffled, but the only conclusion she'd reached was that she had to return the bear. No two ways about it.

Only then could she wash her hands of the whole thing.

Madeira fished the crinkled article out of her pocket, taking a moment to whip a glance around the hallway. She and Simon had just scooped two patients from a minor MVA and delivered them to the ER. While Simon had ambled off to graze through some of the lemon cream cookies that were always available in the police/EMS lounge, Madeira had sneaked off to find a private place to make the dreaded call.

Fingers shaking, she dialed the *Post* reporter's number listed below the most current article. To her surprise the public had caught on to this romantic drivel. From the reader letters the paper had published for the past three days, people seemed just as invested in Grace finding her "Samaritan Soul Mate" as the woman was herself.

So the articles kept coming.

Toro had been right, as usual.

The hunt had become relentless.

Madeira should be running for the hills, but...Gracie loved that raggedy bear. Now that Madeira knew Gracie was alive, she couldn't, in good conscience, keep the thing. Sure, Madeira could mail it to her via the newspaper anonymously, but the very thought made her feel weak. Cowardly. So she'd decided to call the paper, but *only* to find out how to contact Gracie and return her rightful property.

Damn that bear.

If it weren't for Ms. Right, Madeira wouldn't be calling.

Who are you trying to convince?

"Shut up," she muttered to herself, counting the telephone rings. *One. Two. Three.*

New bargain—if no one answered by the fifth ring, Madeira would hang up, conscience clear, her mind absolved of fulfilling this duty.

Four. Fi—

"LePoulet."

Madeira's brain ceased to function at the sound of the gravelly voice on the other end. She cleared her throat, wishing to God she hadn't called, fighting the impulse to disconnect the call and go stuff herself full of lemon cream cookies with Fletch. "Yes. Ah. I've been reading the Samaritan articles and…I have something to return to Gracie—to Graciela Obregon, I mean."

"Is that so?" the voice sneered.

Madeira was making a mess of this. "It's hard to explain. Can you just tell me how to find her?"

A long, impatient sigh carried across the line. "Listen hard, honey. Like I've told two-hundred-some-odd desperate crackpots before you, no way in hell am I telling you where our pretty little Grace lives, okay? Hit the club scene if you want—"

"Wait." *Two hundred women had called*? That same protective emotion flared inside Madeira. "I'm not…I'm—"

"Spit it out. I've got work to do."

Man she'd backed herself into a corner. She didn't want the reporter to think she was just another pervert who found Gracie's picture appealing, but the alternative was…

"I'm the woman who stopped to help Gracie," Madeira blurted, immediately regretting it. Her free hand curled into a fist, which she bonked against her forehead rhythmically.

"You're the so-called Samaritan Soul Mate?" Still skeptical.

Madeira cringed. "I'm not so thrilled with the title."

"Yeah well, alliteration makes for good headlines. If you're the broad, prove it to me," LePoulet challenged. "Grace says the woman who helped her would know the 'magic detail,' if you will. If you know it, whip it on me."

Madeira's mind scattered like windblown leaves for a moment. She didn't know any magic phrase. A reprieve? Maybe Gracie sought some other woman. A firefighter or—

Suddenly, the detail came to Madeira, bright and clear and certain. It was the only aspect of that evening that only she and Gracie would know. Tension buzzed in her ears. "Ms. Right."

Frozen silence.

"What'd you say?"

The man's tone had changed, and Madeira knew she'd hit the phrase squarely. Her stomach contracted with an unmistakable surge of terror, but her mouth kept on talking. "Let me put it this way. *I'm* not Gracie's Ms. Right, but I *have* her Ms. Right. Is that what you needed to hear?"

LePoulet remained silent for a moment, then he guffawed. "Hot damn, sweetheart. What rock you been living under? I was starting to give up hope you'd ever come forward."

Madeira felt light with elation and heavy with dread all at once. "I got it right?"

Hang up!

"Sure enough. Grace said only the woman who'd been underneath that car with her would know about Ms. Right. She'll be surprised you still have that bear, though." The sound of papers shuffling punctuated the statement. "What's your name?"

Don't tell him!

"Madeira Pacias," said her mouth, of its own volition. Madeira caught sight of Fletch searching the hallways for her and shrank deeper into the wall. The last thing she needed was her partner listening in. She'd get this over with, quietly return the bear, make it clear she wasn't any woman's soul mate, and no one would be the wiser. Madeira could get on with her life knowing she'd done the right thing, all the while maintaining her precious independence.

It would work. It had to.

"Well, Madeira. You willing to reunite with Grace?"

"Privately?"

LePoulet barked a laugh. "You got it, dollface. Real private. Just you, Grace, and an intimate little gathering of reporters, photogs, and videographers."

Photographers? Videographers? Reporters? This situation had just plummeted out of Madeira's control. She cast about the hospital corridor for some kind of assistance. Too bad there wasn't a crash cart to treat a critical error in judgment. The blood rushed from Madeira's head, leaving her dizzy and squirming in the trap of her own making.

"Kiddo? What do you say? A reunion?"

Say no!

Run away!

Hang up!

"Sure." Madeira swallowed back an instant wave of nausea. "How about this weekend?"

CHAPTER THREE

Buena es la libertad pero no el libertinaje.
Liberty is good, but not the libertine.

Grace sat behind her desk in the empty classroom finishing up paperwork and basking in the deceptively peaceful silence of the late afternoon. Here in her very own classroom, she could actually forget now and then that her life was in tsunami-sized turmoil. Deep, gold sunlight slanted through the windows along the west side of the room, flashing off the metallic star awards on the bright children's artwork adorning the walls. Dust motes waltzed in the angled beams, and other than the rhythmic hum from the janitor's floor polisher out in the hallway, silence reigned.

She loved it here, and she loved teaching, no matter how tiring it could be to stay "on" all day for the kids. It was only Wednesday, but her leg ached from three long days standing in front of her students. Part of her wanted nothing more than to go home and elevate it, veg in front of the television, maybe with a bag of potato chips by her side and the remote control all to herself. But she'd never lose this limp if she didn't exercise—at least that's what her old college friend and now colleague, Niki Montoya, had convinced her of in the few weeks since the school term started.

Nik taught physical education and held a master's degree in sports rehabilitation, so she should know. Thanks to her encouragement—and the fact that she had agreed to coach Grace—together they had clocked one to two miles around the high school track every day after school since the first week. Just knowing that Nik would be waiting for her every afternoon at four thirty sharp inspired Grace to tie on her Nike walking shoes, whether motivated or not. She didn't want to disappoint her friend by showing less interest in her own recovery than Nik did.

Speaking of her daily walk… Grace flipped her wrist and checked her watch. Cutting it close. Wistful about leaving her classroom now, when everything felt so synchronistic, she nevertheless filed away her attendance book and yesterday's homework sheets and hurried into the restroom to change. As she traded her slacks for sweatpants, Grace ran her fingers along the ridge of the unsightly scar on her leg. It felt numb, much like she did. The past few days had been uneventful, which put her on guard. She couldn't help but wonder if this lull in the upheaval was some kind of a sign. Calm before the storm.

Her thoughts flew to the ongoing search for this "Samaritan Soul Mate," and acid sloshed in her stomach. Her colleagues had been openly curious the first couple days after the story had hit the papers, but the furor had thankfully died down. Nothing new or exciting had been printed recently, which meant no new gossip fodder for the teachers' lounge.

Thank God.

The only good part of the whole debacle was that no one had come forward as her Samaritan. Well actually…*she* hadn't come forward, whoever she was. Lots of women had called the paper, which simultaneously flattered Grace and gave her the creeps, but none of them had known the key detail she'd given to Harold. One thing Grace knew for certain, the woman who'd been under that car with her would know.

Where was she?

Why do you care? another part of Grace's brain rasped.

Ignoring the insidious question, she knotted the waistband tie of her sweats, tucking the lace inside, then sat on the john to put on her Nikes.

Why *did* she care? The question had floated to the front of her mind a lot lately, yet she hadn't quite succeeded in formulating an answer. She figured this elusive woman was probably lying low until the whole thing blew over—and Grace didn't blame her. If she were in the so-called Samaritan's place, she'd probably quietly leave the state. Still… part of her wished that beautiful dark angel would identify herself.

Grace's life had finally jumped back on track, and the last thing she needed was some strange woman coming in and mucking things up. But Jesus…she'd been so sweet. Curiosity consumed Grace—plain and simple. And for some reason she cared enough to explain how this had all come about. Cared enough to apologize for pulling the stranger into this hot mess.

Maybe the woman had been passing through town and would never even see the articles in the Denver papers. Relief and disappointment grappled for the upper hand at the thought. It would save Grace the embarrassment of having the woman think she was in love with her, but it would also deprive Grace of the chance to express her gratitude for all the woman had done on-scene to help her.

Grace laughed softly at her fickleness.

She wanted it all—was that too much to ask?

She wished she could've found the gorgeous woman on her own all those months ago and avoided the humiliating publicity. Damn Lola. Nothing Grace could do about it now.

Dressed and ready, Grace returned to the classroom for her briefcase and backpack. Flipping off the lights and waving good-bye to the tank of fish and the cage of hamsters on the far counter, she hefted her bags onto her shoulders and headed for the door. She had just wrestled her keys from the depths of her backpack when her classroom phone rang.

"School's out. Go away," she whispered, more to herself than anyone. She'd just decided to ignore it when her conscience tapped on her shoulder. She was her grandmother's primary contact, and DoDo wasn't getting any younger. Lately, DoDo's blood pressure had picked up the habit of spiking. Grace wouldn't be able to forgive herself if she missed an important call from DoDo just because answering the phone had been inconvenient. It could be nothing, but was she willing to take the risk?

Heaping her bags on the floor between the door and the jamb, she wound through the desks and snatched up the phone on the fifth ring. "Ms. Obregon, third grade."

"Grace. Glad I caught you. It's Harold."

Harold. A split-second assessment of his tone told Grace he was merely checking in. He sounded the same as always, no more excited than usual. No reason to freak the hell out, even though she did. Automatically. She forced her shoulders to loosen. "Hi, Harold. I'm late for an appointment. Can I call you back?"

"Sure." Computer keys tapped in the background. "Let me ask you one quick thing first. The name Madeira Pacias ring a bell?"

Grace re-tacked a finger-painted rainbow picture that hung from one corner on the wall and straightened some of the art supplies scattered on the counter while she was at it. "Nope. Should it?"

"Maybe not. But I think she's our girl."

Grace froze in the act of straightening a stack of construction paper. Our girl? Our girl! "Are you sure?"

"Let me put it this way. She knew about Ms. Right."

"S-she did?"

"Not only that…" He paused so long Grace felt as if she was underwater and couldn't fight her way to the surface for a much-needed breath.

"Yes?"

"This Madeira woman has her."

"Has…who?" Grace blinked several times, slumping onto the edge of the nearest desk in a flat daze. Stars swirled before her vision, and her mind couldn't seem to grasp a single coherent thought. The wind had been knocked so far out of her, her proverbial future kids would come out gasping. "This Madeira chick?"

"You betcha."

"She has my Ms. Right?"

"You heard me."

"But say it again," Grace gasped, death-gripping the phone until her fingers went cold and corpse-stiff.

His chuckle sounded unpracticed, as though he didn't use it often enough. "Your new Ms. Right has your old Ms. Right."

"Yeah. Let's get one thing straight. Madeira Pacias is not my Ms. Right." Astonished despite the protest, Grace's mouth dropped open, and her hands trembled. All thoughts of her daily walk vanished from her brain. "She kept my bear?" she marveled.

"All this time. Ain't it ironic?"

"It's wonderful. I can't believe—" Suddenly, something didn't seem right. Grace pressed the pads of her fingers to a tension point between her eyebrows and closed her eyes. A puzzle piece was missing.

Somehow, she knew Harold held it. "Actually, wait a minute. Why didn't she give my bear back to me a year ago?"

"You won't believe it if I tell you."

He did have the full story. Blood pounded and echoed in Grace's ears. Her gut told her she didn't want to hear all this, but her brain told her she needed to. "Give it a shot."

"When Pacias called the police department a couple days after the pile-up to try and find you, all she knew was your first name. Grace." He paused, as though that said it all. "You with me?"

"Not yet." Her mind was grasping.

Harold sighed. "The cops told her you were dead, cupcake. They ran the name Grace instead of Graciela and came up with—"

The teen from Lakewood who had died on the way to the hospital. "Oh my God, this Madeira thought I was Grace Mannerly, didn't she?"

"Bingo. Does this story just get more interesting with every layer we pull away, or what? I'm writing a piece about the woman as we speak."

Grace swallowed. "Tell me about her."

"Ah-ah-ah—a good reporter never spills, pumpkin. But the whole story will be out in the paper tomorrow, and for the bargain price of fifty cents or whatever they're charging these days, one of those papers can be yours."

"Gee, thanks." No matter. It was too much to digest, anyway. Details would only cloud the issue. This woman, this Madeira Pacias, had believed she'd died in the accident, and she'd kept Grace's bear *anyway*. For a *year*. A gush of gratitude and emotion closed her throat as Madeira scored a whole slew of points in Grace's mental tally. Madeira had no idea the gift she'd given Grace by keeping Ms. Right. For a split second, Grace pictured Madeira as a scantily clad warrior, riding to her rescue…

Stop it. Grace didn't need rescue. Excitement swirled inside her anyway. She focused on the more important matter at hand. "Did you get her? My bear, I mean?"

"Oh no, sweet cheeks. My job was finding the Samaritan. Retrieving the bear? That's your job." The computer keys clicked on in the background.

"How in the hell am I supposed to do that?"

Clicking stopped. "Don't worry. Pacias is more than willing to give you back your bear."

"Oh. Well, good. You scared me for a minute." Grace grabbed a crayon and flipped over a torn piece of construction paper, scribbling at a deep angle to sharpen the little wax stick's point. "Okay, what's Madeira's number? I'll call her right now."

"Not so fast. Don't forget your old pal Harold and what he needs out of this whole scenario."

"Would you quit being cryptic? What are you getting at?"

He chuckled. "You're going to have to get this bear from Madeira in person."

Grace's heart thudded so hard, she felt certain Harold could hear it. "Fine, then. Jesus. Give me her address, too, but I'll still need her phone number to set up a time for the pass-off." She was still mortified that Madeira might think she wanted—ugh. She couldn't ponder it right now.

"I've already worked that all out. You can meet Madeira Saturday at six p.m., here at the newspaper offices."

Wariness wrapped Grace like a boa constrictor and squeezed. "Can't I just go by her house or meet her at Starbucks, for God's sake?"

"I think the office would be a much better place for the press conference."

The crayon snapped in her quaking fingers. Grace heard the grin behind Harold's words and wanted to pass out.

"Don't you agree?"

"No. Harold? Please. No press conference."

"Oh yes. Big-time press conference."

Grace clenched the phone in her fist, desperation screaming inside her. "Don't make me do this. I'm begging you."

Harold tsk-tsked. "I'm too old to buckle under for a begging woman, gumdrop, even if you are a hottie. Alas, you bat for the other team, and romance ain't my goal. Besides, you owe me."

She frowned. "How do you figure?"

"I'm a newsman, and you're news."

"I'm not news! I don't want to be fucking news."

"Aw, come on, now. I did all the legwork and found Pacias for you. Where's the love, Grace?"

Damn the manipulative old—

The old Grace would've flipped Harold off—or told him off—and said, "I've got your love right here, buddy." The new Grace settled for covering her eyes with her palm and wishing all manner of evils on her sister, Harold, and the world at large. "Fine. Fine. But I'm participating under duress—I want that on the record."

"Duly noted. See you Saturday."

The dial tone droned in her ear like an air-raid siren.

So much for the calm. Here came the storm.

❖

"According to close associates," Lola read, "Pacias is a confirmed single woman known as 'The Thief of Hearts'—"

"Wow, what a catch!" Frankly, Grace thought Madeira sounded like a hotrod car with too many miles on its engine. Fun to look at, hell to own...and one hundred percent impossible to insure. So much for the scantily clad warrior fantasy she'd conjured. She couldn't imagine a woman like the one described in Harold's latest article having enough compassion to hold on to Ms. Right, but...she had. Still, the "Thief of Hearts"? *Gimme a break.*

"Hush. It's cute. She sounds totally exciting."

"Oh, yes. A slut. Really exciting," Grace muttered, rolling her eyes so hard her contact lens curled up on one edge. She blinked rapidly to get it back in place, trying not to recall how sweet and charming she'd found Madeira at the scene of the accident. Clearly, she'd been out of it and idealizing the chick. Grace didn't know why it was such a letdown to learn about the real Madeira, other than the fact she'd conjured a much more admirable image in her mind.

Grace had seen Madeira, and it didn't surprise her one bit that women were willing to test drive this particular hotrod. Grace, however, had gone for all the "test drives" she could stomach in one lifetime. Next woman she took for a ride would be dependable, like a 4x4 truck with extra-strong roll bars. And all hers, free and clear, with no lien, emotional or otherwise. That meant any secret romantic hopes she might have entertained about Madeira Pacias were shot straight to hell. Once and for all. "She sounds more like a bad déjà vu than anything, Lola. I mean, I'm glad she kept Ms. Right, but—"

Lola snatched up a sharp teaser comb and menaced Grace with its pointy handle. "Why are you so pessimistic?"

"I believe the word you're looking for is *realistic*. Trust me, I've been with sluts—"

"Ah, not to mention you've *been* a slut."

"You think I don't realize that?" Grace snapped. "I know what they're like. Ergo, not interested."

Lola pouted. "You're impossible. You'll never find love with this attitude."

"Whatever. I'll buy a dog."

"No, Grace, make it a cat," Lola said, her tone openly sarcastic. "Or ten cats. You can be one of those eccentric cat women. In fact, take up hoarding, too. That way you'll never have to worry about romance and passion as long as you live, guaranteed."

"Can't you just let it go, Lola?" Grace huffed in disgust, glaring at her own black-caped, roller-bound reflection in the beauty station mirror. Giant rollers, of all things! Trapped—that's how she felt. By the situation, her sister, her own emotions. Her initial inclination had been to refuse this trumped-up reunion-slash-press conference, but Harold kept reminding her Madeira had Ms. Right.

Dilemma.

Mama had given her that dime-store bear the final Christmas before she'd died. Every time Grace looked into Ms. Right's mismatched button eyes, she felt her mother's presence, and she'd felt Ms. Right's gouging absence over the past year as if she'd lost Mama a second time. She'd done her best to keep her sadness about the bear inside, but clearly enough of it had seeped out enough for Lola to catch on. Oh well. No sense hiding it anymore. Truth be told, Grace would walk on a bed of nails to get Ms. Right back.

Unfortunately, *that* preferable option hadn't been offered.

To reunite with Ms. Right, she'd have to reunite with Madeira, a wholly unsuitable woman who almost certainly believed Grace fancied the two of them in love, and all in front of the media's invasive eye. How humiliating.

Grace had grudgingly agreed to the reunion after a series of heated arguments with Harold, and then, in defeat, she surrendered to Lola's styling chair coercion. She wasn't up for any more of her sister's pressure tactics, though. Not now. She had to face a confirmed player who believed Grace's goal in life was to be some woman's ball and chain in exactly… Her gaze jerked to the salon clock. Ugh. Less than fifty minutes. Yet all Lola wanted to do was read aloud from the newspaper article Grace had studiously avoided all day long.

Grace didn't want to know about Madeira Pacias. She just wanted to survive the dreaded press interview, retrieve her beloved bear, and return to her regularly scheduled life with some shred of her self-esteem still intact.

Was that too much to ask?

Still, she hated that her realistic, albeit jaded, view of romance always dimmed the sparkle in her little sister's eyes. Grace sighed, feeling martyred. "Lola, do what you must, but please hurry. I'm not Cinderella headed for the freakin' ball, you know."

"Oh, be quiet." Brightening, Lola smacked her on the head with the paper, but Grace barely felt it through the mound of massive Velcro rollers and styling products that increased her overall height by a good five inches. "I'll just read while we're waiting. There's no hurrying a good set anyway."

"Then give me a mediocre set. I've got to get moving and I don't really give a fuck what my hair looks like."

"Well, *I* care. You're my sister and I own a salon. You can't show up in the paper looking like a bad BEFORE picture. Christ. What will people think?" Lola patted the rollers that felt glued to Grace's head. "Beauty is time. Beauty is an investment."

"Blah, blah, blah. Take them out."

Lola pleaded with Grace's reflection in the mirror. "Don't you want to look your best to meet Princess Sexy and Charming?"

Grace's heart performed one deep thunk, hopes dashed, once again. "She's not a princess, she's a player. Whoopee." She lifted one hand from beneath the cosmetologist's cape to twirl her finger. "Been there, done that. Bought the tattoos. Read between the lines, Lola. Madeira is nothing more than the ghost of girlfriends past and I'm not interested."

Lola raised one perfectly arched brow. "You're being pretty judgmental about Madeira's lifestyle, considering."

Grace stared at her own stiff-jawed reflection, wanting to scoff at the irony but unable to drum up the energy to pull it off. Just like a little sister to rattle the skeletons in her closet. So she'd been a wild child herself in bygone days. Big deal. She'd admit it. That insider's view of the player's lifestyle only reconfirmed her lack of desire to fall anywhere *close* to in love with one. Grace's life was finally headed in a new direction, one that left women like Madeira Pacias choking on her dust.

She'd never be able to adequately explain this to Lola. Instead, she flicked a hand at her sister. "If listening to you read that article is the hoop I need to jump through before you'll finish my hair, then read."

Gleeful, Lola turned her attention back to the paper. "Where was I? Let's see. Here. Yadda yadda…a confirmed single woman known as 'The Thief of Hearts,' left her work as a nonprofit project manager with OUR WORLD: Building Communities One Garden at a Time, to pursue a career as a paramedic…"

Lola's voice became a distant buzz in Grace's ears, replaced by the loud rush of blood dispatched by her thrumming pulse. She gripped the armrests of the chair tighter beneath the cape and fought to maintain her disinterested expression, but a surge of adrenaline twirled stars before her eyes and closed her throat.

A paramedic? Her breathing shortened. Since when?

Harold had never mentioned Madeira being a paramedic.

Why hadn't he prepared her for this bomb?

Lola's voice wavered back into her consciousness. Grace held up a hand. "That's enough." She swallowed thickly. "Finish my hair."

"But did you hear the part I just read?"

"Yes, she's a paramedic. I heard." She reached up and touched one of the spiky tubes bending her hair into unwilling submission. "I think these are too tight. I feel dizzy. I might throw up."

"No, I meant the part after that."

Grace blew out an exasperated sigh. "What?"

"Listen." Lola smoothed her finger down the newsprint until she found her spot. "To pursue a career as a paramedic *after*"—she paused for emphasis, pointedly meeting Grace's eyes in the mirror—"after the fateful day her path and Obregon's collided on Interstate 25." Crushing the paper to her chest, Lola fluttered her eyelids, and sighed. "Didn't I tell you? Is that the most romantic thing you've ever heard?"

Yes. Grace gulped. "No. It's just another example of the media sensationalizing the story in search of the almighty buck."

"Curmudgeon."

"Pollyanna."

They made mirror-reflected faces at each other, but inside, Grace's mind reverberated with shock. Wow. If Harold's facts were straight, Madeira had changed her entire career path after the crash. Grace would never have imagined the accident had impacted Madeira's life as deeply as it had her own. She had scars, a limp, and a profound fear of driving to remind her. Could it be Madeira had a few scars of her own? Against Grace's will, the pendulum of her attitude swung in Madeira's favor again.

Danger.

Grace knew herself. She needed to avoid emotionally unavailable bad girls like an alcoholic needed to avoid booze. They were her weakness and her downfall.

Not anymore, Grace. That's in the past.

She tried to convince herself that she'd moved beyond falling prey to another player but failed. She'd changed, but some aspects of her life still needed work, and that was one of them. In spite of herself she cleared her throat and fiddled with the hem of the plastic cape. "What else does it say?"

Lola set the article aside and spoke in a breezy tone. "You aren't interested, remember? We are short on time, after all." With deft motions, she began to unwind the curlers from Grace's crunchy hair, chucking them in the open drawer of her station.

"Don't be annoying. Just this once, I beg you." Grace pleaded with her sister's smug smile in the oval mirror. Lola's iPod was kickin' it old-school, and TLC's "Unpretty" boomed over the salon's sound system. Grace thought it an apt theme song for this moment. "Tell me what it said." So much for avoiding the article.

"Well…three sisters, one older, two younger. Madeira comes from Mexico, been here six years, I think it said. You already know about her job, and she donates to some kind of charity on the side."

Charity? Great. Drop-dead sexy *and* altruistic, to boot. A regular Mother Teresa—just Grace's luck. "Donates to what charity?" she asked, feeling snarky at the fates for throwing this sexy woman in her face and making her weak.

"It didn't really say. Just something having to do with emergency medical services."

"Hmm." Grace didn't know what to think, much less what to feel about this complex-sounding woman. According to the article, Madeira allegedly had a citywide reputation as a big, giant tramp. But she had also gone from one thankless, underpaid job to another, and in her spare time she helped worthy charities. Fuck. This would be a whole lot easier if Madeira didn't have any redeeming qualities.

When it came down to it, why did Grace even care if Madeira was a player? Why was she acting as if it was a personal affront?

I wanted her to be perfect. That's why.

She bit her lip, disappointment curling in her stomach.

"What do you think, Grace? Tell me the truth."

Grace sniffed, striving for nonchalance. "She sounds…"

"Perfect?" Lola released the last curl, snaked her fingers into the stiff mess and began to vigorously—and, oh yeah, painfully—shake the strands free. "It's okay to admit it."

"Not even close to perfect, but—ow! Jesus, stop it."

Her sister shook harder. "Beauty is pain."

"Which is why I'm okay with being ugly. Go easy, or I will punch you." She snaked her hands out from under the cape to grip her sister's wrists, but Lola flicked them off.

"Suck it up." Lola squinted in concentration. "And you aren't ugly, you're just…very raw material."

"Gee, compliments abound in this salon."

Lola shoved Grace over until her hair hung forward, between her knees, then went at the wavy length of it with a styling comb like a bushwhacker with a newly sharpened scythe. "Keep your options open with Madeira. That's all I'm saying."

"There are no options, Lo, beyond hello, thank you for rescuing my bear, and good-bye. Madeira's not my type."

"Anymore."

"That's right."

"Fine. Be that way."

Grace winced as comb met tangle, and tangle won. Through gritted teeth, she added, "But I will admit…"

"What?"

Grace sighed. "I'm looking forward to seeing her. I'm just so incredibly touched that she kept Ms. Right."

"I knew it!"

"Touched enough to tell Madeira thanks, Lo. *That's all*. Now that

I know what kind of woman she is, I'm even less interested than I may have been before."

Lola remained silent for a moment, and when she finally spoke, she sounded dubious. "Well, whatever. At least you'll get to thank her, Grace."

Which she didn't want to do in front of the nosy media, with the entire world thinking she was hot for Madeira Pacias, a woman who had *zero interest in her*. Why couldn't Lola understand how appalling that prospect sounded? If only Grace could explain this debacle to Madeira privately, she might be able to get through this. Whoa. A brainstorm hit.

"Speed it up, Lo. I have to get there before Madeira does."

"Why?"

"Do you have to know everything?"

"Yes. Just tell me."

Grace sighed. "Because. I've got to get her alone before the press conference. I just have to."

Lola's full mouth spread into a Cheshire cat grin. "Now, that's what I like to hear."

Shaking her head slowly, Grace couldn't help but smile at her devious, matchmaking little sister. Grudgingly. "Not like that. You're utterly hopeless."

Lola reached around and patted her cheek. "Yes, but the good news is, I'm beginning to think you might not be after all."

CHAPTER FOUR

Hasta el diablo fue un ángel en sus comienzos.
Even the devil was an angel when he began.

Madeira strode up the sidewalk toward the newspaper offices, almost, but not quite, late. She slowed her pace to an unconcerned saunter, making an effort to lower her shoulders and loosen the muscles of her jaw. No sense looking eager—*which I'm not.*

Maybe a little curious, but definitely not eager.

Unfortunately, she caught sight of her reflection in the windows and realized, with dismay, that she'd dressed precisely like an eager woman. What an idiot. Regret aside, she took a moment to straighten her olive green, Henley-style silk sweater and smooth the creases in her black slacks—a woman had her pride, after all. She might as well look her best now that she'd left herself no other choice. But she wished she'd had the presence of mind to wear her favorite torn and grass-stained jeans and the T-shirt Iris had given her last Christmas that read, *Too Shallow to Love, Too Jaded to Care.*

That would've conveyed her point.

No matter. She could do this and come out unscathed.

She'd prepared herself to face the media.

She'd prepared herself for the public scrutiny, for the taunts she'd suffer at work.

She'd prepared herself to bow out of this soul mate thing gracefully and with style.

What she hadn't prepared herself for, she realized sickly, as she swung the door open and entered, was coming face-to-face with *Grace*.

Madeira stopped short, and her heart made one squeeze before drumming out a rapid warning. Why hadn't she remembered…Gracie? In all her mental preparations, Madeira had simply avoided thinking of Gracie, and for the life of her, she couldn't figure out why. She stood with her arms tightly crossed on the opposite side of the vast lobby. Beyond her loomed a cluster of people armed with notebooks, tape recorders, and cameras. Reporters, no doubt. Gracie was with them, but not a part of them, that much was clear. Bright and beautiful, she stood out from the mass in sharp relief.

Madeira had exactly one split second to replace her stunned expression with one of schooled nonchalance before the door swung shut with a clunk, and all eyes—including Gracie's—turned toward her.

As the breath left her, Madeira was struck with the strange sensation of being one of only two people left on the face of the earth. She remembered that dance scene in *West Side Story*, the first time Tony laid eyes on Maria. Just like in that scene, every single person in the lobby faded to inconsequential, undefined blurs. Everyone except Gracie.

A brief stricken expression moved over Gracie's face before she squared her shoulders like a warrior facing battle. Madeira watched Gracie's long, slender throat work around a deep swallow, remembering the last time she'd seen that motion, remembering all the blood. Remembering *Gracie*, and how she'd stolen inside Madeira and touched something Madeira hadn't even known was there.

A little too late for the memories, don't you think?

"Hi," Gracie said, airy and feminine, equal parts nervousness and challenge.

Madeira stood riveted to the threshold, unable to do more than clench and unclench her fists. "Gracie?"

"That would be me." A ghost of a smile touched Gracie's lips. She started toward Madeira, hesitantly, a pronounced limp giving her gait an unspeakably sultry sway. Her chest rose and fell with breaths that mirrored Madeira's. Anxious, expectant, scared.

Madeira had spent so many months fighting the shock and guilt of Gracie's "death," so many nights telling herself she hadn't known

Gracie anyway, that she'd forgotten how swiftly they'd connected that awful day. Forgotten how, for a handful of minutes, the world had consisted of just the two of them, terrified and tentative, beneath an upturned car. She'd forgotten—or denied—that meeting Gracie had spun her future on its axis, whirling her off in a completely unexpected direction.

A feeling of rightness, of relief, of joy filled Madeira just seeing Gracie, and she couldn't keep the slow smile from her face. For one fleeting moment, Madeira struggled to remind herself, this was the woman who wanted to snatch her freedom. Unfortunately her mind and heart didn't seem to care. Gracie was as sexy as she was off-limits, as intriguing as she was irresistible, and Madeira's mutinous mind slipped into full admiration mode.

Lush breasts bounced gently beneath a short, tight red sweater that screamed, "touch me!" with every fuzzy fiber. Gracie's curves transformed a pair of dark wash jeans into the sexiest thing to hit a pair of female legs since Madeira's own lips. Still, she might've been able to handle the alluring womanly package named Gracie if it hadn't been for those brandy-colored eyes. Eyes that looked at Madeira, looked *into* her and said, "I know you."

No. Madeira absolutely hadn't prepared herself for those eyes.

In two unplanned strides she'd pulled Gracie into an equally unplanned embrace and felt hot breath whoosh out of her. Gracie's body warmed against her own. Soft and pliant, so right. Gracie's spill of hair smelled like green apples, and Madeira could feel Gracie's chest vibrating against her solar plexus. Something akin to fireworks exploded around them; Madeira realized distantly that the photographers were taking the opportunity to capture their reunion on film. Oddly enough, she didn't care. Swallowing back staggering tenderness she didn't want to feel but couldn't help, Madeira said, "God, I can't believe it's you. They told me you were dead."

"I know," Gracie said, her cheek against Madeira's shoulder. Madeira felt Gracie's eyes squeeze shut. "What an awful mistake they made. But that whole situation, it was…it was—"

"Pandemonium. *Claro*. I was there, remember?"

Gracie's body relaxed, and she shifted to look up. Her eyes filled with affection Madeira didn't want to see. "Yeah."

Panicked, Madeira set Gracie arm's-length away but didn't,

couldn't, let go of her. Tucking her chin, she studied Grace Obregon. *Keep it simple. Keep it businesslike.* "How are you?"

Grace gestured vaguely toward her leg. "I'm okay. It's getting better." Her voice dropped to a private whisper, and she peered at her through her lashes. "Thank you for…that day. Thank you so much for—" Her words caught, and she swallowed hard before continuing. "For finding my bear. For keeping her. I know, it's just a silly…toy. But you have no idea, *no idea* how much that means to me."

Madeira's lips parted, but she didn't know what to say. She should be thanking Gracie, no? Madeira's whole life had changed, and for the better, thanks to Gracie and that silly bear. Before she could compose an appropriate response, something heavy landed on Madeira's shoulder. Dazed and disconnected, she blinked, then turned to find an older man who could only be Harold LePoulet invading their private moment, one meaty palm resting atop each of their shoulders. He looked like the rumble of his voice.

"Kids, come on." Harold grinned, releasing Gracie but giving Madeira a wink and one last *way to go* shoulder squeeze. "Let's save some of this great emotion for the interview, huh?"

Emotion? What emotion? How had that slipped out? Madeira glanced from Harold to Gracie, who appeared, strangely, wide-eyed, like a trapped animal. Similar to a bucket of ice in the face, the memory of why they were here hit Madeira. Damnit, she shouldn't have let herself get so caught up in the moment. Gracie wanted something from Madeira that she couldn't give—she had to remember that. Madeira might not want an "I do" kind of woman, but she wasn't in the habit of leading them on, either. She couldn't bear the thought of hurting a woman. Especially Gracie.

Dropping her hands from Gracie's upper arms, Madeira backed up slightly and addressed Harold. "Sorry. It's been a long time since we—"

"Sure, sure. You'll have plenty of time to talk later."

But would they?

Madeira's intention was to return the raggedy bear and make it clear that the so-called *la ladróna de corazones* wasn't and would never be anyone's Ms. Right. If Madeira followed through with the plan, she'd probably never see Grace again.

All of a sudden, Madeira didn't feel ready. Time seemed to be whizzing past her faster than she could grasp.

Clearly oblivious to the turmoil raging inside Madeira, Harold turned and clapped his hands—two sharp alerts—silencing the reporters. When he had their full attention, he raised both arms in the air and pointed sausage-chubby index fingers toward a long corridor behind them. A few people glanced over their shoulders. "If you'll all make an about-face and head down the hall to conference room B, we can get started. Both of the soul mates have arrived," he added, in an amused tone. Excited chatter rose from the crowd as they turned and jockeyed for position.

Madeira eyed Gracie surreptitiously, surprised to find that she looked as nauseated as Madeira felt. She would have thought Gracie would be eager for this culmination of all her publicity efforts. Madeira noticed Harold hurrying to catch up with one of the station managers, and cool gratitude washed over her for the fact she and Gracie were alone. They trailed the crowd, and though Madeira fought for it, she couldn't quite get a handle on how she felt.

"Where's my bear?" Gracie whispered from the corner of her mouth, one eye on Harold steering the crowd toward their ultimate destination.

"I left her in the car. I wasn't sure…" Madeira twisted her mouth in apology and jabbed a thumb in the direction of the entrance. "Should I get her?"

"No," Gracie said, hastily grabbing her forearm, then snatching her hand back as if she'd crossed some imaginary boundary they'd agreed not to breach. "To be honest, I'd rather you gave her to me, you know…later. Just tell them you forgot her at home if they ask."

"Sure. No problem."

Gracie tilted her head toward the noisy crowd of reporters, and her voice took on a protective, almost fierce quality. "Not that I'm embarrassed of Ms. Right, but she's too personal to me for this fucking circus."

Circus? Confusion crowded Madeira's mind. None of this added up. Gracie had caused the so-called circus, so…? "Of course. We can make arrangements later."

Obediently, they followed along, but Gracie's steps slowed even more than the limp dictated. Madeira adjusted her own gait to match Gracie's, wondering how bad the injury had been to leave her with a limp after all these months. She found herself wondering a lot of things about Gracie, like why she seemed so distracted, her eyes scanning the hallway like a woman on her way to the electric chair searching for one last out. Just as Madeira had opened her mouth to ask, Gracie barreled into her like a defensive lineman, and Madeira stumbled to the side, catching herself on a door that swung open beneath her weight. She tripped into a small bathroom, almost ending up sprawled on the shiny black, white, and red tile floor.

Catching her balance on the edge of the gleaming white sink, she spun, just in time to watch Gracie deadbolt the door and sag against it with a sigh. "Jesus, Mary, and Joseph, it worked." She crossed herself.

Hard as Madeira tried, she couldn't keep the frown off her face or the wariness from her voice. "What the hell was that for?"

"I'm so sorry." Gracie shoved off the door and moved toward her, palms raised in the universal dealing-with-an-unstable-person position. "I didn't know how else to do it. I found the bathroom earlier and figured it would be our only chance to…oh, God, it's such a long, absurd story. Look, I—I had to get you alone."

"Alone," Madeira repeated, more to get it straight in her own mind than to confirm it with Gracie. All of a sudden, she wondered if Grace Obregon meant to put the moves on her right up against the red-painted wall. The notion, though unexpected, held a hell of a lot of raw appeal. Before Madeira had a chance to become really enamored of the fantasy, however, Gracie dashed it.

"I have to…explain things, before we go through with this *fiasco* in front of God and everybody."

Huh? First a circus and now a fiasco? One would think Gracie would display a little more enthusiasm for the show of her own making. On the contrary, her eyes seemed troubled, and the strain showed in the tightness of her jaw.

A quick furrowing of fingers through her hair bought Madeira time as she grappled to regain control of this situation. Now seemed like the perfect moment for some charm and levity. Things had suddenly grown serious, and that scared the hell out of her. Madeira had never been adept at handling life's more serious moments, not like her big sister was. "Oh, you want to talk. I see." Madeira flashed her most effective flirtatious grin. "For a minute, I thought you were going to, you know, attack me."

Gracie laughed softly, and the look in her eyes as she shook her head could only be described as a disconcerting combination of pity and patronization.

Not at all what Madeira had expected.

"Why does *that* not surprise me?" Gracie asked in a wry tone.

Gracie barely gave Madeira a moment to be confused and offended before she moved closer and grabbed Madeira's wrists. "Anyway, enough about that. We don't have much time before Harold notices we're gone and comes after us."

Off-kilter, Madeira took a small step backwards, easing out of Gracie's grasp. Jesus, she was never this out of control around a woman. "I'm all ears."

Gracie's mouth opened, but then her bravado seemed to crack. Madeira caught a beguiling glimpse of Gracie's pink tongue as it darted out to moisten her full lips. How odd that the same woman who could steamroll her into a room couldn't quite spit out what she wanted to say...

Madeira raised her brows. "Gracie? I'm listening."

Still struggling for words, she tugged the brief hem of her sweater down like a prim librarian whose virtue had been called into question. Madeira almost smiled, but Gracie's sweater-tugging drew her gaze first to the round, lush promise of her breasts, then to a bright yellow tattoo peeking out of her neckline. Madeira sobered as an arrow of lust shot straight to her center. A tattoo? Hot...but totally unexpected.

Madeira blinked, identifying the design as a yellow caution sign emblazoned with two words. *Easy Vixen?*

Hijole. Madeira's mouth went dry in direct contradiction to other parts of her body, and at the same time, a memory tickled at the back of her mind. What was it Gracie had said about a tattoo on the day of the accident? She couldn't quite remember, but there had been something about a tattoo.

"I...I...I—"

Madeira shoved the elusive memory to the back of her mind, vowing to contemplate it later. None of this made sense. Here stood a chick who wanted to rope Madeira into commitment, yet she sported a tattoo that said *Easy Vixen.* Madeira needed to wrap her brain around what that meant. Grace Obregon shook her confidence for reasons she couldn't quite grasp. A strong need to push her—or scare her—away seized her. "Just say it, Gracie. I don't bite." Madeira leered. "Without an invitation, that is."

Instead of backing Gracie up with the words like Madeira had hoped, the wolfish comment seemed to embolden her.

Gracie straightened her shoulders, leveled Madeira with an unimpressed stare, cleared her throat, and ignored the innuendo completely. "First, I want you to know that I'm so incredibly grateful for all you did for me that day on the highway. And for Ms. Right." Grace implored Madeira with those intoxicating brandy eyes. "Really, I don't even think I can adequately repay you. Please know that."

"*Mira*, you don't need to repay me. I wish I could have done more. After I heard you'd…died, well, no way could I have gotten rid of your bear." *Too close to the surface, Madeira. Too intimate.* "But, really, anyone would have kept her."

"Oh, I don't know about that. But, anyway…" Grace faltered, and her gaze slanted downward.

Uh-oh. The hedging raised Madeira's hackles. Jesus, did Gracie intend to proposition her for a relationship right there in the john, away from the cameras' invasive eyes? Madeira cocked her head, studying Gracie through narrowed eyes. "I'm not sure why you had to get me alone for this."

Gracie cringed and shook her hands. "Hang on for a second. I'm not quite done, I just…don't know how to say it. God, this is humiliating."

A surge of compassion washed over Madeira's bravado like a rogue wave. "Tell me. It's okay."

Gracie took a deep breath, apparently to fuel the stream of babble that burst forth next. "The thing is, Madeira, I owe you an apology. Well, my stupid sister is the one who actually owes you…ugh—" She rolled her eyes, then met Madeira's gaze boldly. "Listen, what I'm trying to gut out is this: my sincere gratitude aside, this whole Samaritan Soul Mate thing is a big…fucking…mistake. Or a lie, actually."

"Ah…okay." An unfamiliar twist of anticipation and dread stretched through Madeira. "Which means what, exactly?"

Gracie sucked in another breath, held it, and answered on the exhale. "It means I don't…Jesus, I don't *want* you"—she cringed again—"or whatever you'd call it. No offense. And despite what you must think after reading those awful, trumped-up articles, no offense to Harold, either. But, holy hell, you're not anywhere *close* to being my soul mate, Madeira, and I'm so sorry, but I'm not actually…seeking you."

The straightforwardness of the admission zapped Madeira like a 220-volt surge. So, there it was. Not a proposition after all, but a pretty epic brush-off. Thank *God*, right?

Right?

Madeira waited for the flow of relief, but to her amusement and annoyance, felt a little sting of hurt pride instead. Still, her shoulders released a bit of their pent-up tension. She raised one eyebrow. "Well, that works out perfectly, because I'm not actually looking to be sought."

"Good. That's what I figured. Then everything's—"

"Forgive me for asking." Madeira held up one hand to stop her. "If this is how you feel, what's with the media coverage?"

Gracie jammed her arms crossed and scowled. "That's where the stupid sister issue enters the picture. My annoying little sis, Lola, set the whole thing up."

Madeira gaped. "I don't understand. Why?"

Gracie blushed almost crimson, and something warned Madeira not to call attention to it. "Because she's…Lola. Hard to explain. She stood in line twice in heaven when they were handing out the romance genes, I guess. Plus, she thought I was"—Gracie swallowed, and forced the rest out through clenched teeth—"lovesick, or some crap like that. For you. It's lame and *so* breathtakingly inappropriate and over-the-top—I get it—but she was trying to cheer me up."

Madeira bit the inside of her cheek to keep from smiling. This was getting weirder by the moment, and watching Gracie squirm was kind of fun. "Whatever gave her the idea you were lovesick…or some crap like that?"

Gracie worried her bottom lip between her teeth, clearly oblivious to the sexiness of the motion. "Do you really have to know?"

"Don't I have a right?"

Gracie conceded the point with a sigh. "I guess I mumbled some things about you during my morphine high after the crash that she took to mean…I was interested." Gracie's arms wrapped tightly around her middle. "In you. I mean, I was whacked the fuck out on narcotics. I don't even remember. But she catalogued it all in her twisted little mind, and when the anniversary of the crash rolled around, she came up with this bright scheme to get us together. She called the paper pretending to be me and fed them the bogus story." Gracie's eyes softened. "I'm sorry."

Okay, Madeira understood the Lola part. But that wasn't what had her intrigued at the moment. She cocked one eyebrow. "So, what exactly did you say about me that led her to believe you were interested?"

Groaning, Gracie flicked a hand as though none of it mattered, but Madeira was gratified to see her chest redden. "You would key in on that part. It was just the ramblings of a drugged woman. I didn't even know you. It's irrelevant."

Madeira grinned. "To you, maybe. I'm kinda curious."

"Madeira," Gracie said, by way of friendly warning. "This isn't about stroking your ego."

"Ouch." Madeira held up her palms to show she'd back off. For now.

"I just wanted you to understand, before we talked to the reporters, that I'm not..." Gracie licked her lips and tucked her hair behind her ears. "Listen, you get the point. I don't know why I'm dragging this out. I am indebted to you for what you've done for me, but as for the rest of it, I'm just not in the market for another woman like you."

Another? "Woman *like me*?" A geyser of amusement bubbled inside Madeira, prompting a huge, ridiculous smile. She wondered if Gracie knew how serious she looked as she unflinchingly slashed Madeira down to size.

Dismay drained her complexion of color as Gracie seemed to become aware of her words. She clapped a hand over her mouth, then slowly dragged it off. "Holy—I didn't phrase that very well. I didn't mean to insult you or imply that you aren't..." She swallowed, rolling her hand as she swept a gaze up and down Madeira's body.

"Every woman's fantasy?" Cocky, but Madeira figured she deserved to shoot one barb after all she'd taken. Hell, her ego had just been destroyed by the hottest woman she'd seen in years. Madeira couldn't help but bait her.

It didn't work.

Gracie rolled her eyes playfully, but emitted the kind of scoff a seasoned player hated to hear from a beautiful woman. "And here I thought I might've hurt your feelings. Geez. I should've figured you wouldn't have the kind of bloated self-image that could be shaken by a little rejection." She sniffed. "Still, I didn't mean to sound so harsh."

"I'm only teasing, Gracie." A laugh started deep in Madeira's belly as she focused on that word—*rejection*. To think she'd been afraid Gracie wanted to trap her. On the contrary, Gracie seemed completely immune to Madeira's usual charms. Almost repelled by them. Too perfect. Gracie was no more attracted to Madeira than Madeira was to the idea of settling down.

She tried, again, to bask in the sense of relief that should've flooded her, but talons of disappointment gouged her instead. She continued to chuckle, but the laughter sounded phony in her own head. Gracie, thank God, didn't seem to notice.

"What's so funny?"

"Nothing. I'm—" Hell, Gracie had spilled her guts. Madeira might as well return the favor and be completely honest. Then again…nah. "Frankly, I'm relieved."

"You are?" Gracie's expression looked hopeful, but just a tiny bit of hurt crinkled around the edges like the black soot around a burned love letter.

Madeira could relate. Still, she nodded. "I just didn't expect you to feel this way. You caught me by surprise." She shrugged, feeling sheepish. "If anything, I thought you might, you know, proposition me on the evening news and make me look like a jerk when I said no to renting the proverbial U-Haul."

Bright color stained Gracie's cheeks. "Yeah? Well, trust me. I'd no more proposition you or any woman than I'd voluntarily re-break my leg."

Madeira's abs contracted with the punch of that statement. "A traditional woman, no? Your perfect woman has to get down on bended knee, I guess?"

"Uh, not even close. I don't have a 'perfect woman.' I just want a woman who wants me, and only me. That's all. I won't settle for less than I deserve ever again, and I don't share." Gracie shrugged. "I don't think that's too much to ask." A stunned expression transformed her face, then she huffed and stared up at the ceiling. "Jesus, why am I telling her all this? She couldn't care less." Gracie groaned with self-derision.

Madeira blinked and crossed her arms over her chest, reveling in the new and uncomfortable feeling of being the dumpee instead of the dumper. Well, sort of. She couldn't be dumped by someone who'd never had her. "Can I ask you something?"

"Sure."

Madeira's gaze narrowed. "Did you ever think of looking me up?"

Gracie bit the corner of her lip and focused on the toe of her boot. "No. I mean, yes, I did. I tried to find out who you were several months ago, but not for reasons of…" She twirled her hand. "I wanted to say thanks, not throw myself at you."

Unable to stop herself, Madeira chuckled again. After a moment, Gracie grudgingly laughed, too, and Madeira pulled her into what was intended to be a friendly, understanding hug. Instead, a curious proprietary feeling overtook her. She had to focus hard to keep from smoothing her palms down the curve of Gracie's back and molding their bodies together in a manner that would only spell CLAIM.

"This is such a mess." Gracie muttered against Madeira's shoulder. "I'm sorry you got dragged into it. If it were up to me, we wouldn't even be having this conversation."

Madeira held Gracie away out of physical necessity, hoping the distance would simultaneously stall her raging sexual attraction and jump-start her brain. "Aw, look. It's not so bad. As long as we know where we stand, who cares what anyone else thinks?" Her palms slipped away from Gracie's shoulders, still tingling from the warm, womanly feel of her.

The absence of touch was palpable.

Madeira wanted to hold her again.

"Are you forgetting we still have to go out there and face those reporters? They seem to care what their readers think about the whole situation. How are we going to survive that?"

How, indeed? Madeira rubbed the back of her hand against her jawline, thinking. A ridiculous thought materialized. "You probably won't like this idea."

"Try me."

Madeira studied Gracie's face a moment, trying to anticipate her reaction. "Let's give them the interview of their dreams, the happily ever after they're salivating for. Once they have a fairy-tale ending for the readers, my guess is they'll drop it."

Grace's brows arched, and her expression said she found the idea intriguing. Thank goodness. "You mean, deceive them? Make them think we're...you know?" A lovely blush rose to her cheeks.

A breeze of excitement blew through Madeira. She liked the idea better the more she thought about it, but tried for a neutral expression. This was one charade she'd enjoy acting out. "Why not? It's what they want to hear."

Gracie crossed her arms, suddenly skeptical. "Hang on. This isn't just some ploy to get me in the sack, right? Because, trust me, it won't work."

"No. It isn't." Madeira didn't want to think about Gracie that way at the moment. It made her blood rush south. "I promise."

Gracie seemed to gauge Madeira for an ulterior motive, but eventually, she flipped her palms. "If you're up for it, I am. Since we both understand *and agree* how completely unsuited for each other we are."

Madeira didn't necessarily share Gracie's opinion on the matter, but she nodded once before lowering her tone to a purr. "Absolutely. Anyone can see we're incompatible."

"Okay, then. This might even be fun." A winsome smile touched Gracie's lips. "I've always wanted to be an actress, though my *abuela* claims I can't lie to save my life."

Madeira nodded. "You'll do fine. And I'm a natural actor."

"Yeah, I bet." Gracie smirked. "Tools of the trade, huh?"

"Something like that." Madeira smiled. "Let's go."

"Hang on. Let me just...check my hair."

"Ah, *mujeres*," Madeira said, with an exaggerated sigh.

"Oh, shut your hole," Gracie said with a wry smile. "I guarantee you check your hair twice as often as I check mine." Grace stepped around Madeira and faced the mirror. A mask of dismay slipped into place. "Lord." With a groan, she bent, flipping her hair over and snaking her slim fingers into it. She shook it almost angrily. "I can't be photographed looking this way. I look like a hooker."

Madeira managed to tear her appreciative gaze from Gracie's luscious ass, albeit reluctantly. "I think you look great."

Grace whipped her hair back and turned, the waves settling around her shoulders in sexy, natural disarray. She looked like she'd just climbed out of bed, and Madeira found she couldn't breathe for wishing that bed had been her own.

"Yeah. I look great if you're into froofy chicks. Which, come to think of it, you probably are," she added, almost as an afterthought.

Madeira's English was perfect after six years in the States, but she wasn't familiar with this word *froofy*. However, if Gracie represented froofy chicks, Madeira could very easily find herself "into" them. "What does this mean, froofy?"

"You know, high maintenance. Totally femme in that unappealing… almost straight way?" Grace glanced toward the ceiling for a better explanation. "It's the whole big hair, fake nails, waxed body, plastic boobs, spray-tan look. Come on, now." One of her brows peaked. "Someone like you has got to be familiar with the concept of a high-maintenance woman."

There Grace went, pigeon-holing Madeira again. She'd be more amused if Grace weren't so on target. Well, after a few mishaps, Madeira had avoided the particular trap of straight women, but she would admit to liking her women on the feminine side of the spectrum. But, still… Gracie's assessment made Madeira sound so shallow. She'd be the first to admit she enjoyed the company of women—plural—but she'd always thought of herself as fun-loving, freewheeling. Not shallow. If she projected that image, she'd have to work on it. "I know the type," Madeira said, keeping it light.

Gracie nodded, as if she'd never doubted her instincts. "Yet another confirmation of our intrinsic incompatibility."

"How so?"

"Because froofy is not me. I prefer simple. Wash-and-wear hair, nails that are ready for football in the park." Grace shook her head, then gave a self-derisive laugh. "Uh, yeah. What am I saying? You don't care about my grooming habits. I swear I'm not usually such a flake. I'm a *teacher*, for God's sake. Well, a brand-new one. But—" She squeezed her eyes shut and clenched her fists. "Stop babbling, Grace, for fuck's sake," she muttered to herself. Her lids fluttered open. "I'm sorry. It's just nerves."

Madeira grinned. Had she ever met a woman who was so naturally adorable and breezily insulting at the same time? She gave in to the urge and brushed the back of her fingers down Grace's neck. "I don't think you're a flake and you aren't froofy, either."

Grace grimaced and turned toward the mirror, putting final touches on her "freshly fucked" hair with her fingers. "Well, thanks. Much to my sister's chagrin."

Madeira stood behind her, thumbs hooked in her front pockets, and spoke to Gracie's reflection in the mirror. "I understand. Sometimes my sister, Torien, expects me to be someone I'm not, too."

"Respectable, you mean?" Those warm-brandy, woman-killer eyes studied Madeira warily, but a hint of mischief spiced her expression.

Madeira laughed, short and surprised, at how unabashedly Gracie cut through her bullshit. Except that her admission about Toro hadn't been bullshit—Gracie just didn't realize it. "That reminds me of the first words you ever said to me. Do you remember?"

Grace gave a little shake of her head and turned to meet Madeira's gaze.

"You opened your eyes and said, 'You aren't Ms. Right.'"

Grace snickered, then smiled behind her fist. "Well, I was probably looking for my bear at the time, but"—one side of her kissable mouth quivered up—"if the teaching thing doesn't pan out, maybe I'll become a psychic."

Madeira laid a palm over her heart and moaned. "Shit, Gracie. You hit where it hurts. Am I that bad?"

"I never said you were bad, Madeira. Of course you aren't. You're just...a player." She hiked one slender shoulder and let it drop, as though that said it all. "Simple as that. Am I right?"

Madeira said nothing for a moment, then lowered her voice to a dangerous rumble. "You know, *fierita*, you can't believe everything you read in the papers. I'm really an okay woman."

"I don't doubt that at all. I remember how you treated me the day of the accident." Gracie bestowed a sweet smile that could crush Madeira's walls if she let it. "It's a simple truth. You're an okay woman who tends to dabble with all the ladies, that's all."

How could Madeira feel so amused and defensive and insulted simultaneously? "Not...*all* of them."

"Clearly not. I'm proof of that. But enough of them."

Madeira opened her mouth to protest, but Gracie held up a hand. "Look you don't have to explain. It's none of my business and really, what does it matter what I think of your lifestyle? It's not as if I'm ever going to be a part of it."

Her *lifestyle*? "I guess it doesn't." But to Madeira's dismay and surprise, it did. It mattered, she realized, because some foolish part of her wanted Grace Obregon to see her in a whole different light, to see *through* her in a way no one else ever had. Madeira wanted to be the kind of woman who would make Gracie feel as if she wasn't settling… which made no goddamn sense at all.

None. Zero.

And yet, and yet, and yet…Madeira yearned to be worthy of Gracie.

Fact.

So…absurd.

Gracie angled her head toward the door. "Let's get this over with and go back to our separate corners of the world, hmm?"

"Sure." Gracie's casual comment stung. Damnit. Something about this woman made Madeira wish their corners of the world weren't quite so separate. What an idiot. She had no idea what evil well these unfamiliar feelings were bubbling up from. A sense of challenge? Because Gracie didn't have the least iota of interest in her and no compulsion for hiding that fact?

No clue.

But as she traipsed toward the conference room by Gracie's side, Madeira said a silent prayer of thanks that she was immune to that crazy little thing called love. If she wasn't, she'd be in *big* trouble with Gracie.

Chapter Five

Él que evita la tentación, evita el pecado.
Whoever avoids temptation avoids the sin.

Ho-ly shit.

Grace was in *big* trouble.

Bigger than big. Huge trouble.

She'd learned a few interesting facts about Madeira Pacias while locked in the bathroom with her, not the least of which was, Madeira was exactly her type—the type she'd sworn off back when she decided to trade bar towels for books in pursuit of her teaching degree: charming, sexy, flirty, and completely unreliable. Madeira was like a well-worn carnival roller coaster—exhilarating…on the condition you survived the dangerous ride.

One of the first steps Grace had taken toward changing the reckless direction of her life was vowing to avoid involvement with women who would break her heart if given the chance.

Women exactly like Madeira.

Too bad Madeira had the Mack Daddy, charm-your-pants-off—literally—thing rockin' full strength, and too bad Grace's weak ass was as susceptible to it as a preschooler was to chicken pox and eating paste. Madeira could be her undoing if Grace let her. *Which I won't.* The smartest thing she could do right now would be to bolt, far and fast, from the unrelenting temptation of this perfect, imperfect woman.

Alas, life wasn't so easy. She couldn't run. At least not now. First she had to sit here cuddled up to danger personified, vamp it up for the media and pretend they were destined for some sort of lesbian happily ever after. Grace—the reformed, and Madeira—the unreformable. As IF. Fake or not, the whole situation felt so promising and real it made Grace want to puke.

In response to something one of the reporters asked, Madeira slung one of those toned arms around Grace's shoulder, one finger absentmindedly playing with her collarbone as she answered. The motion felt so casually possessive, so comfortable. Nipples tight, throat dry, Grace's insides bubbled with pulsing, hot, blinding desire. She squirmed, striving for comfort she knew she wouldn't find from merely shifting position.

Inside, a part of her remained very still, trying to channel her *abuela* into the room to ask whether this whole fiasco was some kind of sign, but DoDo failed to appear. Not that it surprised her. DoDo always encouraged them to figure out their own problems. Maybe Madeira wasn't a sign in Grace's life so much as a test. She'd done a lot of soul-searching over the past few years, and if she knew anything about herself, she knew her weaknesses. Just like a recovering gambling addict took pains to avoid Las Vegas, Grace knew with utter certainty that she needed to keep her distance from Madeira. Maybe Madeira's appearance in her life was a test to see if she could hang tough in the face of—

Jesus Christ, Madeira was hot.

Grace had spent inordinate amounts of energy during the first few minutes of the press conference making sure an inch or so of space separated their bodies, but then she realized two things. One, they had a finite amount of time to convince these reporters they were into each other, and two, this charade would likely be her first and last opportunity to drape herself over Madeira and have a logical excuse for it.

Ah, the Fates were cruel bitches.

Cruel bitches and hard to fight. Despite her better judgment, Grace clung to Madeira like a woman in lust, smiling and doing coupley things like picking imaginary lint off Madeira's clothes—a sure sign of ownership in the secret world of women. The only thing she didn't do, absolutely could not do, was look at Madeira. Way too close for comfort. It would be just her luck to have one of the photographers snap a news photo of her batting her baby browns at Madeira, all adoring and pathetic. Playacting was one thing, but pictures generally didn't lie.

Madeira would take one look at the photo and peg her as another in the long line of starstruck groupies. Thanks, but no thanks.

What am I doing here?

In a motion that belied her inner turmoil, Grace nestled closer to Madeira's firm, warm body, her stomach contracting with lust when she felt Madeira's toned lats flex against her.

God. This wasn't *her*.

Not anymore.

She didn't want to play games.

The desperate need to cut her losses and bail from this situation swamped her. She pressed a hand to her abdomen, tucking her chin as nausea slammed into her, full force.

"You okay?" Madeira had leaned in to ask the question, her hot breath tickling Grace's ear as she spoke. Tingles shot through Grace, the pulse that had been drumming low in her body increasing in both tempo and intensity. All her various physiological signs indicated that no, she was decidedly *not* okay. Far from it.

"I'm fine," she lied, out of the corner of her mouth so the reporters couldn't hear. "You think we're convincing them?"

Madeira's hot gaze swept over Grace, settling a little too long on her mouth. "Damn, *fierita*, I hope so. The way you're molded to my body, we're almost convincing me," she drawled.

"Yeah, well." Grace managed to remain cool and arch a brow. "You do recall this is all for show, don't you?"

Madeira grinned. "Doesn't mean I can't enjoy it."

"Enjoy while you can, darlin'. Tomorrow's articles are going to seriously cramp your social life, and you won't be enjoying it nearly as much then. Mark my words."

"I'm not worried." She leaned in and lowered her voice to a lusty rumble. "The women I date don't usually care if I'm taken or not."

"Gee, just what every woman wants to hear."

"I thought you didn't care?"

"I…I don't." Grace scoffed, jealous in spite of how illogical that was. "Watch out, or you're going to make it impossible for me to even fake the rest of this."

"Ah, my tough-talking Gracie. It's okay to admit you want me, baby," she said playfully.

Grace scowled, forcefully ignoring how her insides spasmed every time Madeira called her "Gracie." God, if Madeira only knew what that nickname meant. Grace would have to tell her eventually, so she didn't blurt it in front of the wrong person and completely fuck her life. "I'm going to kill you when this is over," Grace said, feeling lusty rather than lethal.

Laughing, Madeira patted Grace's leg, then turned toward the throng. Madeira pointedly left her hand there, Grace noted.

"We'd like to finish up as soon as possible, folks. Gracie and I have a lot of catching up to do."

Ugh. Cocky woman.

Harold's eyes crinkled with mirth as he looked from Madeira to Grace, then he turned toward the bay of scribblers. "Okay, last question. Lay 'em out there if you got 'em, folks. Let's cut these kids a break."

The crowd began to holler for attention, raising their hands, notebooks, pens—whatever was handy.

"Mullaney," Harold barked. Most of the journalists settled back, murmuring their disappointment, but the young female reporter Harold had chosen to ask the final question perked up.

Grace watched with bemused interest as the petite, private-school blonde shifted position until one hipbone jutted forward like an "Open for Business" sign. Her eyelids dropped to bedroom mast and she flashed Madeira a full 300-watt, come-and-get-me smile. The entire series of subtle yet pointed motions reminded Grace of a preening cat begging to be stroked, and a twinge of annoyance struck her.

Okay, more than a twinge. She wanted to kick Mullaney's ass.

Another thing she'd always hated about dating a charmer was never feeling one hundred percent secure that the woman wouldn't leave for the first hot little Barbie doll who crooked her plastic finger. Not that Grace was actually dating Madeira. But as far as this rat-whore Mullaney was concerned, Grace and Madeira were in love, and that still didn't stop Mullaney from laying on the "fuck me" vibes good and thick. A ribbon of outrage twisted through Grace. Did women have no shame when it came to Madeira?

What do you care? her mind rasped.

It's the principle of the matter, the other part of her mind snapped back, possessiveness gripping her in its ugly green claws. The angel on her shoulder advised her to blow it off. The devil on the other side whispered, "What good is a charade if you don't play it to the hilt, sister?"

The devil won.

Shocker.

Grace flashed a *dream on, Barbie* smirk at Mullaney and snuggled closer to Madeira, who peered down with amusement that quickly transformed to smoldering recognition. Grace watched the reporter blink several times before her bravado cracked, her pale neck growing blotchy with embarrassment. Victory, Grace realized, could be so very sweet.

"Meow," Madeira whispered, awe in her tone.

"Be quiet. She was totally being a slut, right in front of my face. You wouldn't understand."

"Oh, trust me. I understand only too well, babe." Madeira casually slipped her hand under the hem of Grace's sweater, her warm palm against the small of Grace's back.

"Anyway," began the reporter, tucking her hair behind her ear with the pen she held, "can we have a look at the…uh…the bear that brought you two back together? Maybe a little background on this"—she consulted her notes—"Ms. Right?"

Uh-oh. Grace stiffened, but Madeira gave her back a reassuring caress as if to say she had it under control.

Grace should've known better than to trust her.

"Actually," Madeira began, feigning some sort of modesty Grace *knew* Madeira didn't truly feel, "this is my mistake. When Harold told me Gracie wanted her Ms. Right, I didn't think I had to bring anything other than, well, yours truly." She managed a truly sheepish, yet still sexy shrug. "I'm sure you all understand my error."

Grace's jaw dropped as the crowd roared approval and scrawled notes. Granted, the innuendo-laden answer perfectly suited their purposes, but right at that moment Grace wanted to freaking punch Madeira. Jesus, she acted as if she were a gift-wrapped package from Tiffany's over which Grace should fawn and weep in gratitude. Worse, these reporters were eating it up.

Damnit.

Grace had been holding her own in this media feeding frenzy until now. The last thing she wanted was for the entire Denver population to fall in love with Ms. F-ing Sound Byte, scratch their heads and wonder, "What does Madeira Pacias see in Grace, of all people?"

Goddamnit.

This was one of those moments that would keep her awake at night thinking about all the quippy things she should've said. At the moment, true to form, words escaped her. Her jaw tightened. It shouldn't matter. Truly. But deep down at the seat of her ego, it did. Grace couldn't stand feeling like Madeira's pity date, yet she couldn't seem to cultivate the same level of swagger to effect some sort of damage control.

Closing her eyes, Grace pictured the headlines and stories that would hit the papers tomorrow. It took every bit of her self-control to stifle a mortified groan. What would her students think? Or worse, their parents? Her colleagues?

Unable to formulate a better plan to bring this fiasco to an end, she reached over and pinched Madeira's leg. Madeira jumped, but quickly slid her palm over Grace's hand, to prevent her from inflicting further pain, no doubt. Instead, Madeira only succeeded in pressing Grace's palm flat against her toned thigh, and Grace's inner vixen emerged. She did the only thing she could think of to shake Madeira's unshakable cool. Slowly, she slid her palm higher, higher, until she reached the sensitive top of Madeira's thigh.

Then she squeezed.

Madeira went very still. She slowly turned, and the look on her face imprisoned Grace as effectively as silk ties and four solid bedposts.

Now, why did she have to conjure *that* image?

She swallowed loudly and tried to extract her hand from the depths of Dangerville, but Madeira held it there firmly and addressed the crowd.

"I think that's it for us," she said, sounding and looking amazingly calm, considering the feral look Grace had seen in her eyes moments earlier.

"How about a few pictures?" someone called from the back.

Again, Madeira turned, her lips close enough to nibble, neck close enough that Grace could see the strong, oddly sexual pulse. "You up for some photographs, Gracie? Or did you have other plans in mind?"

The silk ties and bedposts flashed through Grace's traitorous mind again, and she glanced away. "Pictures are fine."

"Where do you want us?" Madeira stood, then held out a palm for Grace. Grace accepted the contact. Madeira pulled her to her feet, obviously mindful of Grace's injured leg, way too close for Grace's peace of mind. "Not that Gracie wouldn't look perfect against any background," Madeira said, her voice a sexy murmur.

"Down here." One photographer, wearing a multi-pocketed khaki vest and a matching baseball cap turned backwards, pointed to a grouping of large plants arranged in bulbous terracotta cauldrons by the entrance.

Madeira kept hold of her hand as they wound their way off the dais toward the spot the photographer had indicated, and Grace allowed herself to enjoy the strong warmth of Madeira's grip, which, on the one hand, felt like a lifeline. Part of Grace knew Madeira was on her team in all of this, just as she'd been since she'd crawled beneath Grace's demolished Explorer and wiped the blood from her face. On the other hand, Madeira was a massive risk, one Grace needed to avoid.

She'd do that.

But later, she decided suddenly.

Right now, she was going to indulge in the sensations, all in the name of giving the paper and news stations their story. What could it hurt?

"How about a couple of the two of you embracing?" the photographer suggested, pulling Grace back into the present. "Or maybe a kiss—"

"No kissing," Grace snapped, emphasizing the words with a dictatorial slash of her free hand. She hadn't meant to bark at the guy, but kisses were definitely out. She'd be a goner if she locked lips with Madeira, even just for show.

Surprise shut the photographer's mouth, and he cocked his shaggy head like a dog trying to understand his owner's unwillingness to hand out a treat.

"I'm sorry, but no way," she repeated, her tone softening.

"Aw, you sure, Gracie?" Madeira's eyes shimmered with mirth, and Grace knew this was payback for the thigh squeeze. "I'll make it as chaste…or unchaste…as you want, darlin'."

Ignoring Madeira and the throbbing in her body, Grace turned to the photographer, crinkling her nose and striving for a good mix of nerves and innocence. "Not in the paper. I'm not that kind of woman." She tugged up the neckline of her sweater as casually as she could. No sense giving her a flash of the VIXEN to contradict her claim.

Madeira slipped a possessive hand against the small of her back and spoke to the photographer in a just-between-us kind of tone. "You heard her, brother. No kissing." She eased Grace against the length of her—Jesus, super-hard—body, wrapping her arms around Grace from behind. Possessively, but with a painful shot of cherishing on the side. "Sorry to disappoint, but a lady gets what she wants when she's with *la ladróna de corazones*. Especially this lady."

Madeira turned toward Grace, a don't-be-afraid-of-the-big-bad-wolf expression transforming her face from merely gorgeous to tummy tightening, lick-your-lips sexy. "And that's a promise," Madeira finished, her tone a husky drawl meant just for Grace's ears.

The photographer laughed, then *Snap! Snap! Snap!*

Flashbulbs everywhere.

When the light show ended, Grace, struck dumb by her own lust, pulled out of Madeira's embrace and shrank as far as she could into the shadows of the plant's large leaves. Madeira—big shocker—stood a bit forward, joking with the photographers and basking in the limelight, completely oblivious to Grace's inner turmoil.

So much for shaking Madeira's confidence.

In a moment of utter clarity, Grace realized with dismay that Madeira held the media, the situation, *and her* firmly in the palm of that sexy, no doubt talented hand.

Definitely a sign.

More like a bad omen.

"Were you just trying to get my attention in there, Gracie," Madeira teased, "or sampling the merchandise?"

Grace should've known Madeira would call her on the thigh squeeze the moment the conference room cleared. What an error in judgment that had been. They'd barely walked out the door before Madeira pounced on the topic like a cat on a lame bird.

"You do remember that was all for show, right?" Grace asked, her tone droll.

As they made their way through the labyrinth of hallways side by side, Madeira grinned at her. "Was it?"

"Of course," Grace murmured, taking an inordinate amount of interest in the drab artwork on the walls.

"Well, you letting your fingers do the walking probably didn't do much good for the show." Madeira paused until suspense made Grace glance over. Madeira grabbed Grace's hand and held it. "As far as I can tell, the only two people who knew what was going on under that table were you and me."

Damn. So much for a good excuse. "I didn't mean anything by it." Grace reluctantly extracted her hand, watching as Madeira peered down at her empty palm, then back at Grace, quizzically. Grace shrugged, by way of explanation. "You don't have to keep up with the charade. The press conference is over."

"Maybe I just wanted to hold your hand."

Whirling, Grace faced her. "Madeira, I thought we'd both made ourselves clear in the bathroom."

"We did, about the whole commitment issue. Neither of us is into it. I'm cool."

"Then you'll forgive me for reminding you that my hand is not yours to hold."

"Okay, if that's the way you feel. But I've been thinking…" Madeira tapped her index and middle fingers rhythmically on her chin.

"Uh-oh. You. Thinking. That can't be good." Grace tried to play it off casually, but inside, all her systems were revved. She crossed her arms—a protective gesture. "Thinking what?"

"I like you, Gracie."

"Well…" Grace moistened her lips and tried not to look like a hungry dog who'd just been thrown a bone "I like you, too. That doesn't alter our basic incompatibility."

Madeira moved forward. Grace backed up. When the wall prevented any further retreat, Madeira braced her palms against it, caging Grace in a position that felt way too close to sexual. "We aren't destined for forever."

"Absolutely not."

"But I can't seem to find any reason why we shouldn't see each other casually. Can you?"

Astonished, Grace's mouth dropped open, and she stared at Madeira as if she'd gone over the edge. She pushed against her hard, flat torso until Madeira backed off. "Uh, yes! There is one very big reason."

"Which is?" Madeira truly looked baffled. Jesus, how could one woman be so sure of herself?

Grace spread her arms. "I have no desire to be your next conquest, Madeira. And don't bother telling me it would be different between us, because I've been there."

"That does present a problem." Madeira studied Grace for a minute then crossed her arms. "Can I ask you one question?"

"Whatever. I guess."

"Are you attracted to me?"

Grace groaned, turning to continue down the hall. "Never mind, you can't ask me a question."

Madeira's knowing laughter taunted her from behind. Catching up, Madeira slipped her hand around Grace's arm until their gazes locked. Madeira's eyes warmed with sincerity. "Don't be mad, Gracie. I'm just playing with you."

She sighed, giving her a grudging smile. "I'm not angry, I just don't want to play. Or be played. You're impossible. Can't we leave things how they are between us and be done with it?"

"That depends. How are things between us?"

Grace pondered this. "We're…friends, I guess."

Madeira nodded. "*Bueno*. Good place to start."

"Good place to *stay*," Grace countered.

Madeira shrugged, ending the nonchalant motion with a sly glance. "Fair enough. But if you ever change your mind—"

"I won't." Grace stopped by the front doors and offered her hand, a firm, businesslike smile on her face. "But, anyway, thanks again, Madeira. For everything."

"Uh-oh, this sounds like good-bye."

"What else would it be?"

Instead of taking her hand, Madeira hiked her chin toward the doors. "Can I at least walk you to your car?"

"Actually, you can't. I didn't drive." She pulled her phone from her purse and waggled it. "I need to call my sister to come and pick me up."

"Oh. Well, I can drive you home."

Alone.

Together.

In an enclosed place.

Dangerous prospect and way too enticing for Grace's well-being. "Ah, no. That's okay. Lola is expecting my call."

"Yes, but aren't you forgetting one very important thing?"

"No." Grace frowned, second-guessing herself. "I don't know… am I?"

Madeira jabbed a thumb over her shoulder. "I'm holding your bear hostage in my truck."

Grace clapped a hand over her mouth. Jesus, how could she have forgotten Ms. Right? "God, where's my brain? I'll just get her from you and then—"

"I'll drop you at home."

"No."

"Come on, Gracie." Madeira cocked her head. "I'm an easygoing woman, but you're starting to insult me. I'm offering to drive you home, not relieve you of your virtue."

As if she could. Grace barely avoided releasing a snort.

"I'm clear on the fact you don't want me. Okay?"

It's not that I don't want you, Grace's rocket-impulsive mouth almost blurted. Luckily, she squelched the urge just short of launch. That would've been a deadly take-off. She blew out a breath and raked her fingers through her hair, knowing deep inside that Madeira was right. It was a ride home. Period. Why did she feel the need to fight so hard?

Why?

She knew why.

She was attracted to Maddee—Jesus, when had she started to think of her as Maddee?—with a ferocity that stole her breath, and if *Madeira*—keep it professional—got an inkling of that, she'd be relentless in her pursuit. Grace had played that game before and lost. The challenge, then, was to remain gracious while preventing Madeira from reading her. They were rational adults. Attraction or not, they could handle a few moments alone together, couldn't they?

"Okay, a ride home," Grace said, holding up a finger and bestowing her most stern teacher look. "But I'm not kidding, Madeira. Nothing more than that between us. Ever."

"Ever?" Madeira smiled. "That's a little extreme. You want to add a loophole for your own peace of mind?"

Despite herself, Grace laughed. "I have an idea. How about you just stop flirting with me?"

Madeira scoffed. "I suppose you'd order a zebra to stop being striped, huh, Gracie? Flirting is my nature."

"Fine. Flirt all you want, then." Grace flicked her fingers in disdain. "But I promise you, it won't get you anywhere."

"Get *me* anywhere?" Madeira held up her palms like a falsely accused woman. "That's a pot-calling-the-kettle-black comment if I've ever heard one. Keep your hands off my thighs, then talk to me about getting somewhere."

After a short exclamation of surprise Grace wasn't able to prevent, she turned and flounced as best she could toward the parking lot. She managed to keep her spine stiffly erect, but her tummy trembled as she walked. Her thoughts flitted from Madeira's damned magnetism, to her own damned Benedict Arnold desire, and to the damned realization she'd probably never recover from this run-in with Madeira Pacias. All the while, Madeira's rich, rolling laughter trailed behind her like a bad reputation.

CHAPTER SIX

Él que algo quiere, algo le cuesta.
He who would have the fruit must climb the tree.

"Well? What do you think?" Madeira stood in the warm kitchen next to Simon, waiting impatiently for Toro's and Iris's opinions of the newspaper articles that had been written as a result of the press conference.

"I think you are at my house way too early on a Sunday morning," Toro told her little sister in a glum tone.

"You know what I mean." Dispatch came over the air, and both Madeira's hand and Simon's went automatically to the volume knobs on their respective portable radios. The morning felt too young for the brash interference from the radio traffic.

Restless, Madeira shifted her weight from one leg to the other. All through the night, Simon had humored her by haunting the newspaper boxes in their district. Madeira had been unable to relax until the Sunday papers hit. They'd collected them all, read the articles, then managed to drive around until the crack of dawn before Madeira couldn't stand it anymore and stopped to place a call to her sister. At Iris's invitation—despite Toro's protests about the ungodly hour—they'd stopped by the house for free coffee, and also to get third and fourth opinions on the news. Madeira had quickly introduced her partner and dispensed the papers to Iris and Toro, who were still drowsy and pajama-clad. Toro was grumpy; Iris was not.

The scent of apple cinnamon coffee cake rose from the oven to spice the air, and gentle fingers of morning sunlight reached through the kitchen window, tickling the household awake.

"They're not so bad, huh?" Madeira prompted, stifling a yawn with the back of her hand.

Iris tucked her hair behind one ear and glanced cryptically into her coffee cup, saying nothing.

"What? Why are you so quiet, sis? I know you must have something to say." Disconcerted by her hesitation, Madeira moved to the coffeepot and topped her mug, turning to lean against the counter, Rocky boots crossed. The position said "casual," in direct opposition to the churning anticipation in her gut.

Iris scooted out her chair and turned to face her. "I have a lot to say, but why should I? You'll just accuse me of being too much of a *romantic* if I give you my opinion. Hit me, Mad." She held out her mug, and Madeira brimmed it.

"I won't. I promise." Madeira mimed a quick X over her heart then crossed her fingers playfully.

Iris shook her head with a smile, set down her mug, then picked up the *Post* article written by Harold. "Fine, you asked for it. It's just, you're so focused on the articles."

"Well, of course. What do you expect?"

"I expect anyone who shares the same genes with my gorgeous partner to be deeper than that." Her eyes scanned the article a moment, then she held it out toward her. "Look at this picture, Mad. What do you see?"

"Me?"

"Don't be a dumbass."

Lips pursed, Madeira bent forward and scrutinized it. It struck her as odd that they'd chosen to publish a hastily snapped shot from when she'd first arrived instead of one of the more orchestrated photos from the press conference. She had to admit, though, this more candid photo really captured the feel of the reunion. At least how it had felt to her.

Inevitable.

Poignant.

So right.

"Well?"

Madeira straightened, unwilling or unable to give in to the feelings. "I'm hugging her. So what?"

"No. Look deeper. Look at your face." The paper crackled as she foisted it toward her. "At your expression."

Madeira knew what Iris was getting at, but she didn't want to address the look of utter adoration captured by the camera's too-perceptive eye. What did it matter? In an effort to evade the topic, Madeira sucked in one cheek and angled her head to the side. "My face…yes. Good-looking *chica*, if that's what you're getting at." She positioned her thumbs and fingers to make a small square box and turned it this way and that, pretending it was a movie frame. "That's a Hollywood face right there." She smacked the paper with the backs of her fingers and postured like a peacock. "Angelina, watch out."

Iris ignored Madeira's posturing, turning the photo back toward herself. "You are *thrilled* to see her, Mad, and you can't deny it. I have never seen you looking like that with anyone. And hell, I've seen you with practically *everyone.*" She shook her head. "First you whine and moan about the reunion, then the camera catches you looking like you couldn't let go of her if you tried. You big faker. I don't care what you say, it's completely romantic."

"That's what I told her," Simon said.

"It's not completely romantic. It's completely staged." Madeira stretched her shoulders, avoiding Iris's gaze and wanting to punch Simon for selling her ass out.

"Do you like her, Madeira?" Iris asked in an almost plaintive tone.

"I don't even know her. I mean, sure I was glad to see her. I thought she was dead, Iris. I'm not a complete cad."

Toro snorted.

Madeira burned her sister a glare.

"That's not what I mean." Iris sighed, perusing the photo as she ran her finger over the angles of Madeira's face as the camera caught her embracing Grace for the first time. "Forget it. You're in denial and it's too early to play shrink."

"Denial?" Why did her entire circle of friends and family seem against her all of a sudden?

Iris ignored her. "I'm going to get an extra copy later and FedEx it to your mother. Won't she just love to see her girl looking so happy?"

"What are you, nuts?" Madeira snatched the paper away from Iris, her eyes immediately drawn to the bright red of Gracie's sweater, the fullness of her lips as she smiled in Madeira's arms. God, she fit so well there. Madeira's chest tightened with the soul-deep, visceral memory. "Send this and Mamá will start planning our forever-after together before the week is out. Before you know it, my life will be ruined."

"Mamá doesn't have to ruin your life," Toro groused. "You do a good enough job on your own with your reckless ways. Damn. You *are* in denial." She glanced at Iris. "My babe is right."

Madeira chose to ignore her grouchy sister's well-placed barbs. Toro had never approved of her freewheeling lifestyle, not that Madeira gave a shit. "Just leave Mamá out of this. She won't understand how this whole thing came about."

"None of us really understand how it came about, Mosquito." Toro rubbed her eyes. "All I know is what *mi hermanita* announces one day." She spread her arms. "She has suddenly decided to become a paramedic so she can 'help people.'" The corners of her mouth tipped down as her shoulders moved up in a shrug. "Okay. Whatever. The sister I know never so much as pondered a Band-Aid before, but who am I to question the impulses of a grown woman?"

"Good point," Madeira almost growled. "It's not your place to question."

"Then, a year later, a woman comes forward looking for my sister. Of course, none of us ever heard mention of a woman."

"What more is there to know, Toro? So I stopped to help on the accident. Later I decided to change careers. What's so mysterious about that?"

Torien shrugged. "Only you and this Graciela can answer that question, Mosquito. Why don't you take a few moments and enlighten us with the truth, for a change?"

Simon loped to the coffeepot, refilled, then nudged Madeira, his gaze knowing but confidential as well. "So, Madeira. Why are you called Mosquito?"

Grateful for the pointed subject change just when things were getting hairy, Madeira opened her mouth to answer, but Toro beat her to the punch.

"Because she's a pest." Toro smiled up at Simon, a conspiratorial expression that said the man would understand the nickname soon enough. "At times a bloodsucking pest."

Madeira pulled an expression of false accusation and flipped her hand palm up toward her sister while staring at Simon as if to say, "See what I have to put up with?"

Simon grinned. "I like it. Mosquito. It fits somehow."

Madeira loomed, as best she could, over the man who stood nearly a foot taller than her. "You start calling me that at work and I'll come up with something worse for you, Fletch. Something emasculating."

Simon and Toro laughed.

"This one makes it sound like you two are an item," Iris said, ignoring the banter going on around her. She'd switched to an article in a suburban journal, concentrating on all the typeset lines and everything in between, all the baffling subtext only a woman like Iris could catch. "I thought you said you'd cleared up all the nonsense about you two being soul mates?"

"Cleared up, handled, same difference." Iris's toothcomb scrutiny of the articles was beginning to make Madeira squirm.

Iris peered up. "Care to elaborate?"

Madeira waved away Iris's concerns with a careless flick of her hand. "Gracie and I decided we'd tell them what they wanted to hear so they'd leave us alone, but don't worry. We aren't an item. She's no more into me than I'm into her."

Simon, Iris, and Toro burst out laughing, but Madeira raised her voice and spoke over them. "We just *handled* things."

"'Gracie and I.'" Iris shared a dreamy gaze with Torien. "Isn't it so awesome to hear her talking that way, sweetie?"

"Yes, *Irisíta mía*." She stroked her hand through Iris's long hair and kissed her cheek. "Listening to my little sister become totally… pussy-whipped is sweet stuff indeed."

"Pussy-whipped?" Madeira tossed out a rapid string of insults in Spanish, cuffing the back of Toro's head.

Toro countered with a whip-cracking gesture and the accompanying sound effects.

"Now stop." Iris smacked Torien playfully, love dancing in her green eyes. "If you tease her all the time, she'll never open up to us." She wrapped Torien in a hug and pulled her face into the crook of her neck, winking at Madeira over her head. "Don't listen to your sister. She's just trying to pay you back for all the trouble you gave her when we met."

"Trouble?" Madeira scoffed. "If it hadn't been for me, Toro would've never come to her senses about you."

"My woman's arms are around me and it's very early Sunday morning," Toro announced to Simon and Madeira, her words muffled as she kissed Iris's neck. "Don't you two have a life to save somewhere in this city?" She nuzzled Iris, who laughed softly, her hair falling over her shoulder in a black cascade as she ducked her head into the love of her life.

Madeira resisted the needle prick of envy she felt watching Toro and Iris. Their love was a palpable presence in the room, the kind of connection singers sang about and poets waxed poetic about. The kind of connection most people looked for their entire lives. People like Toro and Iris were the only ones who actually found that kind of love, though. Worthy people.

A vision of Gracie drifted into her mind.

Gracie was worthy.

Madeira willed away the irrelevant notion. She didn't even *want* something as intense as Toro had with Iris. Not in the long term, anyway. Still, it was difficult to watch them on an empty stomach. She hiked her chin toward the oven, feeling slighted. "We're on a break from saving lives, remember?"

"Break's over," Toro said.

Madeira scowled. Her sister never used to blow her off before she fell in love. And Toro had the nerve to accuse *her* of being whipped. "What about the coffee cake?"

"What about the coffee cake?" Toro repeated derisively. She implored Simon with a disbelieving look. "You married to a woman you're in love with, Simon?"

"Sure am. Lisa and I have fifteen years and counting."

Toro went back to Iris's neck. "Then get my pest of a sister the hell out of my house and explain to her why the coffee cake could burn black for all I care at this moment. Make her understand."

"You betcha. Bye, Iris."

"Bye," she said, her tone distracted by Torien's attentions.

Simon hustled Madeira out of the kitchen, but not before Madeira heard Iris tell Toro, "Mad will understand sooner than she thinks, babe. Trust me. I can sense these things. Your little sister is on the verge of something cataclysmic"—she laughed knowingly—"and she can't do a damn thing to stop it."

Madeira swallowed hard, shaken by the ominous prediction. Did Iris truly have some kind of insight? She'd long believed that women like Iris were a little bit *bruja*. They had the sixth sense. Madeira cast up a silent plea for protection to the patron saint of single women and only avoided crossing herself by clenching both fists.

❖

Wide-eyed in the darkness, Grace heard the small station wagon revving unevenly as it moved up and down its delivery route, the teenage girl chucking papers from the back as her father zigzagged from house to house. Grace jolted up in bed, but waited until she heard the *thunk* of the Sunday paper hitting the stoop before pushing back the covers and slipping her robe around her shoulders. She tucked her feet into shearling slippers, her heart pounding both in anticipation of the article and in fear of waking up Lola or DoDo. This she needed to see alone.

She stealthed her way down the stairs in the darkness, moving far left to avoid the creaking board on stair four and to the far right on stair twelve for the same reason. Thank God her high school curfew-breaking days had taught her how to successfully navigate the noise traps in DoDo's house to avoid getting busted.

At the bottom of the stairs white, bright moonlight reached in through the leaded glass panels in the door like the arms of a ghost. She cringed as the deadbolt snicked back, pausing to peer up the stairwell and listen for movement. Nothing. Her breath released, cold night air making her shiver. Or maybe it was nerves. Turning back to her task, she pulled the door open only far enough to allow her to squat down and ease the thick, rolled paper over the threshold. Carefully relocking the door, she retraced her steps, breathing shallowly until she was in her room, paper in hand, with the door locked behind her. She shed her robe and climbed back into bed.

Holding a penlight in her mouth for illumination, she turned the pages cautiously so they wouldn't crackle. She scanned headlines as she went and had moved through three sections with no luck before she finally saw it.

Holy fuck.

Her stomach contracted. She gasped and the penlight fell from her mouth, rolling across the covers, tossing its meager beam like a drunken searchlight as it toppled. She snatched it up and lit the page once more, her eyes fixed on the photograph next to the headline.

"Oh, God," she whispered. She didn't even need to read the words. That photograph said it all—she and Maddee were connected, now and forevermore, like it or not.

And she didn't like it.

Not at all.

Her gaze traced the strong lines of Madeira's jaw, the look of sheer joy on her own face as Maddee hugged her. Hugged her as if she truly mattered.

A pitiful sigh escaped Grace's lips before she could squelch it, and she frowned at the absurdity. Enough of that. She didn't have time to brood over something that could never be. She refocused on her most immediate problem, glancing at the green numbers on her alarm clock to calculate how much planning time she had before the household arose. She had to figure out how to get this blatant display of raw emotion past her meddlesome sister and perceptive *abuelita*. They'd never let up on her if they saw this picture, and she couldn't bear the thought of the full-court press matchmaking that would follow. The whole thing creaked with tremendous burden.

Buckling under the weight of it, she rolled to the side and pulled open her nightstand drawer, extracting the half-pound bag of plain M&M's she kept there as an emergency stress ration. Clicking off her penlight, she sat in the dark popping the candy-coated medicinal yumminess and running the problem through her mind like a badly edited film.

Facts were facts: her feelings showed in that photograph. Lola and DoDo would catch it for sure. She'd have to be firm with them, letting them know that, despite how it might look, she had no interest in Maddee Pacias. Well…shit.

That wasn't exactly true, and Grace didn't want to outright lie. She wished she could deny her feelings to the bitter end, but the falsehood would eat at her insides. Why'd she have to care so damn much about being honest these days? This was a self-preservation issue, after all. Being slightly left of honest was her only reasonable option. Then again, like DoDo said, she sucked at lying, so what good would it do? The M&M handfuls grew larger in direct correlation to her burgeoning worry.

One part of her yearned to call Madeira and ask how she planned to handle the repercussions…then Grace remembered who she was dealing with. Knowing Madeira, she wasn't giving it a second thought. Too many women, too little time, after all. No sense wasting a minute of her time worrying about a woman she didn't even want. Like Madeira had said, the women she usually dated didn't care if she was considered "taken" or not. On the contrary, this perception of unattainability would probably bump Madeira's sex life into overdrive, all those shameless whore-cats vying for her attention.

Grace's shoulders dropped, and her face felt mulish.

Wait a minute—was she pouting? She snatched up the small hand mirror she'd left lying on the nightstand and scrutinized her reflection in the darkness. Good Lord, she *was* pouting. Over a love 'em and leave 'em woman, of all things. A woman in whom she herself claimed to have not a whit of interest.

Damn. She *wasn't* a good liar, was she?

Thoroughly disgusted, she chucked the mirror aside. You'd have thought a smart woman like herself would learn from her mistakes.

Tipping back her head, Grace poured the remaining half-cup of M&M's in her mouth, crunching the bounty like a squirrel with over-packed cheeks and an eating disorder. Despite her attempts to ignore her inner voice, it kept whispering the truth to her, challenging her to deny it. She liked Madeira. Genuinely. A lot. Madeira Pacias was a woman Grace could fall for. She was also a woman Grace desperately should *not* fall for if she wanted to see her life plans come to fruition.

And she did.

Lust or no lust, Grace was determined to create a future completely removed from her past, which meant Madeira was out. Sorry, Charlie. Draped with sadness and chocolate bloat, Grace glanced down at her crossed legs, bare beneath the Scooby-Doo boxer shorts she used for pajamas. Her gaze froze for a moment on the heart tattoo blighting the smooth skin of her inner thigh; she traced its outline with her pinky. UNBREAKABLE, it read, bold and brash.

She pondered the relative truth of that statement in relation to her current situation, and a picture of Madeira—flirty, charming, *temporary* Madeira—floated to the forefront of Grace's mind. With a strange heaviness in her chest, she covered the tattoo with her palm and bit her lip. Maybe not so unbreakable after all. Not where this bad girl was concerned.

I won't get hurt again.

Flouncing back against her pillows, Grace made a silent vow to herself that Madeira would never find out how Grace truly felt about her. What was the point? It would just scare Maddee off, and when she ran, she'd take Grace's hard-won pride and self-respect with her.

No.

Better that Maddee never knew.

Grace knew she could fool her, though, and resisting her once Maddee had the emotional upper hand would be next to impossible. The only bright side was, now that she had her bear and the newspaper fiasco was finished, she never had to see her again.

Thank *God* for small favors.

CHAPTER SEVEN

Del dicho al hecho hay mucho trecho.
From saying to doing is a long way.

Maddee! I mean, Madeira!" Gracie gaped out the front door of her house at her like Madeira was there to rob her. Despite Gracie's horrified expression, she looked steal-your-breath adorable in old jeans, ripped seam-to-seam at the knees, and a faded-to-gray black CU Buffs sweatshirt that should have been put out of its misery years ago. The yellow logo was peeling, and a large, white bleach spot stood out like a squashed jellyfish near the frayed hem.

Gracie's unbrushed hair had been pulled into a messy ponytail, more strands escaping the band than being held by it. Not a single sweep of makeup touched her skin, but lucky for Gracie, she didn't need it.

"Hey, Gracie." God, it was good to see her.

Gracie's hand flew to her hair. Madeira wondered if she had any idea how telling the gesture was but figured Gracie didn't even realize she'd done it. Madeira swallowed slowly, so incredibly drawn to this woman, in a way she'd never experienced before. And this unfroofy, weekend Gracie was the sexiest version yet.

"W-what are you doing here?"

Madeira smiled at Gracie's unintentional lack of manners. She couldn't blame her. Madeira probably should've called instead of just showing up, but the impulse to see Gracie had overpowered her. One minute, she'd been driving aimlessly. The next minute her truck found its way to Gracie's house and parked. Kismet. Who was Madeira to argue?

Still, she needed an excuse for why she'd come or Gracie might get the wrong idea. Stiving for casual, Madeira cleared her throat and went for light. "What did you think? We were never going to see each other again?"

"Frankly, yes. That was the grand plan."

A breeze tickled the loose hair against Gracie's cheek, and she reached up to absentmindedly brush it away. Madeira's stomach contracted painfully. Since when had she become attuned to Gracie's—or any woman's—every motion? When Madeira was around Gracie, she felt…aware.

Of her movements.

Of her ever-changing expressions.

Of her breaths.

Of her reactions, thoughts, desires.

Of their closeness…and their distance.

This level of awareness actually ached.

"You do remember that big talk we had at the newspaper offices, right?" Despite Gracie's words, Madeira noticed high color in her cheeks and a bright excitement in her eyes. A glimmer of hope?

"Sure. Of course." She stared down at her feet for a minute, head bobbing in a nod even though she didn't agree that their big talk had to be so damned iron-clad. How could Madeira be so aware, so thrown into a whirlwind by Gracie when she was so resistant to Madeira? "But I…I, well, the thing is"—*think, Madeira*—"I just have a question I hope you can answer." Good one.

"Oh." That knocked Gracie off balance. "Well…okay, I'll try." She crossed her arms. "What is it?"

Not so good one. Madeira hadn't thought beyond the excuse. She shifted and racked her brain for a question that would sound time-sensitive or important enough to have brought her all the way across town on a Sunday afternoon without a proper invitation. Nothing inspired came to mind, so she cleared her throat and blurted the first thing that popped into her brain. "Why is the bear named Ms. Right? I-I always wondered what would make a woman name a bear…that."

Gracie cocked her head to the side, her expression incredulous and amused. "You drove all the way over here to ask about my bear?"

Inside, Madeira cringed, but she struggled to keep her expression impassive. Lame was too mild a word to describe her impromptu question. So much for digging herself out. She shrugged, and dug in further. What did she have to lose? "Well, the bear sat on my dresser for a year. She and I have a history. Is it so unbelievable that I'd want to know her background?"

"Ah…" Gracie's bare, full lips quivered up into a smile, which soon developed into a cautious laugh. She shrugged. "Yes. Wholeheartedly unbelievable."

Madeira sniffed. Thought she knew everything, did Gracie? Madeira could be sensitive, interested in bears and so forth. The possibility existed. "Nevertheless, I'd like to know."

"Apparently." Gracie's expression was wry. Smug, even. "And enough to make you drive half an hour to get the answer, no less. Ever heard of a telephone? It would've saved you the trip."

"Are you saying you wish I hadn't come?" A distinct lack of control feeling seized Madeira. She'd never been in the position where she wanted a woman more than the woman wanted her, but life had thrust her off in an unknown direction with the enigmatic Gracie. It sucked. Gracie was definitely driving the bus on this weird journey, and she didn't even want Madeira on it. The sense of rejection, of being discounted, wasn't fun, and Madeira wondered, with a stab of guilt, how many times *she'd* been the cause of such feelings in others. Unintentionally, perhaps, but what did that matter? She toyed with the idea of apologizing to all the women she might have hurt or disappointed in the past, but quickly realized the list loomed too long, the task too daunting.

"Nope. That's not it at all."

Madeira smiled. Five little words grudgingly doled out, and her insides felt light. She needed some serious professional help.

"I'm just wondering why you aren't being up front with me about *why* you've come." Gracie's steady gaze challenged Madeira.

"Okay, fine. You want up front, I'll give it to you." The gig was up. Madeira lifted her arms and let them drop to her sides. She should've known better than to try and snow Gracie. "I didn't have a question; I just wanted to see you."

Gracie nodded, lips pressed flat, a bit of sadness around her eyes. Finally, she sighed. "Oh, Maddee. You understand there's no way—"

"Yeah, yeah. I know how you feel because you've made it explicitly clear. I'm not the woman for you and you're not interested. Believe me. I get it." Madeira leaned one hip against the wrought iron railing. "I'm not here to stand in the way of your grand life plans, Gracie, I just wanted to see you for a few minutes. Is that a crime in this country?"

"No. I just don't get why you wanted to see me."

"*Hijole madre,* are you always this skeptical?"

"I am these days," Gracie said.

Madeira laughed, a playfully exasperated sound. "Maybe I think you're cool."

"No question there, but that's beside the point." Gracie picked at some lint on her sleeve. "I'm trying to figure out your motive."

"People don't always have motives, *fierita.*"

Her expression droll, Gracie leaned her head to the side. "Uh, yes, they do. Not always bad ones, mind you, but motives nonetheless."

"Okay, then maybe I came to talk about the articles, I don't know. Maybe I came to talk about the accident."

"Did you?"

Madeira shrugged, looking into her eyes and trying to reach her, to locate and hold on to that vulnerable woman who'd clutched her pants leg and whispered, "Don't leave me," while they were trapped under the car. She was in there, beyond Gracie's impenetrable protective shell. Madeira knew it. "Maybe I came because it doesn't feel like we're finished and I just wanted to find out why. And you call me Maddee. No one—and I mean *no one*—calls me that."

For a minute, Gracie's face softened. The vulnerable woman peeked out, her expression hopeful and raw, then ducked into hiding again. Tough Gracie scoffed. "Good line."

Madeira didn't even feel like joking. Why could she see Gracie so clearly when Gracie remained so blind to Madeira? "It wasn't a line. I meant it." Frustrated, hurt, Madeira ran both hands through her hair. "Look, maybe I shouldn't have come. Maybe it was a mist—"

"No, I'm—" Gracie hung her head a minute, then leaned against the jamb and crossed her arms, offering a sheepish smile. "I apologize. I didn't mean to imply you aren't sincere."

Madeira's eyebrows raised in disbelief. "No?"

"Well, you can't blame me for being a little wary where you're concerned." Gracie's expression sobered, but her tone remained kind. "You do have a rep."

"We all have reps, don't we? What do they matter in the reality of it all?"

Gracie bit her full bottom lip and slanted an uncomfortable glance away.

"But you're the one who said we could be friends." Madeira softened her tone. "Remember?"

Gracie laughed nervously. "Doesn't 'let's be friends' usually mean 'don't call me, I'll call you' in player-speak?"

A pang of real hurt struck Madeira's middle. Hurt and annoyance that Gracie felt justified in calling Madeira a player when she was the one being played with Gracie's false offer of friendship. "Is that the way you meant it, Grace? As a kiss-off?"

"No," Gracie said quickly. "Not really. Not at all, actually." She sighed, removing the hair band and working her hair back into a slightly neater ponytail. "I don't know what I meant, Madeira. I just can't figure you out."

"Then don't try. Life doesn't have to be so intense."

"Easy for you to say."

"Maybe it is." Madeira shrugged without apology. "I have never agreed with people who take life so seriously that it passes them by. I have fun, Gracie, but that doesn't make me a bad person."

Gracie didn't reply, and something inside urged Madeira to continue, to *make* Gracie understand.

"Let me ask you this, and please be honest with me." Madeira narrowed her gaze on Gracie, intent on picking up every nuance of her body language. "If the newspaper thing had never happened, if you'd just looked for the woman who had crawled under your demolished car that day and found me, would you be this opposed to our friendship? Do you find me that unlikable?"

"I don't find you unlikable at all."

"No?" Madeira stepped back and feigned fear. "What do you do to your enemies? Shoot them on sight?"

Gracie regarded her drolly. "Do you want an answer to the question or not?"

Madeira inclined her head, allowing Gracie time to formulate an answer. She watched a cloud move over Gracie's expression as she pondered her question. Finally, this enigmatic woman sighed. "No."

Madeira blinked with confusion. "No, what?"

"I guess I wouldn't be opposed."

Arms spread, Madeira smiled. "Then forget it ever happened that way. Let's start over, Gracie. As friends."

Gracie studied Madeira from beneath thick, black lashes. "Just friends? You ever been friends with a woman before?"

Madeira's heart leapt, and she jacked up the flirt-o-meter a notch or two to test Gracie. "Sure. Just friends…or whatever you want. I aim to please. If I fail to please, I re-aim."

Gracie's gaze tangled with Madeira's for a few seconds before she huffed and shook her head. "You're persistent."

"And persuasive, no?" Madeira grinned.

"Don't push your luck," Gracie said, playfully vehement. "Friends or not, flirting will get you nowhere with me."

Madeira laughed, relieved they'd released some of the tension that stretched taut between them. "Fair enough." She glanced over Gracie's shoulder into the house. "So…can I come in? Hang out? Get this friend thing started?"

"Oh, um…" Gracie straightened, as though suddenly remembering where they were. Shooting a worried glance over her shoulder, she worried the corner of her lip between her teeth. Easing out onto the porch, she pulled the door mostly closed. "Actually, you see, I'm in the middle of cleaning house."

Madeira shrugged. "So? I'm not an inspector. See?" She held up her hands. "No white gloves. I can even help if you want."

"No, that's okay." Gracie seemed to cast about for a logical explanation.

"Then take a break from cleaning."

"Well, if you must know, Lola and I moved back home when my grandmother started having health problems, to care for her. This is my grandmother's house."

"That's good of you and Lola. But what's your point?"

"Well, they're both inside, and after all the excitement over the articles this morning, now's not the best time to—"

"Graciela?" The door squeaked open. A tiny, brown-skinned, white-haired woman peered out as she wiped white flour from her palms onto her apron. She reminded Madeira of her own *abuela*, and Madeira warmed to her immediately. DoDo's gaze widened as she took in Madeira, her remarkably smooth face showing surprise for a moment before her lips spread into a grin.

Madeira smiled back, bowing slightly. *"Buenas tardes."*

DoDo started to answer then turned a chiding look on her granddaughter. "Graciela Inez, where are your manners, making this young woman stand out on the porch when she comes to call at our home?"

The chastisement came as a surprise, and Grace's face flamed. Wasn't it enough she had to face Madeira looking like a bag lady who'd gotten rolled for her best clothes and had to resort to these? Now DoDo had to point out her rudeness. "I wasn't—"

"You should be ashamed of yourself. Did I raise you in the penitentiary?" She harrumphed and smacked Grace lightly in the shoulder. "And look at your clothes, *m'ija*. She's gonna think you're from the streets."

Affronted, Grace blinked down at her outfit, then looked helplessly from her grandmother to Madeira. Maddee merely stood there grinning—no help at all. Grace felt compelled to defend her questionable fashion choice. "But, DoDo, I was cleaning hou—"

"Oh, never mind. I'll deal with the hospitality." DoDo bestowed a weary, conspiratorial glance at Madeira. "You want something done right, you gotta do it yourself, *m'ijita*, no? *Oy yoy yoy*." Shedding her apron in record time, DoDo balled it in her able hands as her deep blue eyes studied Madeira. She smoothed the skirt of her housedress, then propped her fists on her rounded hips and released a decisive breath through her nose. "Now. Let me get a look at you."

"Ah, me first," Madeira said.

Grace watched in mute horror as Madeira flashed her octogenarian grandmother a brashly flirtatious once-over, ending her perusal with a grin. "This must be Graciela's sister, Lola, *verdad*? I can see the family resemblance."

Grace winced, expecting DoDo to call down all manner of punishment on Madeira for her lack of respect, but it didn't happen.

"Oh, you silly thing, flirting with an old woman." DoDo ducked her head and tittered behind her hand. "Your *mamá* ought to tan your shameless hide."

Grace froze, gaping at her grandmother.

DoDo *tittered.*

She actually stood there in the doorway fucking tittering while a lovely girlish blush rose to her face. This was insane! Realizing that the ball had already been set in motion, Grace slammed her jaw closed, swallowed,then mumbled her way through the common courtesy thing. "DoDo, this is Madeira Pacias, the woman who helped me after the accident."

"Of course, Graciela," DoDo reprimanded gently. "I recognize Señora Pacias from the news."

"*Por favor*, call me Madeira." Maddee lifted the older woman's fingers and bussed her knuckles with her lips.

Grace actually felt a coil of jealousy that Maddee's mouth wasn't on *her*. How twisted was that—jealous of her own grandmother? On the other hand, part of her was pleased at the way Madeira treated DoDo with extreme deference. DoDo seemed to like her. Too much for Grace's own good, actually. She flipped her hand toward her grandmother. "Anyway, Madeira, meet my *abuela*, Dolores Obregon."

Madeira inclined her head. "*Mucho gusto en conocerla, Señora Obregon*. The honor is all mine, I assure you."

"Oh, you." DoDo kept hold of Madeira's hand in her iron grip, tugging her over the threshold into the house. "Come on. And call me DoDo, *m'ijita*," she said, beaming as brightly as if the Pope had come calling. "Family calls me DoDo, and from now on, after the help you gave our Graciela, you are *familia*."

"Yes, ma'am. Again, I'm honored." Madeira tossed a bewildered but amused glance over her shoulder. Grace just shrugged in defeat and made desperate shooing motions with her hands to indicate it was out of their control now, and Maddee should simply follow DoDo. She supposed this was inevitable. Might as well get it over with.

DoDo fawned. "It's so wonderful to finally meet the woman who snatched my Graciela from the jaws of death."

Grace trailed helplessly behind, rolling her eyes at her grandmother's gushing melodrama.

"Ah, actually Graciela was the brave one that day, not me."

Grace blinked, surprised to find that Madeira seemed uncomfortable with the praise. How odd. Madeira might not have snatched Grace from death, as DoDo had romanticized it, but she certainly had kept her calm that day. Maddee deserved the praise. She'd earned it.

Still…brave? Grace?

Grace smiled. It pleased her to know that Maddee hadn't thought she'd acted like a big baby that day. She continued on behind them, a little lighter in her limp.

DoDo led them into the living room, jabbering all the way, and stopped by the arched entrance into the dining room. "Excuse me a moment," she said, pressing the button to the totally outdated intercom she'd had installed when Grace and Lola had been in high school. She'd used it mostly to order them to turn down their music whenever it threatened to vibrate her precious knickknacks from their wall-mounted, shadow-box displays.

Finger on the button, DoDo leaned toward the box. "Lolita?"

"Is lunch ready, DoDo?"

"No," DoDo said, her tone almost singsongy. "But Graciela's friend is here."

"Grace's who—ohmigod!"

Grace groaned. Brrrrother, here came the tornado. Just as she expected, Lola's footsteps pummeled the stairs as though death itself nipped at her heels. She skidded to a stocking-footed stop on the hardwood landing at the bottom.

"Ohmigod!" she squealed again, hands pressed to her cheeks. "You're even hotter in person! You're an absolute goddess. Grace, why didn't you tell me that the pictures didn't do her justice?"

Madeira laughed, meeting Grace's gaze pointedly. She straightened her collar with a smart snap of her wrists. "Now there's the way a woman likes to be greeted."

Please. Did Maddee have to flirt with everyone, including her sister and her freaking grandmother? "Lola? Show some class. And, Madeira? Have you no shame? This is my sister, you'll recall. The one who practically destroyed our lives?"

"Oh, what do *you* know?" Lola flicked her nails at Grace, her close scrutiny never leaving Madeira. "Clearly not a good woman when you see one."

Madeira glanced at Grace in surprise.

"Hey, I warned you about her." Grace peered at Madeira with a "you're on your own, babe" expression, then walked over to the couch and sank onto it. This little impromptu visit might actually work in her favor. Sure, they'd agreed to be friends, but how realistic was that? Her heart couldn't handle palling around with a woman to whom she was so attracted. Only the worst could come of that arrangement.

Don't picture it.

But the beauty? None of it mattered now that DoDo had busted them on the stoop. Once Madeira was exposed to a full-blast dose of Lola and DoDo, she'd be ass over teakettle in her urgency to escape. Then and only then would Grace be safe, she decided. Smug, she sat back to watch Madeira craft her exit.

Instead of stammering her excuses and fleeing from the house, Madeira grinned at Lola. "Little Lola Obregon," she drawled, spreading her arms for a hug. "The woman responsible for reuniting us. Come here and let me thank you properly."

Lola laughed and accepted the embrace, mouthing "Oh my GOD," to Grace over her shoulder and shaking her hand as though to convey Madeira's "hottie" status.

Grace wanted to flip Lola the bird, but DoDo was watching, and she didn't relish the thought of getting her ears boxed. Instead, she cleared her throat. "Maddee can't stay. Right?"

Madeira turned toward her and bestowed a glittery smile, despite the fact Grace's announcement had been rather rude. "Actually, that is right." She peered down at the face of her watch. "I just stopped by to see if Grace had seen the articles."

"We all saw them. I thought they were terribly romantic," Lola offered.

"Gee, what a surprise," Grace muttered.

Lola made a face. "Killjoy."

"Flake."

"Pessimist."

"Sap."

"Mule."

"Whore."

"Girls!" DoDo dispensed with a glare that shut them down immediately. She peered down her nose quite effectively at Grace, despite her four-foot-ten stature. "*Con esa boca comes,* Graciela? You can eat with that mouth?"

"I'm sorry, DoDo. I got carried away." She probably shouldn't have resorted to calling her sister a whore, not in front of DoDo.

"I'll say. Using such language in front of guests," DoDo muttered. "Street urchins." She pointed at Grace, then at Lola. "You two apologize to Madeira."

Grace felt ten years old and now *really* regretted her word choice and immature display. But Lola started it! What the hell, it wasn't her job to impress Madeira Goddamn Pacias. She wasn't the most mature woman in the world either.

"Maddee doesn't care."

DoDo loomed ominously. "*I* care. Unless you wanna be on the outside lookin' in, you start spouting the apologies."

With a sigh, Grace glanced at Lola. Lola shrugged. "Sorry," they chimed listlessly, in stereo.

Madeira simply stood there, lips twitching, doing her best not to laugh.

The tiny general turned toward their guest, all sweetness and adoration. "Now that we've cleared that up." She knotted her gnarled hands. "Please stay for lunch so we can get acquainted."

"Oh. Well. I don't know."

Grace could tell Madeira felt supremely uncomfortable disappointing DoDo. Part of her wanted to pity Madeira until she reminded herself, *Madeira* brought this on herself stopping by uninvited and stirring up her life. So there.

Still, Grace watched Madeira, wondering how she'd get out of it. The more she watched her, the more it became about watching her. Grace sighed. Lola was right—the pictures didn't do her justice. With her work-honed muscles and carefully casual clothing, Madeira made Halle Berry look like a BEFORE picture. That took some doing.

Had Madeira really stopped by just to see her? Her stomach toppled with flattery. She'd been so surprised, so psyched, so dismayed, so elated, so scared when she'd opened the door and seen Madeira standing there. None of it made sense. Madeira was a dead end. Grace knew she shouldn't see her, as friends or otherwise, yet deep inside it just felt right.

"Idiot," Grace muttered to herself.

Everyone turned toward her. DoDo's face reddened, and looked ready to dole out a few head smacks. "I can't pop my nitro like candy, you know." She patted the left side of her chest as if to remind Grace of her heart problems.

Grace smiled wanly. "Sorry, I was just thinking aloud."

Madeira watched her thoughtfully for a minute, then turned back to DoDo. "I appreciate the offer, but I have to work in a little bit."

"It's okay, *m'ijita*. No need to apologize. Work comes first. You'll just have to come back for a proper dinner sometime next week, yes?"

"DoDo," Grace warned her gently. "Maybe Maddee has other plans."

"Every night?" DoDo arched her brows.

"I think dinner is a great idea," Lola interjected, drawing out the *r* in "great" like Tony the Tiger. She watched the situation with amusement, taking advantage of the opportunity to dish out paybacks to Grace. "We owe it to you anyway for helping Grace, and I'm *sure* she'd love to have you over, right, Grace?"

She glared at Lola, trying to decide between Nair in the shower cap or itching powder in the underwear drawer.

"Graciela?" DoDo prompted, in a tone that said she would stand for no further rudeness.

Grace forced a saccharin smile. "Sure. Come on over."

Appeased, DoDo patted Madeira's arm. "*Sí*. It's the least we can do. What do you say? Will Wednesday evening work?"

Grace buried her face in her hands for a moment before looking up again. Much as she loved DoDo, and despite the fact she hadn't thought twice about selling her condo and moving back in to care for the woman who had raised her, sometimes she wished she had her own place again. Like, right now, for example, and she wouldn't mind if it was in Costa Rica.

"Actually, I work evenings all this week," Madeira said.

A reprieve! Grace bounced up from the couch and grabbed her elbow, herding her doorward. "Bummer, sorry we couldn't work it out. I'll walk you to your truck."

"Next Sunday, then," DoDo insisted, ignoring her granddaughter. "Do you work then?"

"No, I don't. But really, it's not necessary."

"What, necessary? What does necessity have to do with anything? It's a simple dinner invitation," Lola said. "You can't disappoint DoDo. Plus, she's a really good cook."

"I bet she is." Madeira hedged, and Grace had the sudden impression Maddee was doing so on Grace's behalf. Either that or the whole thing was getting too domestic for Madeira, which was the more likely scenario. Still, she felt unduly touched.

Madeira looked her way and their gazes locked. Once again she had that eerie feeling of being a team, Grace and Madeira against the world. Madeira *did* mean to respect her wishes about this dinner thing, and that pleased her.

"What do you think?" Madeira's husky tone touched her like a rough-soft hand on naked, heated flesh. "Is dinner an imposition for you, Gracie?"

Lola and DoDo gasped simultaneously, their eyes round with wonder and shock.

Grace flinched. Oops. Fuckity-fuck. She'd meant to speak to Madeira about tossing around that nickname before Madeira met her family. Or actually, she'd meant to keep her away from her family altogether, but whatever. Madeira had caught her by surprise, and now Grace was screwed.

Madeira blinked at them, a small worried frown bisecting her forehead. "What's wrong?"

"Nothing, *m'ija*," DoDo breathed, her expression dreamy.

Madeira shared a perplexed frown with Grace, splaying her palm on her chest. "Did I say something?"

"No. It's nothing," Grace lied. Damnit, why hadn't she remembered? Probably because she loved the way her name, Mama's special name for her, sounded on Madeira's tongue. "It's just that… well, to be honest, no one has called me Gracie since…since—"

"Since our mama died," Lola told her.

Madeira startled.

"It was her special nickname for Grace. No one calls her…that… except Mama."

"And now our Madeira," DoDo said, in a reverent whisper, her eyes shinier than usual. "It's a sign."

"No, it isn't," Gracie insisted. She turned to Madeira. Her smile was meant to reassure, but it felt like more of a grimace. "Don't worry. It's not a sign."

"A sign of what?" Madeira became more baffled by the moment, totally out of her element.

Grace kind of liked Maddee looking that way. "Nothing," Grace said, just as Lola said, "Destiny."

"Not freaking destiny, you idiot." Grace jabbed a finger toward Lola, a warning scowl on her face. "It's not even a sign."

"Destiny," DoDo reiterated, nodding. She smiled benevolently at Madeira. "And don't you listen to our foul-mouthed Graciela, *m'ija*. It's definitely a sign."

After escaping the funny farm known as her house without any of the inmates following, Grace shuffled Madeira into her truck and leaned against the doorjamb. "Look, don't feel obligated to come to dinner next weekend. I appreciate your gracious handling of my psychotic relatives, but you don't owe Lola or DoDo anything. They always put people on the spot."

Madeira's eyes narrowed, and for a moment she didn't speak. When she finally did, her tone was hard to read. "I like them. I just didn't want to step on your toes. If it's okay with you, I'd like to come."

"Oh." The single word had sounded disappointed, so Grace vied to pep it up a bit, even managed a smile. "Really? I'd have thought you'd be dying to get away."

"Not at all, Gracie." Maddee looked slightly affronted. "I miss my sisters and mother, and DoDo reminds me of my *abuelita*. Plus, you heard her. I'm *familia* now."

Grace shrugged, trying to play it off that she didn't care if Madeira showed up or not. In truth, the very prospect of seeing Maddee again in seven days made Grace go crazy inside. Crazy-good, and crazy-bad—an even mix. She didn't want to want Maddee, but if she kept showing up and insinuating herself into Grace's life, what choice did that leave her? "Okay, then I guess dinner next Sunday." At least she'd have a full week away from her to batten down her emotional hatches. Maybe she could find a suitable decoy date by then to throw her off.

"Perfect." Madeira drummed her hand on the door of her car. "Hey, what was all that stuff about the signs?"

"Just a bunch of cosmic *curandera* woo-woo crap. Nothing to worry about." Grace brushed a little road dust off Maddee's side mirror, then wiped her fingers on her tragically worn-out pants. "DoDo believes the universe sends us signs, and that it's our duty to notice them if we want to live the lives we were meant to."

Madeira pursed her lips. "You don't believe it?"

Grace laughed, a little nervously, unwilling to admit how often she'd wondered if Maddee and the whole weird path of their "relationship"—term used loosely—was some kind of a sign. "Well, I try not to. But sometimes she makes me wonder."

"Signs." Madeira toyed with the idea, then feigned a shiver. "Makes me want to go to church and confess."

"I'd urge against it," Grace teased. "Shocking a priest to death won't serve you well in the afterlife."

Laughing, Madeira switched on her ignition, and Grace stepped back, slipping her hands into her back pockets, feeling Maddee's absence already, like the kind of wound that sent a reminder twinge now and then. "See you Sunday, Gracie."

Grace opened her mouth as if to speak, then closed it again.

"What?"

"You can still change your mind and not come. It's okay."

A faint line of annoyance bisected Madeira's brow. "I have no intention of doing that. I made your grandmother a promise, and regardless of what you think of me, I'm honorable. I intend to stick by my word."

"I never meant you weren't—" Grace sighed. "You realize that this changes nothing between us, right? Friends, okay, but my sister and DoDo have other ideas."

A small huff escaped Madeira's lungs, and for a moment she just stared forward. "Gracie, do you want to get married? The commitment ceremony, the rings, the whole thing?"

Grace blanched. A split second passed where she thought Madeira was suggesting they take this inconceivable route. She came to her senses quickly, realizing it was more of a survey question, but how to answer now that she could barely remember her own name?

Wait—she had nothing to hide from Madeira. "No. I mean, possibly yes. Someday I want to commit to a partner. But not until I get my career under way and find the right person. I'm in no hurry and I'm not going to settle."

Madeira draped her arm along the window well. "So, that's out for you right now?"

Grace nodded. "Totally."

"Then why do you continue to fight so hard against us?" Madeira gave her what Grace assumed was supposed to be a calming smile. "I'm not trying to claim you forever. It's just a casual thing."

Grace shook her head sadly. Could Madeira be any more clueless? "That's exactly why we're so totally wrong for each other, Madeira."

"Huh?"

"Trust me, I've had more than my fair share of *casual things* and I'm not in the market for another one." A beat passed. "Not even with you."

Understanding dawned in Madeira's eyes, veiled with even more questions. "How will you know if something's right if you don't start with casual?"

Grace shrugged. "I'll just know."

"I thought you didn't believe in signs?"

"Well…I'm hopeful."

Madeira ran her fingers through her hair, looking rumpled with confusion and frustration. "So, let me ask you this, then. If I *were* serious, if my intent was to make you mine forever, would you be more willing to date me?"

Grace's chest heated, and she stared off down the street, the breeze lifting her hair. "No. It's not that easy."

"*Híjole.* I don't get you. Why not?"

Grace sighed. "Look. I like you. I really do. And after the whole accident and everything else we've been through, I do feel a sense of connection." She chewed on her lip.

"But?"

"But even if you were supposedly trying to get me to the commitment stage, I wouldn't date you. Because, frankly, you aren't the commitment type." She paused for effect, then dipped her chin, gently challenging her to deny it. "Are you?"

Madeira didn't answer the question Grace asked. A muscle in her temple jumped. "Are you dating someone else? Is that it?"

"Maybe."

"Are you?"

"That's not the point."

Madeira stared straight ahead for a few moments before turning to face Grace. "You never told me why the bear's named Ms. Right."

The abrupt change of subject threw Grace, and she swallowed a few times before answering. "Mama named her. She said she wished she could promise me I'd find my Ms. Right—"

"She knew you were gay back then?"

Grace nodded. "Most of the women in my family have this… stupid sixth sense. But anyway, Mama said a so-called Ms. Right most likely didn't exist, so the bear would have to do." She smiled wistfully. "Lola has a little dog named Princess Charming for the same reason."

Madeira's gaze warmed. "So, your mamá was, ah, a little jaded about love?"

"You could say that."

"Even about your father?"

Grace sniffed, as if it didn't matter. "Don't know. I never knew him. He skipped the instant she peed on the stick and their relationship stopped being about *fun*. See? Mama had valid reasons for being jaded."

"Hmm. Looks like Gracie is following in Mama's footsteps."

Her startled expression told Madeira she'd never looked at it that way. "I'm not jaded."

Madeira scoffed, but her expression sobered. "Yeah, sure. And I don't want to pull you through this window and kiss you breathless right now."

Her engine gunned, and with one staccato squeal of her tires, Madeira left Grace standing in silence, trying to deal with the impact, the promise of those words.

CHAPTER EIGHT

Él que nace para mulo del cielo la cae el arnés—policía del cielo le cae el bolillo.
He who is born to be hanged shall never be drowned—you can't escape your destiny.

Madeira sat sprawled on a plastic chair in the back of the training room, barely paying attention to the president of the EMS Benefit Committee, who addressed the group from the podium up front. On duty or off, they'd all come together to discuss the upcoming EMS Singles Auction. In exactly one month, Madeira, along with every other "unattached" EMT and paramedic, male or female, would be auctioned off as a one-night "escort" to raise money for new rigs, which they badly needed. The whole thing was in good taste and for a worthy cause. She'd show up, she'd charm the elderly philanthropists, and she'd do her best to live up to the donation she brought in. But the only thing on Madeira's mind at the moment was Gracie and her latest rejection.

When Madeira thought hard about it, the thing that hurt the most was that Gracie *did* want to find the right woman, but Madeira wasn't in the running. Not even close. She had a good sense Gracie would consider the Singles Auction yet another strike against Madeira in the suitability department, and that bummed her out.

"Pacias? Yo, Madeira," called the president, Buzz Willmont.

Simon threw Madeira an elbow and hiked his chin toward the front.

Startled out of her brooding, Madeira sat up straighter. "Yes?"

The man's eyes sparkled with mischief. "You still in for the gig?"

Confusion pulled a frown into Madeira's forehead. "Of course. Why wouldn't I be?"

A ripple of amusement moved through the room, and Madeira glanced around to find all her coworkers leering at her.

Buzz garnered support for his ribbing from the laughter. "Well, we all know the newspaper doesn't tell the whole truth and nothing but—"

"That's no lie," someone hollered.

"Still, it seemed clear that your, ah, hot little accident victim had staked her claim. We didn't want to be stepping on any pretty toes with this thing. Unattached medics *only* on the auction block. That's the rule." More chuckles and muffled jeers.

From a place of pure political correctness, Buzz made eye contact with various female medics in the room. "No offense to any of you women with that hottie comment about Madeira's girlfriend, but we all saw her."

"HAWT," someone yelled.

Madeira's throat tightened to hear Gracie referred to that way. Girlfriend. She wished.

Wait—no, I don't.

Do I…?

"Yeah, we're used to you," one of the married female medics said, wryly. "You never mean offense, do you?"

Buzz grinned, then looked back at Madeira. "So, you a bought and paid-for woman now, Ms. Pac-Man, or what?"

Madeira stifled a sigh, flashing Buzz what she hoped was a nonchalant smile. "No. That was just…" She didn't want to explain this thing with Gracie to her coworkers. She couldn't even figure it out in her own mind. "Whatever. Anyway, Buzz. I'm in for the auction."

"Does that mean Grace is available?" someone else yelled.

A blinding blaze of red filled Madeira's head. "Not for you," she said with a dead calm, not even knowing who had called out the question. Didn't matter. No one in this room was good enough for Gracie. Probably not even Madeira herself. She finished the retort with a benevolent smile, not wanting to antagonize a colleague. She was still a probie and valued her good working relationship with people.

Buzz ignored the banter volleying around the room. "In that case, if you're sure you're in and you don't mind, we'd like to exploit you a bit."

The hair at the back of Madeira's neck prickled. "How?"

Buzz crossed his arms and spread his legs wide. "Not to make you sound like a hooker, but we think we'll be able to get top dollar for you with all this publicity, which is a good thing."

"I feel like a piece of meat," Madeira muttered to Simon, "not that I'm complaining."

"Damn straight," Simon said. "All you singles are meat that night, and don't you forget it. Meat that's gonna buy us five new rigs, if we're lucky."

"Okay. What did you have in mind?" Madeira asked Buzz, casually slouching in her seat, adjusting her trauma shears so they didn't dig into her thigh. She and Simon were on-duty, but the radio was silent.

"We'd like to take photos of you and then print up some promo posters with you front and center. Grimson came up with a great slogan to tie in with the newspaper articles. It'll be laid out like an old west wanted poster, your picture with 'The Thief of Hearts' at the top. Then, on the bottom"—he spread his hands as though displaying a marquee—"will be Grimson's slogan: Some hearts can't be stolen, but they can *all* be bought. Find out how at the First Annual EMS Benefit Singles Auction."

Madeira had to admit, the slogan was clever. It would likely draw in people who had never intended to show up. Gracie would smirk when she read it, thinking Madeira had eagerly volunteered to be marketed in such a way, but truthfully? Madeira had all but given up hope of changing Gracie's attitude toward her. "Sounds good," Madeira said, without much enthusiasm. "Say when, and I'll be there."

"Tomorrow. Noon."

Madeira nodded. The meeting moved on to other topics, and Madeira slumped back into her chair, lost in thoughts about a pretty third-grade teacher who made her want to get schooled.

As though reading her mind, Simon leaned in. "I bet she'd pay top dollar for you if she could afford it."

Madeira huffed a decidedly humorless laugh, not even attempting to pretend she didn't know who Simon meant. "Gracie wouldn't even come to something like this, Fletch."

"I bet you'd be surprised. Invite her."

Madeira gaped at her paramedic partner. "Bring a date to a bachelor/bachelorette auction? When I'm on the auction block?" Madeira laughed and gave him a look that said the idea wasn't just bad, it was flat fucking crazy. "Fletch, buddy, you've been out of the dating game too long if you think that ploy has a chance in hell of working."

"Yeah, thank God I'm out of that game."

Madeira did a double take.

Simon shrugged. "What? I love my comfortable life and my comfortable wife. I know you think you've got it made with your… ways, but you don't know what you're missing, Mad. I can't imagine having to get used to a different woman all the time." He shuddered, propping one booted ankle across the other knee.

Come to think of it, that was one downfall of prowling the scene. The variety was great, but no one ever seemed to get close. Then again, until she'd met Gracie, Madeira had never wanted anyone close.

Why was that?

"Look," Madeira said, staring straight ahead. "Gracie already thinks I'm a player—"

"Which you are."

"Granted. But Gracie also has zero interest in dating me, even for one night, even for a good cause. She wouldn't come to the auction."

Simon didn't answer for a long time. Madeira peered over. "Did you hear anything I said?"

"Shh." Simon held up a hand. "Aren't you listening?"

Madeira glanced toward the front, then back at her partner. "No, I'm talking to you."

"Well, I can multitask. And if you ever want to make it through P-school, you need to master that skill, too."

Madeira tried to catch up on the conversation. "What's up?"

"Sounds like they have a problem with the auction that you, and you alone, can fix. Hang on." Simon held up his hand, and Buzz acknowledged him immediately.

"You have an idea, Fletch?"

"Yes, the best idea. Madeira's…" Fletch angled a glance downward, as though choosing his words carefully "Grace Obregon used to tend bar for a living. I'll bet Madeira can convince her to bartend for the auction for a reduced fee or free, and that will further tie this thing into the newspaper articles—"

"Are you out of your damn mind?" Madeira rasped, gripping Simon's arm.

"Mad, we don't have a bartender," Simon said in an urgent whisper. "Which could ruin this whole event. And we need those rigs."

Madeira didn't argue.

"This is a great way for you to get Grace to the auction without asking her on a date."

"I don't *want* her at the auction."

"That's a great idea," Buzz said, loud and enthusiastic. From the rumbling through the room, her colleagues agreed. "Some of us married guys can work as bar backs and waiters, but we really need a professional to head everything up." Buzz hiked his chin toward Madeira. "Think you can talk her into it?"

Madeira seriously wanted to hurl. Buzz stared back. Slowly, other medics turned, until almost the whole room of hopeful faces had turned her way.

With effort, Madeira managed a sick smile, wondering how the hell she was going to convince Gracie to do this *and* survive her presence while Madeira strutted her stuff for high dollar bids. Still, Madeira knew she couldn't let the other medics down. Knew she wouldn't, no matter how horrible the task, how much it would prove to Grace things about Madeira that just weren't true. "Can't hurt to ask, right?"

❖

"Hey, Grace."

Grace looked up from her desk where she sat grading papers to find Niki's much-welcome face in her doorway. She had been enjoying the solitude since school let out. Try as she might to keep the focus on her lessons these first two days since the articles hit, all the pupils wanted to talk about was the newspaper articles, the crash, and the Thief of Hearts. She couldn't blame them. They were just kids. From the questions they asked, she figured many of them were fronting queries for their curious mothers anyway. Still, it was good to see a friendly, unquestioning face. She smiled and set aside her pen. "Hi, Nik. What's up?"

"Tanforan has called a quick faculty meeting in the cafeteria. I'm rounding everyone up."

"Oh." Grace stood, trepidation loosening her limbs, though the reaction made no sense whatsoever. Tanforan was an abstract thinker and a brilliant man. He often called impromptu meetings when an idea struck him. Grace pulled her cardigan off the back of her chair and stooped to lock the bottom drawer of her desk where she kept her small backpack. Picking up her planning calendar, she glanced at Nik. "Is something wrong?"

Nik shrugged. "Don't know. He didn't seem upset, though. If anything, I sensed a little excitement in the air."

"That's good news. Maybe we're all getting raises."

"Ha."

They hurried down the hall, and Grace found herself taking larger steps than was comfortable. She flinched when her leg twinged, slowing immediately.

Nik peered down, steadying her with a hand on her elbow. "You okay? How's it feeling?"

"A little overworked, actually. It's been bothering me since our walk yesterday." Bent forward, she kneaded the scar tissue for a moment, then peered up at Nik. "Can we skip the walk today?"

"No problem." Nik patted her back. "I'll even give you a lift home after the meeting, if you'd like."

She flashed a grateful smile as they filed into the cafeteria behind the three sixth-grade teachers. "I'd appreciate that."

Niki had been a good friend to Grace ever since her first day of college, when she'd been more overwhelmed than anything. After attending her first class, she realized with dismay that the majority of the other freshmen were about six years younger than she, and most of them treated her like an oddity rather than a classmate. Niki never treated her as if she were different, because *Niki* was different, too. Despite their seven-year age gap—Nik had graduated from high school at seventeen—they'd both come to college to study and learn rather than party. That set them apart *and* threw them together, and they'd been pals ever since.

Not to mention, they were both lesbians.

Nik had always been a bookish, unassuming type. Theirs was a solid friendship built on mutual acceptance of each other's true selves more than anything else.

Nik had been valedictorian of her high school class and finished college at age twenty with a slew of honors and infinite possibilities.

When she'd chosen teaching instead of a more prestigious, lucrative field, most of the people in her life were scandalized. Nik's parents believed she'd thrown away her potential, but Nik was the rare sort of person who realized that a good teacher early in life could set even the most disadvantaged child on the path to greatness. She wanted to be that teacher, that conduit, to inspire as many children as she possibly could.

Grace respected that goal more than she could even say. Nik, in turn, respected her—tattoos, bad rep, and all. Other than Lola, Niki was probably the only person who knew all about Grace's wild past and poor life choices and didn't hold them against her or use them to place her in some sort of mental box. She saw the person Grace wanted to be, and how rare was that quality in a friend? Two friends, actually. Nik's longtime partner, Bree, was a welcome part of the friendship package.

Nik had been with Bree since the day they graduated from high school. The two planned to marry in Canada as soon as Bree finished her education, which would be years down the road since she'd just entered med school with the goal of becoming a pediatric neurosurgeon. Nik always joked that she and Bree were perfectly matched, because Bree wanted to get into kids' heads and Nik had chosen to get into their hearts. Grace just felt lucky to have the two of them in her corner.

Niki had helped her get this job, and she'd been instrumental in helping her keep it after the accident. She owed Niki…so much.

They took seats at the cafeteria tables, chatting with the other teachers until Wes Tanforan swept in. He greeted everyone as he moved toward the front, pausing to pat Grace on the shoulder.

"How's the leg?"

"Fine, thanks. Niki's been helping me rehabilitate."

Tanforan patted Niki as well, then headed to the front table. "Thanks for gathering, folks. I know I tore some of you away from your favorite task, paper grading," he said wryly, garnering some soft laughter. He smoothed his windblown hair. "I wanted to see how these first couple days went…but I've decided we need to address the media coverage of our own Miss Obregon with the students."

Grace's stomach plunged, and the mild smile froze on her face, transforming into something garish. Was Dr. Tanforan going to fire her right in front of her peers?

"Don't worry," Nik whispered. "You're fine. Just breathe. He wouldn't bring you in front of everyone to burn you at the proverbial stake."

Grace couldn't even nod. Her heart rattled, and tension pulled the skin on her head taut.

Tanforan held up the *Post* article and another couple from smaller papers. "The kids can't stop talking about this, as I'm sure you all know." The teachers laughed and commented, and Grace said a silent but fervent prayer that she would be zapped into vapor and whisked out of the room on a breeze.

She finally managed to clear her throat. "I-I'm sorry if this has disrupted your classrooms," she stammered, glancing around at the teachers without really seeing any of them.

"No, no, Grace. You misunderstand. I just think it's the perfect opportunity to incorporate this experience into our lesson plans," Tanforan finished.

Gracie's racing thoughts screeched to a dead stop. She replayed the man's words. Had he said "the perfect opportunity"? Her jaw slackened.

"That's a great idea," said one of the sixth-grade teachers, jotting a note in her calendar. She turned and smiled toward Grace. "It's a fantastic chance to focus on a media lesson, now when the kids can truly relate it to themselves."

"Exactly."

Grace eased a breath through her lips and laid her hands in her lap to steady her quaking legs. Okay, maybe this wasn't quite the end of the world she'd imagined. *Chill, Grace. Just listen to the man.*

"Told you," whispered Nik, as though reading her mind.

She flashed a small but grateful smile.

Tanforan uncapped a marker and flipped over a fresh sheet of paper on the large easel to his left. "Let's brainstorm some ideas on how to do this school-wide. I really want it to be a team effort. Grace? Do you have any ideas to start us off?"

She swallowed. "Well, this comes as a bit of a surprise. Let me think for a minute."

"I could focus on sports and exercise to overcome injuries," Niki offered.

"Super. That's just the kind of ideas I want to hear. Think past the media coverage itself, to the bigger picture." The Magic Marker squeaked as Tanforan listed Niki's idea on the paper in angular drafter's printing. Grace found the sound both familiar and comfortable.

"I'd like to do something on the power of the media, though," said one of the English teachers. "It fits in with the propaganda lessons I have on schedule."

"Of course." Tanforan added it to the list.

As the ideas flew, Grace became caught up in the excitement of the faculty, grateful that the media coverage hadn't blown up in her face. She had just begun to feel all sappy emotional and swamped with gratitude over her wonderful job and supportive colleagues when the health teacher raised her hand.

"Yes, Betty?"

She shot a glance toward Grace. "I think this would be a splendid opportunity to teach the children about accident prevention and first aid. Maybe Grace could ask the, uh, Samaritan to give a school-wide presentation on the topic."

Excited chatter drifted up from the assemblage. Grace wanted to puke.

"She and her partner could bring the ambulance," Betty added. "The kids would love it."

"We can even use it to segue into a discussion about the importance of helping others," offered the school nurse.

Tanforan beamed approval as the brainstorming picked up speed. Grace slumped in her chair. Just what she needed—another reason to be around Madeira. And yet, they'd expect her to pull this off. All the teachers, with the exception of Niki, no doubt believed what they'd read in the papers, that she and Madeira were romantically involved. It would only stand to reason, then, that Madeira would accept such a request. Grace couldn't very well tell everyone she didn't have any such significant other–type clout without coming clean about having duped the media. What kind of example would that set for the kids? What would her colleagues think of her?

The thing was, Madeira would probably jump on the chance to invade this part of Grace's life, too, persistent bugger that she was. Childish as it sounded, Grace didn't want Maddee encroaching upon school, the only Madeira-free haven she had left.

From the enthusiastic murmuring moving through the cafeteria, she got the distinct impression she was the only person who thought this visit from Madeira was a monumentally bad idea.

For the second time during the relatively short meeting, Niki leaned toward her and whispered, “You’re okay. Just breathe.”

Tanforan held up a hand to quiet the crowd. When the mumbling had dwindled, he glanced toward Grace and raised his brows. “What do you think, Grace? Can you talk her into it?”

Grace managed a sick smile, wondering how the hell she was going to convince Madeira to bow out of this gracefully. Then again, she didn’t want to let the other teachers down, so maybe she should just suck it up and suffer Maddee’s presence. Oh, who knew, anymore?

She hiked a shoulder. “Can’t hurt to ask, right?”

“We’ve always been honest with each other, haven’t we, Grace?” Niki kept her eyes on the road.

“Of course.” She peered curiously at her longtime friend. “What’s up?”

Nik paused, as if searching for the correct words. “I’m having a hard time figuring out why you’re fighting against this Pacias woman so hard.”

Grace bit back her surprise over the statement and laid her head back against the headrest. “You know why, Nik. She’s the kind of woman I’ve sworn off of.”

“But is she really?” Niki flashed Grace a quick glance, then returned her focus to the winding pavement ahead.

“What do you mean? The chick has dated, like, a million women. A long-term relationship for Madeira is one where she remembers the woman’s name after she makes her breakfast.”

“You know this for certain?”

Grace sniffed. “Maddee doesn’t deny it. And she’s a big flirt.”

“Yeah?” Nik nodded sagely. “Well, I know this really great woman who has also dated, like, a million other women and she can be a big flirt when she wants to. Granted, she has had a few longer-term relationships, but I also know for a fact that she went through a serious biker phase during which she dated women named Lurch, Mongrel, and Rat. And despite all that, I wouldn't hesitate to fix her up with my best friend."

Grace warmed with the compliment. "Rat wasn't *that* bad."

"Are you talking about the same Rat I'm thinking of?" Nik stopped for a red light and pinned her with a stare. "I guess you've blocked out Rat's late-night motorcycle repair parties on your living room carpet. You know, the ones that got you evicted? Or the fact that her favorite Harley-Davidson T-shirt said 'If you can read this, the bitch fell off' on the back?"

"Hmm." She crinkled her nose. "I did hate that shirt. And, okay. Getting evicted wasn't a walk in the park."

"Exactly." A pause. "Has Madeira pulled any such egregious acts?"

Grace let the moment stretch silently. She wrapped her hand around the shoulder strap of her seat belt. "Well…no."

Nik inclined her head, as if to say she didn't think so. "Do you want my impressions of Madeira, just from the newspaper articles and what you've told me?"

No. "I guess."

Nik turned off the main thoroughfare into Grace's neighborhood. "She and her sister moved to this country to make money for their family back in Mexico."

"Pretty common."

"Sure, but they turned a grassroots community gardening project into a nationwide nonprofit, and Madeira worked as a project manager. My guess is not for much money."

Nik paused.

Grace said nothing, so she continued.

"Then Madeira stopped to help you on the accident scene, put herself in harm's way by crawling beneath your demolished car, soothed your fears, right?"

"Yes." Grace focused her gaze out the passenger side window. She wasn't sure she liked having Madeira's good points laid out this boldly. It made the damn woman sound perfect.

"She kept Ms. Right *for a year*, even though she thought you were dead. And apparently the accident—indeed, meeting and trying to help *you*—impacted her so deeply, she left her job to pursue a career in paramedicine."

Grace held up her index finger. "We don't know that for sure. Maddee's never talked about it."

"Well"—Nik hiked one shoulder—"what else could've prompted such a life change? It only makes sense."

"Okay, I'll give you that."

"According to you, she's charming, likable, kind—"

"And a big flirt."

"Your family likes her. You like her—"

"Not like that."

"Grace," Niki said, her tone droll. "Was I born yesterday?"

Grace quirked her mouth to the side. "Practically."

Niki grinned but ignored the playful barb. "Anyway, don't you see how different Madeira is from, say…Rat?"

"Well, sure. But—"

"Or Lurch. I mean, honey, her nickname was *Lurch.* And how many times did you bail Lurch out of jail after she drove drunk?"

That memory still pained Grace. It had been a real low point in her life, and bailing out a drunk driver would always be one of her biggest regrets. She bit her lip. "Three times."

"Three times. Three bail bonds and one eviction. And yet, you put Madeira in the same category with those…choices."

"Not exactly the same category, Niki, and not for the same reasons." She sighed, running fingers through her hair and pulling it away from her forehead. "Madeira is great in a lot of ways, sure. But I can't see her ever being faithful to one woman. Epic fail. She's automatically out."

"Grace, babe, when I first met you, I couldn't see *you* being faithful to one woman."

Heat suffused Grace's skin. "What are you trying to say?"

Niki reached over and covered Grace's hand, flashing an apologetic smile. "I say this with the utmost love and respect because you're my second best friend next to Bree." Niki paused, and Grace held her breath. "Don't be so hypocritical as to judge Madeira more harshly than you'd judge yourself. She doesn't sound at all like your ex-girlfriends." A beat passed. "She sounds exactly like *you.*"

Defensiveness stiffened Grace's spine. "But I've changed."

Nik squeezed her hand and smiled. "Ah, yes. And I guess you're the only person in history to have accomplished that, hmm?"

Grace shook her head, equal parts sheepish and defensive. "Not the point."

"You're fighting too hard, G. And as your friend, as someone who loves you, warts and all, that tells me you're afraid. Probably because Madeira's perfect for you, and you just can't accept the fact that you deserve her."

Grace stared at Niki's smooth, angled profile, and had just opened her mouth to explain that she didn't *want* Madeira, deserving or not, when Niki turned onto her street.

Nik's expression morphed into one of panic, and she accelerated. "Holy crap," she said.

"What?" Grace glanced toward her house and saw an ambulance idling in the driveway. The front door to the house stood open. Her pulse took off at a gallop toward a murky, desperate destination she didn't even want to ponder. All thoughts, all worries, all considerations fled, except one.

DoDo.

CHAPTER NINE

Amor no respeta ley, ni obedece a rey.
Love laughs at locksmiths.

Niki threw her shoulder under Grace's arm to help her rush up the sidewalk toward the house without further straining her bad leg. Grace burst through the door, breathing heavily, with Niki at her side in much the same state.

"DoDo! Lola!" Grace hollered, whipping a glance around the foyer and living room. Lola shouldn't be home from work yet, but maybe…? Thinking she heard some noise from the kitchen, Grace took off that way, praying DoDo had remembered to slip her nitroglycerin bottle into her apron pocket this morning. Sometimes she forgot.

Oh, God. Please not today.

"DoDo!" Grace yelled again, and then the sound of laughter stopped her short in the middle of the dining room. Niki slammed into her back with an "oof!"

"Graciela?" A healthy-looking DoDo peered out the doorway of the kitchen to where Grace and Niki stood. "What are you bellowing about, *m'ija*? Oh, hello, Nicole, honey." DoDo absolutely glowed in the presence of guests. "So nice of you to stop by."

"Hi, DoDo," Niki said, confused. "It's good to see you looking so…well."

Grace blinked, her brain not quite processing this new information quickly enough. Her chest rose and fell in quick trembles of panic and adrenaline. "What the hell? Are y-you okay?"

DoDo's forehead crinkled. "Of course. Why wouldn't I be?"

Grace pointed vaguely toward the front of the house. "The—the ambulance. I thought…I thought you were—" To her horror, tears choked her words and blurred her eyes. "I thought s-something had happened to you or that you w-were ill, *Abuelita*."

DoDo's face softened, and Niki moved forward to console Grace with a hug. Grace turned toward her friend and fell into the embrace, grateful for the comfort. She struggled to rein in her emotion, but a rogue tear escaped and rolled down her cheek anyway.

"Oh ,*m'ija*, your old *abue* isn't as fragile as that. Our good Lord knows if She comes for me before my girls are paired up and settled, I'm digging in my heels, anyway." DoDo came closer and rubbed her back, the same way she'd always done when Grace had cried for her mama in the years right after she'd died.

"Then why is there an amb—" Grace heard chairs scraping back in the kitchen and turned her head toward DoDo.

"The ambulance? Oh, honey. Madeira and Simon stopped by to talk to you. That's all." Madeira appeared in the doorway behind DoDo, her expression moving from pleasant welcome to surprise, to sparking jealousy at the picture of Grace in Niki's muscle-roped arms. Madeira's gorgeous eyes went dull just as tall, redheaded Simon appeared behind her, waving a hello.

"Oh." Grace spun. "Oh! I didn't even think…"

"Hey, Gracie," Madeira said, her tone reserved, wary.

"Maddee, Jesus! You, too, Simon." She laid a palm on her chest and shook her head as if to rattle the stupid out. "Y-you guys scared the crap out of me." She wiped at her cheek with the back of her hand, laughing self-consciously. "DoDo has heart problems. I worry."

"You worry too much, *m'ijita*," DoDo said. "I'm a tough old bird, you know."

"I'm sorry to have frightened you." Madeira laid a hand gently on DoDo's slight shoulder. "DoDo said you'd be home soon and offered us some cookies and milk while we waited. How could we refuse cookies and milk?" Madeira's gaze flickered toward Niki. "But perhaps this isn't the best time to talk." Moving forward, Madeira extended a hand stiffly toward Niki. "I'm Madeira Pacias."

Nik grinned, shaking the proffered hand warmly. "Hey, it's great to finally meet you." Madeira didn't reciprocate the enthusiasm, Grace noticed. "Niki Montoya."

Grace glanced curiously between the two women, just as Madeira turned to her partner. She jerked her head toward the front of the house. "*Vamos*. Grace is busy. We'll come back later."

"No, wait," Grace, Niki, and Simon all said at once. They glanced around in surprise at one another and laughed. Simon leaned in and introduced himself, and the group exchanged handshakes.

Niki jabbed her thumb over her shoulder. "Look, don't let me interrupt. I just gave Grace a ride home. I'm not staying."

A muscle in Madeira's jaw jumped. "Don't leave on our account."

Niki held up both palms. "I'm not. Really." She touched Grace's shoulder. "Don't forget to ask them, Grace."

"Ask us what?" Madeira said.

Niki leaned forward and kissed DoDo on the cheek, then waved at the medics. "Nice to have met you both."

"Thanks for the ride, Nik."

Nik kissed Grace on the cheek. "See you tomorrow. Rest that leg, and don't forget to *ask*."

After Niki had ambled off toward the front of the house, DoDo clasped her hands together at the waist and beamed. "Come. Have cookies with our friends. Your leg is hurting today?"

"A little bit, yes." Grace shed the backpack that still hung on her shoulder and limped into the kitchen, drained now that the adrenaline rush had waned. "You two needed to talk to me?"

Madeira nodded. "But first, what were you supposed to ask us? Your…*friend*…told you not to forget."

They all took seats around the tile-topped, wooden table, Grace accepting a glass of milk from DoDo with a smile. She set it down and looked from Simon to Madeira. "It's about a favor, actually." She sighed. "I don't know how to ask except to come out and simply…ask."

"Uh-oh." Simon grinned. "That sounds ominous."

Madeira, she noticed, still had that stormy look on her face. Hang on. Was she jealous? Of Niki? The thought made her tummy quiver with a sense of her own innate feminine power, but she ignored it and stuck to the matter at hand.

"The kids at my school can't seem to stop talking about the newspaper articles."

"Sounds like the ambulance bay," said Simon, with a snort.

Grace commiserated. "The principal got the bright idea to have you two come to the school and give an assembly about safety and accident prevention." She grimaced and flipped her hand. "Don't feel obligated."

Simon leaned in, his eyes bright with excitement. "Odd that you should need a favor from us, because we need one from you as well, so this could work out dandy." He smacked Madeira in the back, urging her, with a quick jerk of his chin, to elaborate.

Grace raised one brow. "Oh, yeah?"

Madeira planted her elbows on the table and ran her hands over the top of her head, a tired motion. "We're having a benefit to raise money for new ambulances, and we haven't been able to find a bartender. Simon suggested we ask if you wouldn't mind throwing in for the cause since you used to tend bar. All the other medics went in for it big time."

And how do you feel about it, Madeira? She didn't look too thrilled about the prospect. Grace sat back in her chair. She supposed if they agreed to help her, she could reciprocate. Even if they didn't. She did, after all, owe a huge debt of gratitude to the paramedics who had helped her at the accident scene. To Madeira herself, for that matter. But it had been a few years since she'd mixed. "Oh. Well, I don't see why not. Actually, I'd be glad to pitch in."

Both of them smiled, Madeira in relief, it seemed. "Really?"

"Sure." She tucked her hair behind her ears. "I'm a little rusty, you realize. How big a benefit are we talking about? What is it, some kind of dinner dance?"

Madeira swallowed hard and looked down at the table.

"Ah, a little different from that." Simon pulled a folded piece of paper out of her shirt pocket, smoothed it, and shoved it toward her.

Grace grabbed the flyer. It looked like a wanted poster featuring… Madeira. An advertisement for—oh, well, she might have known. Despite her efforts to remember this was all for charity, her stomach sank a bit. No wonder Madeira didn't want her there. After all the publicity, Grace would cramp her style. "Well, well. This ought to bring in some money," she murmured.

"The flyer was their idea," Madeira said, an air of defensiveness in her tone. "And all the single EMTs and paramedics will be auctioned, not just me. It's for new rigs."

DoDo moved in close to read over her shoulder. She erupted into cackles. "If I wasn't on a fixed income, *m'ija*, I would bid on you myself. You're a looker."

Madeira winked at her, truly appreciative.

"Okay, I'll tend bar at your event." Grace cleared her throat. "As long as you two can get it cleared with your department to do the safety assembly and bring an ambulance for the kids to see."

"Shouldn't be a problem," Simon said, pulling out a pocket calendar and leafing through the pages. "When are you looking to host this thing?"

"The faculty thinks this Friday would be best, while the news is still fresh in the kids' minds." She grimaced with apology. "I know it's short notice."

"We can work it out, Gracie," Madeira said, her words seeming to have a deeper meaning than what they conveyed on the surface. Or maybe wishful thinking had Grace reading meaning into a simple statement. Still, Madeira's level whiskey rumble went down like a much-needed shot.

Their gazes met.

Held.

Pulled away.

Grace swallowed with some difficulty. "Does late afternoon work? I know you two work nights."

"They'll let us flex our hours," Simon said. "Something like this is great PR. Maybe we can pass out some auction flyers to the faculty while we're there. Got any cute teachers?"

"None as cute as Gracie, I'm sure," Madeira said, in that too calm voice that stole Grace's breath.

"W-we have a whole school of attractive teachers," she said, ignoring the velvety compliment, trying not to be so attuned to the woman who'd delivered it.

"You think Lola would put flyers in her salon?" Madeira asked.

Grace smirked. "If *you* asked her, she would. I mean, if you asked her to jump off the Golden Gate Bridge, she'd probably at least consider it."

Madeira smiled.

"You leave some of those flyers with me, kids," said DoDo from the sink, where she rinsed dishes and placed them in the dishwasher. "I can hand them out to the women in Peacemakers. My quilting bee," she added with a smile.

"Really, DoDo?" Grace asked. "You think they'd be interested in this?"

"Hey, it's for a good cause. Don't discount us older women. We may have a few wrinkles, but some of my friends made out like bandits when their husbands passed, God rest their weary souls." She crossed herself, and everyone laughed.

"Okay," Simon prompted, clapping his large hands together once, then swishing his palms against one another decisively. "That wasn't half as difficult as you thought it would be, eh, Ms. Pac-Man?" He grinned at his partner.

Grace cocked her head questioningly.

"I wasn't sure you'd do it," Madeira said, looking sheepish.

"Well, of course I'll do it." She tried to convey her appreciation with her eyes. "Without EMS, without *you*, I'd still be under that car."

Grace's attraction to Madeira jacked the tension in the room to a near-unbearable level, and Madeira's energy reciprocated. Grace wondered if DoDo or Simon noticed.

"Then it's all settled. One hand washes the other and everything gets clean," DoDo said, closing the dishwasher door and starting the cycle. She scuttled to the table and nudged the cookie plate more to the center. "Now, eat. Eat!"

Grace and Madeira reached for cookies, and their hands collided above the plate. Both of them pulled back as though the connection burned, then their eyes met and held. Little zaps of desire moved between them, and Grace couldn't look away, didn't want to. Madeira's eyes remained hard, though. Almost sad, and yet she seemed unable to break the spell.

The whole interaction made Grace's stomach flutter with worry.

Madeira wasn't flirting at all, and that just didn't seem…normal.

The EMT radio crackled and Simon pulled the pac-set from his equipment belt, moving to the other side of the room to reply to dispatch's query. After a moment, he returned to the table.

"We've got a transport, Mad, but non-emergent. I'll head out to the rig and fire up the run sheet. You take your time, though." Simon's gaze conveyed some kind of meaning Grace couldn't grasp.

"I'll be right out."

Simon turned and gave a mock salute to DoDo. "Most sincere thanks for the snack, Mrs. Obregon. I haven't had milk and cookies in a long time, and it rocked."

DoDo radiated pleasure at the compliment. "I'll walk you to the ambulance and get some of those flyers. You kids come back any time you want. I'm here all the time, and I so enjoy visitors," she said, her voice drifting off the farther they got from the kitchen.

Attraction still crackling between them, Grace stared at Madeira. The clock ticked, the dishwasher hummed and sloshed from the other side of the room, and hot blood drummed a sensual rhythm in her ears. Other than those sounds, the kitchen remained cloaked in a heavy, expectant, uncertain silence.

"Maddee, what's wrong?"

"Who's Niki?" she asked, pushing out the words in a voice that sounded way too calm to be safe.

Grace's skin tingled with understanding, but she wanted to play it cool. So, that's what she'd seen in Maddee's eyes—some kind of feminine possessiveness she couldn't rein in.

Interesting.

Flattering.

Alarming.

"She's that woman who drove me home," she said, using Madeira's favorite defense mechanism: humor.

Madeira's eyes narrowed and she smiled. Controlled, measured. "You know what I'm asking, Gracie."

"She's a friend." She picked up a cookie, took a bite, chewed, and swallowed, her eyes never leaving her face. "A very good friend."

Madeira's lips pressed into a grim line. "Are you dating her?"

"Why would you think that?"

In a swift, frustrated movement, Madeira pushed back from the table and stood up. She shoved her hands through her hair and paced the width of the room, looking like a freshly broken stallion, yearning to gallop off the excess energy that quivered her sleek muscles.

Grace had never seen her like this, and it stunned her. She thought they had been playing.

"You have to ask, Gracie?" Madeira clenched her fists, flashing a dark glance that looked almost tortured. "Because I want you and you don't want me," she growled, almost ashamed. "I'm trying to figure out what this Niki might have that I don't."

"She has a partner, for one thing," Grace said softly, surprised enough by Madeira's pained outburst that she wanted to put the suspicions to rest as swiftly as possible.

Madeira spun, toned arms standing out from her work-tapered torso.

Wow, seeing Grace with Niki had sincerely bothered Madeira. Grace would've never imagined…

"Excuse me?"

"Bree." Grace took a sip of milk, mostly to steady her own voice. "The woman Niki's going to spend the rest of her life with, her one true love."

Madeira cocked her head to the side, her stance rigid, body flexed. "I don't get it. You'd rather date a woman who has a girlfriend than one who is single but has been around the block a couple times? Of all the convoluted logic, Gracie, I—"

"Of course not." Grace stood and crossed the room to stand before Madeira, stunned by the power of the tension radiating from her body. She gentled her tone. "When I said Niki was my friend, Maddee, I meant it." She paused to let that sink in. "I wasn't being coy. Niki and I went to college together and we teach at the same school. She's helping me rehabilitate my leg, and she gives me rides home now and then." Grace shrugged, flipping her palms up at the same time. "That's it. Friendship, and not with benefits. Nik's seven years younger than I am."

Madeira blinked a couple of times, then moistened her lips with her tongue. "Oh."

Fearing she'd explained herself into a corner out of which there was no escape, Grace cleared her throat. "To be clear, I'm not dating Niki, but that doesn't mean I wouldn't date someone else if that perfect someone came along." She reached out and touched Madeira's forearm in a gesture that was meant to take the sting off her words. She didn't expect the warmth of Madeira's skin, the firm musculature beneath, to flash white heat straight to her core. But it did. "If you truly want to be my friend, Maddee, you've got to drop the jealous act."

"I don't want to be your friend, Gracie," Madeira said, though clenched teeth, "I want to be your lover. Not that I have any say in the matter."

Grace couldn't speak for a moment, could hardly draw breath. "I…I'm not looking for a lover, Madeira."

"Unless that *perfect someone* came along, no?" Madeira's tormented gaze searched Grace's face for a moment before she reached out with both hands and grasped the sides of Grace's torso. Gentle-rough, Madeira pulled Grace's body against her own. Madeira's face bent toward Grace's, close enough that Grace's mouth tingled in anticipation of their lips touching. A hot, painful ache throbbed low in Grace's body. Her nipples tingled and yearned for Madeira's touch, her tongue. Her.

Madeira's thickly lashed eyes traced Grace's lips, breaths heavy and barely controlled. Their bodies melted together from knee to stomach, and Madeira's palms spanned on the curve of Grace's waist radiated heat and need, deliciously… Dared she say it? Possession. But not in a bad way, not how Grace was used to it. With Maddee, it felt good. Right.

Dangerous.

"And if I date someone else, *fierita*, will you be okay with that as well?" Grace felt the rumble of Madeira's words through her chest, her breath in warm puffs on her face.

Her stomach went sour, and she swallowed past a catch in her throat. *No!* Grace wanted to yell. She couldn't pinpoint the moment it had changed, but she couldn't bear to think of Maddee with another woman, much less a slew of them. How could she want to avoid Maddee and restrain her at the same time?

Don't look away, Grace. If you do, she'll know.

She steeled herself for the lie, using every available energy resource in her body.

"Of course, I'll be fine with it," Grace managed, sounding surprisingly calm and together despite the storm of mixed emotions raging inside her. "I have no hold on you."

Madeira studied her for a moment longer, then set Grace carefully away, smoothing her sweater in a curiously care-taking motion. One corner of Madeira's mouth lifted, that rueful, sad-edged look back in her eyes. "Now, see, that's where you're wrong, my little *vixen*," Madeira said in a deceptively soft voice. "Dead wrong." With that, Madeira brushed past Grace...and was gone.

❖

Grace wanted her to date, she would damn well date.

To hell with it all.

Madeira stood before the mirror, straightening her perfectly faded and fitted jeans and V-neck black tank top. A bergamot candle burned in her bathroom, and the Cuban salsa music wafting in from the stereo set the tone for the evening's agenda.

Wednesday.

Ladies' night at Karma.

Checking her hair—perfect—she shrugged into her favorite black leather jacket, exquisitely tailored to fit her body and made of butter-soft Spanish lambskin. It had always made her feel like her game was on—way on—but tonight the combination of black leather and angry desperation in her eyes depressed her. She glanced away from the mirror, stopping to slap some musky cologne on her neck.

If she were taking Gracie out on the town, maybe...

No. Gracie didn't want her, and Madeira had grown tired of the futile chase, the constant rejection. Beneath her devil-may-care bravado lived a tender place that had always somehow known Madeira Pacias wasn't good enough. Gracie had been the first, the only woman to see through her act to the truth of her, and instead of setting her free, she'd unflinchingly confirmed what Madeira already knew: she wasn't the kind of person a woman could depend on for life, not like her *hermana*. When all was said and done, Madeira simply wasn't a keeper.

Toro took after Mamá, whereas Madeira took after Papá. Not that she hadn't loved her father—she had. Still did, even in death. But the man had always been a rolling stone, the kind who should've known better than to marry a good woman and create four children who needed him, children who would always be disappointed by his shortcomings as a father and husband. Too much of her father's blood pumped through

Madeira's veins, and that left her of little long-term use to any woman. She'd accepted that so many years ago, it hardly mattered anymore.

Still…Jesus. Madeira needed acceptance from someone.

Why not Gracie? Why couldn't Gracie accept her, faults and all, embrace the woman she was despite everything? Wasn't there supposed to be one perfect person for everyone? Why, in God's name, couldn't Madeira's someone be Gracie?

Sick to death of the melancholy, the yearning, Madeira gave herself a vicious mental shake. What had happened to her? She'd always been able to shrug it off when a particular woman wasn't interested, and she'd do it tonight, too. There was bound to be a woman at Karma who wouldn't judge her and find her sorely lacking, a woman who'd be glad for the company of *la ladróna de corazones*. A woman who wouldn't see her in quite so much ugly detail…

She still won't be Gracie, her mind whispered.

Madeira set her jaw.

Good.

She didn't want a woman who reached deep inside her and tore her guts out every time they saw each other, a woman who consumed her thoughts, swirled her brain. A woman whose very name squeezed her heart until Madeira couldn't take a full breath and didn't even want to if the two of them couldn't be together in this life.

Madeira had never wanted that.

She didn't want it now.

How had she gotten so off-track, anyway?

Blowing out the candle, Madeira palmed her keys, left the house, and stalked toward her truck—a woman with a mission. Her friends, Kita and Carmen, were meeting her at the club in half an hour, and Madeira's goal for this fresh Wednesday was to party.

Hard.

It would be good to get back to the old routine of carefree nights with willing women. She needed to forget Gracie and her damned teddy bear, to release herself from this inexplicable hold Gracie had over her, if only for one night.

Please, Gracie. If you don't want me, let me go.

❖

They needed to talk. She knew it.

Grace rolled over and punched her pillow, but it didn't increase the comfort quotient one bit. She squinted at her alarm clock and settled back into the mattress, sighing in frustration.

Midnight.

Freaking swell. She'd been tossing and turning for two hours, and she had to be up and alert in another six to start the grind all over again. So much for turning in early to recharge after an already long work week that wasn't even half over.

Her discomfort, she had to admit, wasn't so much from the bed as it was from the fact that her gut told her she'd somehow managed to hurt Madeira's feelings. Maddee didn't deserve it, and in truth, the fact Grace even had the ability to hurt her was a shock. Weren't players immune to the emotions of commoners?

Then again, she'd once been considered a major player herself, and if anything, her emotions had been magnified. Maybe she had judged Madeira unfairly, as Niki had so tactfully suggested yesterday afternoon. Guilt pricked at Grace's conscience. Even when she'd been dating…let's call it *heavily*, she'd always felt like a good person inside. Had someone implied she was unworthy, it would have hurt. A lot.

God…had she made Madeira feel that way?

If so, what a total asshole she'd been.

Ugh. She couldn't bear it. Grace sat up, unsnarling her hair with her fingers. She wouldn't be able to rest until she spoke with Madeira and got a feel for her emotional state. If Maddee deserved an apology, Grace wouldn't hesitate to give it. The last thing she ever wanted to be was cruel. To anyone, but God…especially to Maddee.

How had that happened?

Pulling back the covers, Grace padded across her room to retrieve her backpack. She had both Madeira's and Simon's cell phone numbers programmed into her phone, and if her calculations were correct, they'd be at work right about now. It couldn't hurt to call.

She dialed Madeira first, but the phone rang repeatedly and went to voicemail. She listened to the whole message, just to bask in the exotic rhythms of Maddee's accent, but then hung up without speaking. Maybe they were on a run. Or perhaps when Maddee and Simon rode the rig together, they shared a phone. She dialed Simon, and the phone picked almost immediately.

"Fletcher."

Grace cleared her throat. "Simon? This is Grace."

His tone warmed immediately. "Hey, Grace. Is everything okay? What's up?"

"No, everything's okay. And nothing's up, really. I was just... hoping to speak with Madeira for a minute. I called her phone, but she didn't answer."

"I'd love to let you talk to her, but she's not here."

"She isn't?"

"Nope, she took a comp day. As far as I know, she had plans to go out with some of her friends."

Grace went cold inside. Madeira took a comp day to party? Grace's heart began to thud. "Oh...that's right. I think she mentioned it and I just spaced it," she fibbed. "Where was it they went again?

"Karma, baby." Simon's grin came through the line. "Wednesday is Ladies' Night at Karma, after all."

Grace's stomach lurched with something green and sticky and unhealthy. Jealousy. She immediately wished she hadn't even called, much less asked where Madeira had gone. Why was human nature so fucking cruel? Why was she always compelled to seek out information she didn't really want to know? "Oh, yes." She laughed lightly, feeling anything but. "To think I'd forgotten about Ladies' Night. Where's my brain?"

"Can I let her know you called?"

Like a desperate, sniveling woman who would swallow her pride and chase her while she went prowling around for anonymous sex on Ladies' Night? Not a chance in hell. "No, actually, don't bother. I'll call right back and leave her a message on her voicemail," Grace said, knowing she wouldn't. It wasn't as if Madeira had lied to her or committed some other transgression. She hadn't. In fact, Grace had as much as *told* her to go find someone else yesterday afternoon.

Still.

The one solitary romance gene that had gone into her chromosomal makeup instead of Lola's wished Madeira was at work, or better yet, sitting at home pining. Ha.

"Okay, sounds good. Hey, see you at the school on Friday."

"Yeah." Grace dreaded it more than ever now. "Can't wait."

They said their good nights and disconnected, and Grace sat in the darkness of her room marveling at her damned gullibility. Madeira could pour on the emotion and the sex appeal, lace it all up neatly with vulnerability and say she wanted to be Grace's lover one day, then head out to the most notorious lesbian meat market in the city the next. It was the principle of the matter, and it just confirmed the fact that, sadly, Madeira wasn't the woman for her.

Grace's whole body ached, and she curled into herself.

God, she was stupid. What's more, she *never* learned.

Possibly didn't even have the capacity to learn when it came to her Kryptonite: delicious, irresistible, unattainable women like Maddee. Which was why she needed to steer clear of her from here on out.

Climbing back into bed without any hope of a good night's sleep, Grace made a couple difficult but firm decisions. One, pain or not, she was getting these tattoos removed. Clearly Madeira had seen the one on her chest, or she wouldn't have tossed out that "my little vixen" comment so directly. Grace had grown weary of the false impressions her tattoos conveyed. She wasn't that person anymore.

More importantly, she would date suitable women from here on out, period. Starting now. Blind date, mercy date, whatever the hell it took. Before she saw Madeira again, she'd have a date with a decent woman if it killed her. And judging from the squeezing of her heart and the moisture at the outside corners of her eyes, it just might.

Madeira set a personal record that night at Karma. Two, actually. Longest time nursing one tepid, tasteless beer and most women turned down in a single evening. Whooey, what a stud.

She snorted in disgust. This was getting ridiculous. To the pre-Gracie Madeira, any number of these women would've been perfectly acceptable. Agreeable, even, she thought, as a voluptuous redhead undulated past her table in a cloud of promise and pheromones. Madeira's gaze tracked the redhead's seductive movement dispassionately; she couldn't even manage a full smile when the woman turned back and cast her a calculated, challenging glance. Post-Gracie Madeira couldn't even drum up enough enthusiasm to fake interest in a gorgeous redhead. What a damned shame.

Madeira pushed her warm beer aside and sought the crowd for

Kita and Carmen, finally locating them deep within the gyrating crowd on the dance floor. Each of them was draped in willing woman, yukking it up in a fashion that used to be second nature for Madeira, too. Not anymore. She felt out of place in the club, a poser intent on convincing the world she fit in, but failing miserably. If she believed more strongly in mystical nonsense, Madeira would almost imagine that Gracie had cast a spell on her, completely destroying any charm or charisma she might have had at one time.

Gone.

Poof.

Just like that, she'd been rendered useless.

God, she didn't want to be here.

Placing her pinky fingers in her mouth, Madeira let loose with a short, sharp whistle—a signal she and her friends had devised years ago. Kita heard and glanced over. Through a series of hand motions, Madeira managed to convey the fact that she was outta there, and Kita signaled back that they'd talk soon.

Madeira climbed into her truck and drove, punching the radio buttons almost angrily to interrupt the plethora of romantic ballads that all seemed to apply too poignantly to her miserable situation with Gracie.

Broken heart, this.

Lonely nights, that.

Bah.

She wasn't even sure where she was headed until her truck pulled up outside her sister's house. She checked her watch and cringed, sitting for a moment to listen to the hot, ticking engine. One thirty in the morning and darkness cloaked the house. Toro wouldn't be pleased.

Too damn bad.

Madeira lit from the truck and slammed the door, ready to face her sister's wrath or any other adversaries who might stand in her way. She hadn't come to speak with Toro, anyway. The only antidote for what ailed her at the moment was a heart-to-heart talk with the closest female friend who actually understood her. Iris.

Chapter Ten

El remedio puede ser peor que la enfermedad.
Sometimes the remedy is worse than the disease.

Leave her alone," Iris said half an hour later, after Madeira had spilled her guts about her so-called relationship with Grace.

"Huh?"

"You heard me. If you want to be with Grace, leave her alone." Iris curled her feet beneath her on the wicker love seat and regarded Madeira with what looked like sympathy in her emerald eyes. "Your usual modus operandi isn't going to work with this one, Mad. The stronger you come on to her, the faster she'll retreat. Mark my words."

"I know this only too well. And you think the remedy is—"

"Leaving her alone. Yes. If you really want her, you're going to have to back off and trust that fate will guide you."

"Fate." With a rough sigh, Madeira scrubbed her palms over her face. Fate was just another one of those *bruja* concepts designed to trip up her and her ilk. Fate, kismet, signs from the universe, all if it. It only made life more confusing. She regarded Iris. "I guess you've never heard it said, *él que no mira, no suspira*?"

"Long absent, soon forgotten?" Iris asked. "I've heard it. But you've got to trust me. That only happens when the person is wrong for you. So"—she shrugged—"if Grace is wrong—"

"She isn't," Madeira said. "That's the whole problem. She's the only woman I've ever met who is exactly right for me. But it doesn't matter because I'm completely wrong for her—I know that. The few times I've tried to forget, she never hesitates to remind me."

"Wow. I'd love to meet this woman."

In spite of herself, Madeira smiled, picturing Gracie in her mind and going soft inside. "You'd love her. She's a beautiful tangle of contradictions wrapped up in a fireball package."

"Uh-oh. You're sounding way too poetic to be the Madeira I know and love," Iris said gently.

"Be quiet."

Iris laughed. "Listen, it'll work out if it's meant to. You want my opinion?"

"Would I be here if I didn't?"

Iris conceded the point. "I think it *is* meant to, because you deserve a woman like her, Mad, despite what you might think."

"Yeah. Right." She wished she could share Iris's serene confidence. It felt as if Madeira's only good shot at happiness was slipping through her fingers like fast-running water, and there she stood without even a Dixie cup to catch the flow. She stood and crossed to a window that looked out over the dark backyard, still mired in feelings that made no sense.

Behind her she heard the rustle of Iris's robe as she shifted positions. "You know, I'm wondering something."

"What's that?" Madeira turned to her.

"What exactly makes you think you aren't right for her?"

Madeira huffed and spread her arms, hoping to convey her "gee, I wonder" feelings that roiled inside like poison. "Iris, have you ever met any of my girlfriends?"

"Nope."

"Do you know why?"

"Because you'd have had to introduce them and you couldn't remember any of their names?"

Iris's playful comment stung because it hit damned close to the truth. It also sounded like a barb Gracie would wing at her. Madeira clenched her jaw against the wave of pain.

"You know I'm just kidding," Iris added. "Tell me."

"Kidding or not, you're on the right track." Madeira shook her head with self-derision. "I haven't brought them to the family because I've never had a relationship that wasn't superficial."

It pained her to say this, but she had to come clean with someone. She knew Iris wouldn't judge her. Still, Madeira flicked her hand, not quite able to meet her eyes. "I didn't truly care about those women. Not a single one of them. I had a good time with each and every one, but that's all they were to me—a good time. You know what that makes me?" Madeira searched Iris's face in the moonlight. She pounded a fist against her own chest. "It makes me an asshole. *I* wouldn't want me, Iris. I'm like candy. Good when you have a craving for sweets, but no substance. Nothing to hold on to. So how can I expect someone like Gracie, who deserves the world, the moon, the stars, to want me?"

Sadness moistened Iris's eyes. "Oh, honey. Come here."

Madeira crossed to the love seat and slumped next to Iris, grateful to lean her head on Iris's shoulder and accept some sisterly nurturing.

"You're so wrong, Mad. You have a lot to offer, you just weren't meant to share it until you found the right woman."

"Is that another way of saying I'm an asshole?"

"How did you get to be so hard on yourself?"

"Try having a perfect sister like Toro. That's a lot to live up to."

"You're not Toro, Madeira. No one expects you to be."

Madeira pushed out a humorless, listless laugh, lifting her head off Iris's shoulder to lean against the opposite corner of the sofa. "Hard on myself, you say. Shoot, I've been telling myself and the whole world of women that I'm the best invention since the wheel ever since I was old enough to date. Lots of them believed me, too. Hell, I'd even convinced myself. Until I met Gracie." She crossed one ankle over the other knee and picked at the sole of her boot. "She saw through the crap to the real me. Unworthy."

"No, Mad. Wrong. *This* is the real you. My crazy little sis who gets so worked up about a woman, she risks waking her—let's face it—sometimes grouchy older sister in the middle of the night because she desperately needs a heart-to-heart with someone who understands." Iris cocked her head to the side. "Those women from your past might have just been good times, but it's obvious you don't feel the same about Grace. You may not have cared for the others, but you care for her."

"Yes. I…I…I—" Madeira didn't even know the proper words to describe how she felt about Gracie. She'd never felt it before. "You're right."

Iris leaned forward and cupped Madeira's cheek. "You're not letting her see your true heart, Mad."

"What do you mean?"

"You're showing her the same face you've put forward for those women who didn't matter. Only this time, you're using that world-class charm and devastatingly sexy grin to shield your heart, not to win a woman into your bed." Her chin lowered along with her tone. "I'm not judging. I'm just saying…if you truly care about Grace, put your heart behind your charisma. Take a risk. Be vulnerable."

Madeira hiked one shoulder, not agreeing, not disagreeing.

Iris smiled sweetly. "Trust me. Show her the woman who's talking to me tonight. If she sees the real you—all of you, *this* you, honey—Grace won't be able to *not* adore you."

But suppose I put my heart and soul into Gracie and she stomps them both?

How will I survive then?

Madeira blocked out Iris's wisdom and her own persistent, unanswerable questions. She couldn't bear to get her hopes up. She stood, putting distance between herself and Iris while she paced the width of the room. "I don't understand what's happening, Iris. Something's got to be wrong with me. I feel sick and on edge almost all the time now."

Iris crossed her arms. "Go on."

Madeira ruminated for a few laps. "Sometimes it seems like I'm holding my breath, breathing shallowly just to stay alive, you know? To exist." She turned, watching Iris in the lamp light. "And then I see Gracie, and I exhale"—she closed her eyes and blew a long, slow breath through her lips—"and at that moment everything is right again and I feel…home."

"Ah, yes." Iris's eyes glittered.

Relief flowed through Madeira that Iris seemed to understand her convoluted explanation. "You know what I'm trying to say?"

"Of course." A beat passed, and Iris's lips spread into a Cheshire cat smile. "It's the same way I felt from the first moment I saw Torien and every day since."

Madeira stopped short. She could almost feel all her systems shutting down one by one until there was absolute stillness in her body, utter clarity in her mind.

No lightning struck.

No thunder clapped.

No volcanoes erupted.

No meteors struck the earth.

Yet, at that moment, the gravity of the situation hit Madeira with the force of the most massive natural disaster imaginable. She hadn't wanted it, didn't know how it had happened. But, Jesus, nothing had ever been more obvious to her than this thought, at this split second, of her life.

Madeira didn't simply want to date Gracie Obregon.

She'd somehow managed to fall in love with her.

Love.

Madeira Pacias, *la ladróna de corazones*...in love. Surreal...but true. Truer than anything she'd ever known.

A surge of determination straightened her shoulders. If it took backing off to make Gracie understand how she felt, Madeira would damn well grit her teeth and do it. Well...after the safety assembly at Gracie's school. And after DoDo's dinner. Not to mention the Charity Singles Auction, which wasn't for another six weeks, but still.

Aw, hell. So much for simple solutions.

Madeira smoothed her palm slowly down her face. How could she back off, give Gracie space, if situations kept forcing them together? Madeira would never blow off the commitments she'd made, but at the same time, those commitments would prevent her from following Iris's advice. Or would they? Perhaps this necessary distance was more than merely physical. Removing herself from the situation emotionally might be enough.

Could she do it?

Could she see Gracie and not touch her?

Could she mask her feelings so as to draw Gracie closer rather than send her skittering away? She gave a derisive laugh.

"What's so funny?" Iris asked.

"Look at me." She spread her arms, feeling nothing but self-scorn. "*La ladróna de corazones*, unable to steal the only heart she's ever really wanted."

Iris joined her in laughter. "It is pretty ironic, sweetie."

But as they laughed, a thought stole into her brain like a cat burglar...quickly, quietly, unexpected. The best thieves were silent and unobtrusive, no? Something she'd never been before. Something she'd never believed she could be, had never wanted to be. Perhaps it was past time she gave it a try.

Difficult, yes, but Gracie was worth it.

❖

Grace had been distracted all day by the impending accident prevention assembly and by the thought of seeing Madeira. Last time she'd seen her, they shared an almost-but-not-quite kiss, the memory of which she could almost-but-not-quite evict from her brain for a few moments at a time. But after learning Madeira had spared no time beating feet to the club the night following the not-quite-kiss, Grace had set up a hasty dinner date with Layton Fair, the art teacher at her school and the most attractive single woman in her current circle of acquaintances.

Dinner with Layton. Tomorrow night.

In her mid-thirties, studious Layton was conservative, soft-spoken, approachable, and good-looking in a nondescript kind of way. She'd been surprised and pleased by Grace's invitation, but Grace had had to convince her that she and Madeira weren't a couple before Layton finally agreed. She had a monogamist's conscience—just the kind of woman Grace needed.

Madeira, on the other hand, was Layton's polar opposite—flamboyant, gregarious, untouchable, and way too damn sexy for her own good. Honorable, for sure, but with an agenda behind her manners. Tomorrow night at dinner, Grace was sure she'd have Layton's undivided attention, and there wouldn't be random women flinging themselves at her every time Grace turned away. She couldn't honestly say she felt that physical pull to Layton, but that wasn't what mattered in a relationship…was it?

Still, it almost felt as if she was cheating on Madeira—pure insanity—and every time she remembered she'd be seeing Madeira soon, she lost a few more minutes of her life to stress. Oh well, it couldn't be helped. She needed to wean herself from this senseless crush she had on Madeira by spending time with more suitable women, and Layton was a primo candidate. No sense dragging her feet.

A quick glance at the clock told her D-day had arrived, and her pulse revved. She looked around at the children, who'd been reading so quietly for the past twenty minutes she'd almost forgotten they were there.

Standing, she nonchalantly stretched out her stiff leg. "Okay, kiddos. Books in your desks, hands on top, faces front, mouths closed so we can head down to the auditorium."

After a flurry of supercharged activity and high-pitched chatter, twenty-two faces of various colors and shapes grinned dutifully at her from behind their numbered desks. Teeth, she noticed, were optional. She experienced a moment of true affection for her students and smiled back.

"Okay, when I say go, I want you to line up by the door, numbers twenty-two to one." She held up her hand to tick off the rules on her fingers. "No running. No poking. No antagonizing. No talking. No pushing. No complaining. No gross noises. Is everyone clear?"

"Yes, Ms. Obregon," they chimed together. But unless she was mistaken, one of the students in her class had undergone a very rapid maturity cycle. Her gaze shot to the door and her stomach dropped to the industrial flooring below her feet.

"Madeira." She white-knuckled the edge of her desk. How could she dread seeing Madeira for two solid days, but when they actually came face-to-face, she felt lighter and happier than she had in...well, since the last time she'd seen her? She had really turned into such a total flake since Madeira had reentered her life.

The children strained and scrambled to see the visitor, and little Sean Santiago, the spitting image of his tattoo-exposing brother Steven, bolted from his desk to greet the uniformed medic that no one had expected in the classroom. And, *damn*, did Madeira look sexy in her uniform, or what? Excited prattle spewed a mile a minute from Sean's little mouth, and Madeira had bent forward to try and catch it all. The other kids remained in their seats, but a bouncing, manic, blabber-wrought kind of pandemonium ensued.

After recovering from the shock of seeing Madeira standing in her doorway, so brashly female and strong and utterly sexy, Grace raised her hand—the quiet signal. Most of the kids glanced forward; third graders in general were still eager to please authority figures. She did her best not to raise her voice, because experience had taught her quickly, the louder she got, the louder they got. "I need appropriate behavior before we can go, kids. Feet together, hands on your desks, eyes forward, please, looking at me."

As the class settled, she made her way toward Madeira and Sean, catching the tail end of a very one-sided conversation. Sean finished one tale, sucked a quick, deep breath, and said, "And then this one other time, me and my brother—"

"Hey, little Mr. Santiago." She jostled his spiny shoulder, and Sean peered up at her. "Back to your desk, buddy."

Sean pointed toward Madeira, excitement putting sparkles in his chocolate-brown eyes. "Did ya see, Ms. Obregon? She's a cop!"

"Not a police officer, *chavalito*. I'm an EMT. I help sick people."

"Cool," Sean exclaimed. "I get sick sometimes. So does my brother and my sister, too. Once I even throwed up on my brother at dinner. And this one time—"

"To your desk, Sean," Grace interjected, in a soft, firm voice, "or we'll miss the assembly."

"Aw, man!" Sean slumped off, but not before Madeira had chuckled and ruffled the boy's hair. She straightened up, and her eyes met Grace's.

So much for breathing. "Hey." Grace crossed her arms. "You sure know how to rattle some cages. I couldn't have worked these kids up any more if I'd released a truckload of freaked-out chickens in the room." Grace smiled at Madeira's playful look of dread.

"Do you know it took me six months before I could eat chicken again?" Madeira said in a confidential tone.

Grace laughed softly and made a "yuck" face, sticking out her tongue. "I still don't eat it."

One corner of Madeira's mouth lifted. "Anyway, sorry about the class. I forgot how easy they are to agitate."

"Speaking of that." Grace touched Madeira's arm to stop her for a moment and turned back to look at her kids, who waited obediently for their next instruction. "Okay, same rules about lining up by the door. Quickly but quietly, please."

The kids began to file into a long queue, and she turned back to Madeira, lowering her voice. "What are you doing here? Shouldn't you be in the auditorium preparing?"

"We got here early. We're all set up." She reached up and wrapped her hands around both ends of the stethoscope that hung around her neck. "I actually wanted to talk to you for a few minutes, if that's possible."

Grace consulted the wall clock. "Not much time. Hang on." She stepped around her and opened the door to her classroom. Peering out, she caught the eye of Eula Washington, the teacher in the adjacent room. Eula taught the Special Ed students, and her class was considerably smaller. "Eula."

"Hey, Grace."

"Would you mind walking my kids down with yours? One of our speakers needs to, ah, discuss something with me for a moment."

Eula gave a knowing smirk. "Yeah, you go, girl. I bet I know which one needs you, too."

Ugh. They all thought she and Madeira were an item.

Grace offered the other woman a rather sick smile, choosing not to comment on the innuendo. "Thanks. I owe you." Turning back, she addressed her kids. "Mrs. Washington is going to walk you down to the assembly, and I expect she'll tell me you were the most perfect kids in the whole school. Right?"

They nodded, amongst giggles and bounces.

"If not"—Grace pointed toward the restrictions list she kept in a neatly-written DO NOT box on her white board—"we all know what happens, right?"

"No fun privileges," Sean Santiago said.

She nodded. "That's right. Okay, out you go." They filed past like a little train, each child studying Madeira unabashedly. After Mona Clay, the little girl who occupied desk number one, exited, the door swung shut. Grace released a breath.

"You're really good with them," Madeira said.

The compliment warmed her. "Thank you. I love children. They're tiring, though."

"I bet you're a great teacher."

"I try. I'm still feeling my way a bit since I'm a greenhorn." Grace offered a wry smile. "I've always wanted to be a teacher, but I chose to trash a few years of my adulthood with self-destructive behavior and dead-end jobs before college."

Madeira laughed. "Yeah, well. I'm sure you'll be a better teacher for the life knowledge and street smarts."

She'd never thought of it that way, but the kind words made her brim with confidence.

"Kids are cool," Madeira said. "I can't wait until Torien and Iris start providing me with some nieces and nephews to corrupt."

"They want them?"

"Yep."

"That's awesome for them." God, Madeira looked edible in her navy blue uniform pants and fitted white shirt. The short sleeves hugged her muscular biceps in a way that made Grace want to trace her fingers over the ridges. And that accent...Grace could listen to Madeira talk for hours.

Years...forever.

Grace scurried to refocus. "How long have they been together?"

"Long enough to get busy and figure out the insemination part."

They both laughed, and Grace wished Eula had been right and Madeira had come by early to sweep her into her arms and kiss the breath from her lungs. She licked her lips, and her gaze dropped to Madeira's mouth. Suddenly self-conscious, she crossed her arms, realizing, yeah, she could talk to Madeira all day, but the entire school awaited the infamous hero's arrival. "So, what's up?"

Madeira paused for a moment, then blew out a regretful breath. "I wanted to apologize for how I acted in your kitchen last Tuesday, Gracie. I had no right to ask about Niki, or to grab you..."

An apology? And here Grace had hoped for a repeat, flighty wench that she was. So much for Madeira kissing her breathless. "Oh. Hey, it's okay."

"No, it isn't. You've made it very clear that you only want to be friends, and I mean to start respecting that."

Ah, Madeira must've met someone at the bar, Grace thought acidly, then immediately checked herself. Niki's admonition rang in her head. She had no right to scrutinize Madeira's choices unless she put her own life under the same microscope. She knew it was true, and inside, she softened. "Well, thank you. I appreciate that."

"You do?" Madeira stood a bit straighter.

"Of course." She thrust out her hand. "You and I are a lot alike, Maddee. Something I may not have admitted even a few days ago. But being friends is a good compromise. Who makes a better friend than someone who really gets you?" *Who makes a better lover than someone who really gets you?* Grace shoved the traitorous thought away.

Madeira took her hand and shook it, but didn't let go right away, allowing her thumb to caress Gracie's silky skin. "Someday you should meet my sister Torien and her partner, Iris. You'd like them."

"Someday I just might," Grace said. "Actually, I'd love to."

"How come none of my teachers were as beautiful as you, Gracie?" Her half-mast gaze damn near rendered Grace speechless.

She willed a casual tone into her voice. "They probably saw you coming."

Madeira dropped her hand, grinning. "You may be right. Torien claims I've been incorrigible since elementary school."

Grace gave a little sarcastic snort. "My guess is you were an incorrigible infant." She managed to walk calmly to her desk to palm her keys, then joined Madeira again at the door. "Let's go. All I need is to make you late to the assembly. There's enough gossip going around about us already."

"Sounds interesting," Madeira mused.

Grace tossed her a droll, silent stare and led the way to the auditorium.

Twenty-five minutes later, Madeira and Simon had finished their presentation. Madeira had absolutely charmed the audience—big surprise—and Simon's wealth of knowledge and his ability to convey it in simple terminology the children could understand was admirable. Gracie glanced around and noticed that the other teachers and the hundred or so parents who'd shown up seemed mesmerized, too. Partway through, Eula had leaned forward and whispered, "Grrrrl, lock that one up, otherwise back off and give me a crack at her. Mmm-mmm-mmm."

Grace shook her head with amusement and shushed her friend. Eula had flawless skin the color of a perfectly mixed latte and eyes the cerulean blue of the water around her birthplace—Jamaica. The last thing Grace planned to do was introduce this island beauty to Madeira. If only Grace could lock Madeira up, she would. Yeah, right. That would be like caging a lion. Some wild animals were meant to be free, she realized, a pang of respect-tempered sadness striking inside her.

Simon smoothed his palms together. "All righty then, ladies and germs"—the kids laughed—"are there any other questions before we head out to take a quick look at the ambulance?"

A dozen hands shot up. More.

Simon acknowledged one of the fifth-grade girls.

"I have a question for her," she said shyly, pointing a stubby, sparkle-polished fingernail toward Madeira.

Madeira moved forward and smiled. "Go ahead."

The girl giggled behind her hand for a minute until her friends started to elbow jab her from both sides. "Are you gonna, like, marry Ms. Obregon, or whatever?"

Grace went rigid, and Eula's hand came forward to squeeze her shoulder. Madeira, she noted, looked similarly stricken. Her gaze sought and found Grace's, like an S.O.S. She managed a subtle, useless shrug. The only bright spot in the whole thing was the fact Madeira was on the spot instead of Grace, which wasn't a very nice notion for her to entertain, but there it was.

The little Disney star clone went on. "Because my mom said that stuff in the paper about you guys was the most romantic thing she'd ever seen since Luke and Laura's wedding on *General Hospita*l, like, a zillion years ago. I don't know what that means, but anyway, my friends think so, too, even though none of us have a clue who Luke and Laura are 'cuz, I guess, we were babies then. Or maybe not even born."

Several of the teachers and many of the parents laughed.

Madeira managed a nervous heh-heh-heh as a prelude to her big hem-haw. "Well, now, a lot goes into a relationship before it gets to the, um…happily ever after question, little one." *Stammer stammer.* She cleared her throat. "But how about a question or two on the topic of accident prevention or safety or…yes?" She acknowledged a boy off to the left, the relief clear on her gorgeous features.

"How come you kept Ms. Obregon's bear if you thought she was dead?"

God almighty. Grace closed her eyes to stave off the wave of nausea and knocked off a few desperate Hail Marys in her head. The entire assembly went downhill from there. Despite repeated attempts by Simon and Madeira to keep the kids on topic, the questions ranged from "Did you fall in love at first sight when you crawled under the car?" and "How are you and Ms. Obregon going to have kids since you're both girls?" to "Could you see the bone sticking out of Ms. Obregon's leg when it was broken? Was it cool?"

They should have anticipated that the children would be more interested in the sensational aspects of the situation. Live and learn. Oddly enough, none of the teachers or parents made attempts to rein in the questions, and Gracie spent the rest of the Q&A period sweating beneath her blazer and avoiding the million or so pairs of eyes that kept settling on her. Everyone wanted the skinny on her life, it seemed.

Finally, Simon stopped the interminable questions and led the long, snaking line of children out the side door of the auditorium for a quick walk through the rig. Grace limped dutifully alongside her class, holding shy little Mona's hand, but frankly she wanted to perish on the spot. When her class made it to the front and began entering the business end of the boxy ambulance in groups of five, she stood to the side. Madeira spoke in an animated voice to the children, but Grace could feel her awareness like hot rays of the sun.

No sunscreen.

So, naturally, Layton chose that moment to approach, because Grace's life just sucked that way these days. "Hi, Grace." She looked nice in a pair of khaki pants and a loose-fitting shirt, untucked, and she carried her jacket and briefcase.

Grace wouldn't cower. She didn't have anything to hide. "Hi, Layton. Heading out?" Since art was considered a "specials" class, Layton didn't have regular students.

"I am." She ran her hand over her curly light brown hair. "Say, I just wanted to make sure we're still on for dinner tomorrow night."

In her peripheral vision, she saw Madeira's full attention snap to their conversation. Perspiration began to bead on Grace's upper lip. She whisked it away. "Of course. Seven, right?"

Layton cleared her throat. "Yes…well, because after the assembly, I got to thinking about not wanting to step on anyone's toes again, and—"

"You won't," Grace insisted, her tone more firm than she'd intended. She tried to soften it with a smile. "I'll see you tomorrow night. I'm looking forward to it."

Layton's face spread into a relieved smile. "As am I."

After Layton had ambled off toward the faculty parking lot, Grace eased out a sigh and pressed two fingers to the stress point between her brows. She closed her eyes, wanting desperately for this evil day to end.

"Need an aspirin?" Madeira whispered, her breath warm as an angel's caress on Grace's cheek.

Startled, Grace jerked her hand away from her face. She offered a weak smile, gauging Madeira for any jealousy and finding none. She didn't quite know how to feel about that, but she appreciated the effort nonetheless. "Screw aspirin, I need a drink."

Madeira nodded her agreement. "So…who was that?"

Uh-oh. Here it came. Grace chose to answer the question Madeira had asked, rather than those she hadn't. "Layton Fair. She teaches art."

"You going out with her?"

Grace met her gaze levelly. "I am," she said, her tone intentionally breezy. "To dinner. Tomorrow night."

Madeira's throat tightened on a carefully controlled swallow, but she did manage a mildly disinterested smile. "That's great. She seemed like an all-right woman to me."

"Well, thanks for your approval."

Madeira ignored that, gazing off toward the faculty lot. "I hope you have a good time."

Grace couldn't have been more stunned. *Well, what did you want her to do, nitwit? Pound her chest and demand you cancel?*

No.

Maybe.

Oh, shut the hell up, she ordered her conscience.

She felt oddly deflated in spite of herself and took a long gulp of air before answering. "T-thanks. I hope so, too. It's just dinner."

"Mmm."

Noncommittal.

Silence yawned between them, growing more uncomfortable by the moment. Grace didn't want the day to end on that note, so she touched Madeira's arm "Thank you, Maddee. I really mean that."

Madeira gave her a devastating, dimple-pulling smile, but her eyes were unreadable. "No sweat, Gracie. What are friends for?"

CHAPTER ELEVEN

Las penas con pan son menos.
With bread, all grief is lessened.

"You do realize you just inhaled my entire fifty-dollar box of Godiva truffles, right?" Lola asked, glaring at Grace's reflection in the beauty station mirror. Grace had stopped by to drop off the stack of flyers for the bachelor auction Madeira and Simon had given her. Lola guilt-tripped her into a trim by claiming the sight of Grace's dry ends made her physically ill.

"Fifty bucks of Godiva isn't that much chocolate."

"Yeah, right! If you were a dog, you'd be dead right now."

Grace stole a shamefaced glance at her sis. "You offered."

"I offered *one*."

"I don't recall negotiating a specific limit."

"What are you now, a lawyer?" Lola took a threatening stance. "Don't cross a woman who has your hair in one hand and shears in the other."

Grace rolled her eyes. "You don't scare me. Your reputation is too important for you to give me a heinous cut."

Lola didn't deny it, but she continued to pout over the half-pound of chocolate working its way into full bloat mode in Grace's stomach. "Do you have any idea how many fat grams you just threw down your gullet?"

"As if I care. Look, I'll pay you back when we get home, if you're going to be a big, stingy whore about it," Grace mumbled as she sucked the decadent brown nectar of the gods off her fingers. "I needed a fix. You know how I am when it comes to chocolate."

"Hmph." Lola gave new meaning to the word "snippy" with her stiff-backed clipping of Grace's locks. "Next time, satisfy your cravings with Hershey's, okay? And buy it yourself."

"Fine, Jesus. Some loving sister you are, hoarding chocolate in my time of need." Grace waved her sticky fingers. Truth? She loved bantering with Lola, even though it drove DoDo absolutely nuts. Lola thrived on their snark wars, too, and neither of them ever meant true harm. DoDo paid no mind to that. She just thought arguing was unseemly, especially for women.

Which made Grace want to do it more.

Evil granddaughter! Thwack! Thwack!

"Just cut, will you? I have math papers to grade." Her least favorite task.

"Quit cracking the whip, or I *will* pull a Britney-freaking-out-on-the-paparazzi-with-an-umbrella on your head. Trust me, I wouldn't be the first stylist who yearned to shave an annoying client's head."

"You would not shave my head."

"Risk it, then, if you think you're woman enough." Lola's perfectly arched brow raised in cool challenge. "I'd become a hero among my peers and you'd become a hat lover, PDQ."

Grace studied her reflection and pondered how she might look bald. Not great, she decided, not with these ears. She laid off the nagging, settling back to sluggishly metabolize some truffles. Really, she trusted Lola implicitly to do the right thing with her hair, but she liked keeping baby sis on her toes.

"What's up with you and the chocolate anyway? PMS?" Lola's scissors snip-snip-snipped away at Grace's split ends.

"Close. FWS," Grace said. "Frustrating Woman Syndrome."

Lola drew up long strands of Grace's hair until just the uneven ends showed between her fingers, then sliced them off with the very shiny, very expensive scissors she kept in a locked safe when the shop was closed. "I thought you said you and Madeira were getting along better? Hell, the woman gave her blessing for this travesty of a date you're going on, what more do you want?"

A lot more, answered Fickle Grace, the evil twin who lived inside Sensible Grace just to make life more difficult. "How do you know I'm even referring to Madeira?"

Lola paused mid-trim for an exaggerated "puh-lease" look.

"And anyway, it's not a travesty of a date." Grace sniffed. "Layton is an awesome woman."

"I'm sure she is." Lola paused for effect. "That doesn't mean she's the right woman for you."

"How do you know she isn't?"

"Because Madeira is, dipshit, and women aren't like truffles—eventually, you have to pick just *one*."

Grace smirked. "Clever. Point-maker."

Lola grinned, then grew serious again. "Come on. You saw the sign as clearly as DoDo and I did. She called you Gracie," Lo stage-whispered. She set her shears on the station and pulled her fingers through the sides of Grace's hair and down to her collarbones, checking that the lengths matched. "You're just too stubborn to admit what that truly means."

Grace stared at the little wet hair clots spotting the cape that covered her, trying not to wish *too fervently* that Madeira's use of the revered nickname had been a sign. "All it means is that she was being sweet to me, trying to make me feel better under that car. Nothing more than that."

"Maybe. But *why* would a stranger call you Gracie when you told her your name was Grace? Did you ever stop to wonder who sent her underneath that car?" She caught Grace's gaze in the mirror and waited until realization began to dawn before adding, "We both know Mama is our guardian angel."

Oh my God. An eerie recognition skittered up Grace's spine, and she shivered violently.

Lola lifted up Grace's hair and checked her nape for goose bumps, glancing back up with an incredulous expression. "You hadn't thought of that, had you?"

"Actually…no. So what?"

Lola did a little "I rule" dance in back of the chair, then wrapped Grace in an awkward hug from behind. "Grace, Mama's always with us. It totally makes sense."

"Matchmaker from beyond the grave," Grace snapped. "Yeah. That only makes sense if you read the *National Enquirer*."

"Admit how uncanny it is that Madeira happened to show up at that pivotal moment in your life."

Grace clamped her bottom lip in between her teeth.

Lola went on. "You think angels in heaven don't have to enlist the aid of angels on earth now and then?"

Ugh! It sounded so impossibly possible. Grace covered her ears with her hands, singing, "La la la la, I don't hear you," but Lola wrestled them off.

Hands entwined, they engaged in a little isometric struggle while Lola continued pleading her point. "Listen to me. Mama always did want to give you your Ms. Right. Hence the bear. But once Madeira came along…well, maybe this was Mama's way."

Grace had to admit, it made a freakish kind of daytime-talk-show sense. She stopped resisting, and they released each other's hands.

Lola pulled open the Velcro closure on the plastic cape and whisked it from Grace's shoulders with flourish. "The only problem is, Mama forgot to give you the brains to recognize a good sign when it shows up."

"Would you stop?" Grace rasped, feeling off-kilter and tingly and wishing with her whole heart that Mama could pop in and either confirm or deny the hypothesis. She glanced around as though someone might overhear, even though the salon had emptied an hour earlier. "Maybe it is a sign. Maybe not. But I have a date tonight and it's not with Madeira. I can't have this on my mind. It's not fair to Layton." She glanced frantically around the cutting station, lifting brushes and shoving aside bottles and tubes, opening and closing drawers.

"Okay, but think about it after the date. Promise me."

"I promise." A paddle brush spun off the edge of the counter and hit the floor with a crack.

Lola frowned. "What are you looking for?"

"Something else to eat," Grace muttered. "I'm suddenly in desperate need of a therapeutic binge."

As she'd suspected, Grace had a perfectly fine time on her date with Layton, despite being a tiny bit uncomfortable due to an unusually tight waistband—go figure. But Layton had been kind and attentive, and the small Italian restaurant she'd suggested provided ambience, great food and service, and just enough seclusion to make it perfect for a first date. She'd even refrained from comment when Grace had asked the waitress for a third basket of garlic knots.

They had teaching in common, and the conversation was easy. Layton listened to her, really heard her, even laughed at the correct moments. Conclusion: Layton Fair was a nice woman. In the world of New Grace, Layton was perfect on paper.

So…why did it feel as if something was missing?

Layton pulled her Honda Accord up to the curb in front of Grace's house and slipped the transmission into park, pulling Grace out of her bleak thoughts. Layton smiled in the darkness. "Home safe and before the witching hour. You seem tired, Grace."

Grace glanced at the clock on the dash, really truly wanting to adore this woman, because it would make things so easy. Eleven o'clock. She wasn't tired, she was brooding. Layton didn't deserve that. "It is early, and I'm really not all that tired." She smiled. "Please come in for coffee. I'd like that."

Layton twisted the key in the ignition. "I'd love coffee."

As they traversed the walk, Layton settled her palm at the small of Grace's back, much like Madeira had done. Grace waited for the electricity to heat her skin, but felt nothing. She bit her lip, consumed with remorse. She had initiated this date, and she owed it to Layton not to continually compare her with Madeira. It made no sense—Layton and Madeira were two vastly different women and this wasn't a competition.

This whole thing was Lola's fault for filling her head with thoughts of divine intervention just before she had to prepare for her date. On the porch, she paused to fish her keys from her pocket. Tossing back her hair, she regarded Layton in the gold glow of the outside light. "I'm sorry if I've been distracted. It was a beast of a week for me."

"If anything, Grace, you're distract*ing*." She smiled. "No need to apologize."

Grateful and guilt-ridden both, she unlocked and pushed through the door, then flicked on the overhead light, stopping to take both her coat and Layton's and hang them on the hall tree. She saw the undulating blue glow of the television set from the otherwise dark living room and hoped it was Lola. She didn't like to think she'd kept DoDo up all this time.

But when she peered around the corner, it turned out to be neither of them, and in the split second it took her to recognize who sat sprawled on the sofa with her feet on the coffee table, Grace learned the true meaning of curdling blood.

"M-maddee?" Surprise and outrage rendered her speechless for a moment, and Layton appeared at her shoulder.

Madeira smiled innocently, pausing to flick the television on mute. "Oh, hi, Gracie." She glanced at Layton, then sprang up from the couch to offer her hand. "Hey, nice to finally meet you. Layton, isn't it? I'm Madeira Pacias."

"Yes, I know." Layton bestowed a genuine smile. "I teach at Grace's school, too. Great assembly."

Madeira snapped her fingers. "Oh, that's right. Gracie mentioned that. Thanks." Madeira slipped her hands in her pockets and rocked on her feet for a moment, smiling placidly, looking for all the world as if she'd never heard the phrase "third wheel."

Grace sputtered out of her shock-induced silence, finally. "Maddee, what are you doing here?"

Madeira blinked in bafflement before a understanding dawned. "Oh, hey. I can turn off the movie and go hide out in your room for a while if you'd like, Gracie."

"M-m-my room?"

"So you can finish your date, of course." She spread her legs into a comfortable but very sexy stance and crossed her well-defined arms over an equally toned chest. Maddee's thin T-shirt only emphasized the perfection of her physique.

"You still haven't answered my question," Grace said.

"Right, sorry. Lola called me and asked if I could come sit with DoDo until she got home."

"W-why? Where did she go?"

"Out." Maddee shrugged. "I don't know. But DoDo was having some mild chest discomfort earlier, so Lola didn't want her alone. I've checked her vitals every hour, and she's doing fine."

Grace blinked several times, trying to digest it all and not believing half of it. Still, she didn't want to handle news about her grandmother's health in a cavalier manner. She smoothed her fingers through her hair, struggling to sound calm, to stay focused on the most important matter. "DoDo's having chest pains?"

"Not full-on chest pains." Madeira gave a little maybe-so, maybe-not shrug. "It could be indigestion. She claimed to be fine, but Lola didn't want to take any chances."

"It was really good of you to sit with her," Layton said.

Madeira grinned broadly. "My pleasure."

Yeah, I'll bet, Grace thought. At a loss for what else to do, she started toward the kitchen intent on making coffee but whirled to face the two women at the entrance to the dining room. She couldn't quite make eye contact with either of them. "Madeira, thank you for coming. I hope we didn't spoil any plans you might have had."

"Not a one. My schedule was blank."

And on a Saturday night, even. Interesting. She cleared her throat. "You can head out now. I'll look in on DoDo until Lola gets home."

"Great." Madeira smoothed her palms together, then jabbed a thumb over her shoulder. "I've got my equipment here. I'll just take her vitals one more time."

Grace paused, but what was she going to say? No, don't check on my grandmother who's been having chest pains? "O-okay. Thanks."

Madeira gave Layton a companionable clap on the back, then disappeared up the steps.

Grace released a breath and glanced at the Layton, dismayed to find her looking as open and accepting as she'd been the whole evening. Poor woman. Grace shouldn't have dragged her into this nightmare. "Layton? Why don't we have our coffee in here?" She pointed to the kitchen.

"Ah…look, Grace. I think I'll just head out."

"No, please. I'm sorry this—" She didn't quite know how to apologize, so she simply shrugged and let her arms fall against her thighs, pleading her forgiveness with her eyes.

Layton crossed the room. "Don't. It's fine. I can see you're upset about your grandmother—"

A fresh pang of guilt struck Grace—as if she hadn't suffered her share of the acrid stuff all night long.

"—and like you said, it was a long week."

She nodded, touched that Layton would be this understanding about an interloper ruining the end of their date. She truly was a great catch, spot-on girlfriend material, and totally wasted on a fool like Grace.

"You're right." Grace sighed, smiling as she tilted her head to the side. "You're awfully sweet, you know that?"

Layton inclined her head. "Thank you."

"No. Thank you. For a wonderful evening." Grace walked her slowly to the door and handed over her coat.

"We'll have to do this again soon."

"Sure," Grace said, feeling like a louse.

Layton leaned forward and kissed her softly on the cheek. "I'll see you Monday?"

She nodded. "Yes." Grace watched her out to her car, then shut and deadbolted the door. Sagging, she rested her forehead against the cold, solid wood. How could she go out on a date with a seemingly perfect woman and end up at home with Madeira, and why did it feel so goddamned right…and wrong…at the same time? Lifting her head slightly, she clonked it on the door a couple of times, hoping blunt trauma might rattle out the demons of reckless stupidity.

"That good a date, *fierita*?" Madeira asked wryly from the top of the stairs. She wore a sympathetic expression, as though Grace's current state of discombobulation had anything whatsoever to do with her evening.

Grace turned and watched Maddee descend, too drained to deny, too glad to see her to keep the fires of annoyance stoked beyond a simmering blue flame. She couldn't blame Madeira. Lola had clearly set this up, and to Madeira's credit, she hadn't pulled the jealousy scene Grace had feared when she first saw her sitting there. "Don't even get me started."

Madeira paused on the landing and regarded her with sympathy. "I'm here if you need to talk."

"I don't want to talk." She limped toward the kitchen, not wanting anything except to get away from the distraction of Madeira, the allure of her comfort.

"Okay, but if you change your mind—"

"I won't."

"I'll be here. What are friends for?"

Gracie ignored Madeira, but she trailed Grace like a regret.

Yet another regret.

"Layton wasn't mean to you, was she? Or was it just boring?"

Grace spun to face Madeira wanting, needing to dispel her false impressions. "Layton wasn't mean or boring or anything else. She's an amazing, kind woman and the date was"—she flipped her hands, palms up—"perfect," she finished, in a funereal tone. Reaching out, she turned Madeira toward the front door and propelled her that way. "But, like I've *said*, I don't want to talk about it. My week has been hell. I'm tired. And I'm perfectly capable of caring for DoDo, so you're free to leave."

Madeira went willingly, almost cheerfully. "Okay. But I have to say, it makes me happy to know you had a perfect date with a perfect woman, Gracie. You deserve that."

"Thanks," Grace said, thrown off guard and not quite trusting Madeira's heartfelt admission. That really idiotic part of her didn't want Madeira to be this happy she was with another woman, either.

A pause. "You going out with her again?" A silence ensued while Madeira gathered her belongings, not looking at her. Bag packed and secured with its plastic clips, she slung it over her shoulder and cocked her head. "Gracie?"

Grace sagged against the wall. "Probably not."

Madeira looked completely baffled. "Why not? I thought you said she was a great—"

"She is," Grace said, heading toward the stairs. Halfway up, when her foot creaked loudly on step twelve, she turned and met Madeira's gaze. "Layton *is* an awesome catch." *She's just not you*, Grace thought traitorously. "Good night."

"I'm sure it will work out if it's meant to. A smart woman told me that once."

Grace gave her a listless smile. "Yeah."

"Anyway." Madeira blew her a kiss. "Sleep with the angels."

Gripping the railing, Grace gaped at Madeira while shock swirled black stars in her vision. Her heart sprang up to lodge firmly in her throat.

Sleep with the angels?

No way. It couldn't be.

When the door snicked shut behind Madeira, Grace collapsed onto the step, dumbfounded, hand still clutching the smooth wooden railing. Her breaths shallowed, part pain, part wonder. Would Lola be so cruel as to set her up like this, suggesting Madeira use that particular meaningful phrase? Mama had bid her and Lola good night with those exact words every night of their way-too-short life together. Grace pondered it and decided…no. No matter how much matchmaking Lola thought Madeira and Grace were meant for each other, she wouldn't stoop so low as to manipulate Grace's emotions in such a painful way. In which case, it could only be…a sign?

Another sign?

No.

Grace threaded her fingers into her hair, staring at the door and toying with the abstract concept of angels on earth. She didn't want to believe it. The whole thing was fetched so damn far, not even Jerry Springer would believe it. Still…there had to be an explanation, and Grace meant to find it before she lost any more of her sanity.

Madeira sat in her truck for a few minutes struggling to slow the blood thumping through her temples. She'd done it. She'd survived seeing Gracie with another woman despite the fact it had nearly killed her on the spot. She knew this wasn't the politically correct response, but she'd wanted to tear Layton to shreds, bang her own chest, and drag Gracie off to some cave where she could brand her permanently.

Mine.

Wouldn't Gracie just love that? She laughed with scorn, then scrubbed the heels of her hands into her tired eyes. Okay, focus. Starting with her tight forehead and jaw and working down, she concentrated on relaxing each and every one of her muscles, one at a time. She needed to chill before turning her key in the ignition, or she'd be as much of a hazard on the road as that semi driver had been a year ago.

This backing-off plan was going to be harder than she'd ever imagined. Granted, Gracie had said she didn't intend to go out with Layton again, an admission that had provided a moment of satisfaction. But that didn't mean she wouldn't go out with someone else, and maybe the next woman would be the one who made Gracie's face light up with love.

And then I'll die inside.

Madeira's grip convulsed on the steering wheel. Wasn't gonna happen. Call her a blind optimist, but she couldn't make herself believe fate could be that cruel. She jabbed the button to roll down the window, in desperate need of a slap of cool air to bring her to her senses. Closing her eyes, she leaned toward the open window and inhaled deeply. The night smelled of fallen leaves and the promise of cold, the kind of scents that made Madeira want to find a creative way to keep her woman warm all night long. Who would be keeping Gracie warm when winter came? Madeira's fists clenched automatically, but she made an effort to relax them.

Stay calm. She'll come around eventually.

God, Madeira prayed it were true. She had a hell of a lot banked on this plan of Iris's, despite her reservations. She also hoped that Lola and DoDo had had the right idea tonight, thrusting her in Gracie's face like they had. She felt a twinge of guilt for the manipulation, then figured she'd do just about anything to keep from losing Gracie forever, even if it meant pretending DoDo was ill—which had been the wily old *abue's* brainstorm in the first place and one Madeira had argued vehemently against. But DoDo would have none of it. The idea was to keep Madeira fresh in Gracie's mind without any pressure, without Madeira tipping her emotional hand. She'd managed pretty well until just before she'd left.

Madeira snorted and revved the idling engine of her truck.

What on earth had made her blow Gracie a kiss and bid her good night with that sentimental phrase her mother had used when she and Toro had been little girls?

Sleep with the angels?

Madeira hadn't thought of those words in a decade or more, and suddenly POOF, there they were on the tip of her tongue, clear evidence that seeing Gracie stripped her of what little sense she had left. If Madeira wasn't careful, Gracie would pick up on the fact that Madeira wasn't as objective about the whole thing as she pretended.

And then she'd be back at square one.

No Gracie. *No chance.*

Madeira's resolve hardened. Tomorrow night at dinner, she'd be more careful, more distant. No matter how difficult it was, Madeira told herself as she pulled away from the curb, she wouldn't let her love for Gracie trip her up. She'd be so damned platonic at dinner, Gracie would wonder if Madeira was the long-lost sister she never knew she had.

❖

After getting ready for bed, Grace clutched her pillow to her chest and crept down the hall, acting on pure sisterly instinct. She eased open the conniving little ho's door, absolutely certain she'd find Lola snoring beneath the covers. And if she *did* find her there, she'd be compelled to beat her inert form with the pillow until Lola begged for mercy and 'fessed up.

Grace held her breath until the hall light cast a cone of illumination into the dark room…slowly…slowly…and onto the bed.

Empty?

Huh.

She relaxed against the doorjamb, one foot atop the other. So maybe it hadn't been a set-up. A wave of relief washed over her, followed quickly by a rough slap of tension. If the whole thing hadn't been a ruse, what had prompted Madeira to use Mama's favorite tuck-in phrase?

Divine intervention?

Grace hugged her arms around her middle.

There was only one way to find out for sure. Padding back toward her room, Gracie made herself a promise. The next time the opportunity presented itself, she'd ask Madeira point-blank what made her say it. If she didn't lose her nerve, that is. She shivered at the prospect of hearing the answer, unwilling to believe it had been anything but a coincidence. Never mind that DoDo insisted there were no coincidences in this life, only signs.

Graciela Inez Obregon did *not* believe in signs.

CHAPTER TWELVE

Hacer de tripas corazón.
What can't be cured must be endured.

Dinner on Sunday started out as a pleasant surprise considering the tumultuous evening that had preceded it. Madeira made no mention of Grace's date with Layton, instead regaling her, Lola, and DoDo with interesting tales from her work while they ate one of DoDo's special meals—paella. She tried to tone down the stories, but DoDo would have none of that. She kept pressing for gory details until Madeira relented. By the time the homemade caramel flan was served, Madeira had all three of them equal parts engrossed and grossed out, and Grace had finally relaxed.

And then the other shoe fell.

"So, let me ask you this, Madeira, because it's been on my mind," said DoDo. "Is it true what they said in the papers about you becoming an EMT because of Graciela's accident?"

Grace tensed, but the only one who caught it was Madeira. She reached beneath the table and covered Grace's quaking hand with her own as if to reassure. Their eyes met, and Grace gulped back a moan at how tingly one simple touch made her feel. Maddee had been completely hands-off lately, and Grace had missed the feel of her.

What a loser.

How was it Grace could go out with a perfect-on-paper woman one night and feel nothing beyond friendship, and the next night sit in her kitchen with her grandmother, sister, and a woman she claimed she wanted no part of and feel…everything? Grace didn't get it. Was she destined to be attracted only to women who would hurt her? Maybe she did take after Mama more than she'd figured.

"Yes," Madeira said finally, tearing Gracie out of her ruminations. "It is true." She looked down at her flan, lips pressed together.

Everyone waited with bated breath for her to continue.

"The truth is, I felt so helpless under that car. Gracie was"—she shook her head at the painful memory—"really hurt. I could see that, but I had no idea how to help."

"What are you talking about? You did great," Grace insisted.

Madeira shrugged as if to imply she disagreed, then looked back at DoDo. "After the police told me she died"—she broke off, her throat working over some emotion that etched brackets of pain around her mouth—"I couldn't help but think she might have lived had I known what to do."

"But I didn't die."

"Didn't matter. I thought you had, believed it with my whole heart." She met and held Grace's gaze, eyes warm and full of enough affection that Grace's stomach contracted. "I became a medic so I'd never feel that lost, that useless again."

DoDo and Lola sighed, but Gracie just stared, feeling so mixed up and emotional, so grateful their paths had crossed yet still desperate to escape Maddee's spell. It seemed like forever since she'd seen that old familiar flame in Maddee's eyes, and Grace basked in its warmth like a backpacker with only one log, bellied up to a campfire that would dwindle to ashes far too soon. "You weren't useless," Grace said, trying to convey the depth of that statement with her gaze. "I'm sorry you felt that way. I would've been lost and panicked without you."

To Grace's surprise and dismay, Maddee tossed off a carefree smile and released her hand beneath the table. "Eh, don't sweat it. If it hadn't been for that day, I wouldn't have my current career, which I love." She took up her fork, as though they'd just been discussing nothing more important than why she'd chosen cargo pants instead of blue jeans that day. "I have you to thank for leading me to a very fulfilling job."

Okay, now Grace was completely confused. Face aflame, she followed suit and lifted her fork, concentrating on her dessert. Maddee's explanation had seemed so heartfelt, but Grace had to admit, other than that, Maddee had been overwhelmingly platonic the entire night.

Maybe wishful thinking had her reading subtext into what Maddee had intended as nothing more than a straightforward explanation.

Clearly she had made Maddee uncomfortable with her emotional display.

Had she gotten over Grace so easily?

Grace bit her lip.

Served her right, she supposed.

The four of them spent a few minutes eating and exclaiming over the flan, and thankfully, the awkward moment passed. Maybe, Gracie thought, the awkward moment had been hers alone. The possibility depressed her. Nothing worse than wanting a woman more than *she* wanted *you*. How quickly the tables turn, Grace thought, suffering a fresh bout of self-disgust.

"DoDo," Madeira said, after finishing her flan. "I noticed you have a couple squeaky steps in the staircase."

DoDo uttered a sound of defeat. "*Ay*, those stairs. They've groaned since the girls were little." She passed a knowing look to Grace and Lola. "These two even learned how to avoid the looser boards in high school so I wouldn't know when they were sneaking in past curfew… or so they thought."

Lola laughed. "Told you she knew."

Madeira chuckled, too. "Mothers and grandmothers always know."

"That's right," DoDo said.

Swear to freaking God, the tension of this pleasant, innocent small talk was going to make Grace snap into a psychotic frenzy. It was bad enough she had to sit there next to a woman she'd pushed and pushed and pushed away until Maddee didn't want her anymore, but now Grace had completely lost her ability to read her. Confusion reigned. Grace felt like a wishy-washy jumble of lust and neediness, unanswered questions and uncertainty. If Madeira could hear her thoughts, she'd run. Fast and far. Who wanted to be with an indecisive flake? "What about the steps?" she asked.

Madeira cleared her throat, addressing DoDo. "You know, I've done a bit of carpentry. I'd be glad to fix them for you." She gave her an indulgent smile. "I'm pretty good with my hands, if I do say so myself."

Grace's lungs squeezed, and in a moment of poor judgment, her gaze flew to her sister. Lola read into her startled look, sucking her cheeks into a blatantly innuendo-laden, *hubba-hubba* expression. Grace scowled a warning, but thankfully Madeira and DoDo ignored them both.

"Oh, *m'ija*, that would be wonderful. You know how it is with an old house." DoDo gestured widely. "Always too many things to fix and not enough time or money."

"*Sí*, I do know. Only too well." Madeira leaned in. "*Mira*. Why don't you make me a list of things that need repairs? I enjoy fixing things, and it's the least I can do to repay you."

"B-but, you're so busy at work. Won't it be too much trouble?" Grace asked, praying Maddee would rescind the offer.

"Not at all." She glanced at her and then shared a private smile with DoDo. "It's the least I can do for the three women who helped me feel less homesick for *mi mamá* and my baby sisters."

Swell.

Now Maddee thought of her as a sister! Grace glanced down at her utensils and pondered…suicide by butter knife? Nah. Not quick or efficient enough. The table blurred before her eyes. Life had never sucked with quite so much force, not even the day Burn had done the inner thigh tattoo. She'd thought that was the worst pain she would ever feel.

Wrong again, Grace.

"I'll pay you, of course," DoDo said.

"Nonsense. All I ask in payment is a good meal like this now and then." She patted her stomach and her mouth pulled ruefully to one side. "Living alone, with my schedule, I must admit I don't eat as well as I should."

"That's so generous of you, *m'ija*," DoDo gushed, hands clasped at her chest.

"What you need is a wife. Or a partner—whatever terminology you prefer," Lola said.

Grace didn't even glance up from the pit of resignation into which she'd descended.

"Ah, but with all of you, what do I need with a partner?"

Grace couldn't help but flinch. Ugh. It just kept getting better, didn't it? "DoDo, do we have any Kahlúa? I think I'd like some in my coffee." *Like a whole bottle, for example.*

"Good idea." DoDo bustled up and refilled all the coffee cups on the table, adding a small dollop of liqueur to each mug. After she'd set down the heavy brown bottle, Grace picked it up and added a second generous *chug-chug-chug* to her mug, needing all the liquid courage she could guzzle. She stirred the concoction with her index finger, then sucked down a generous mouthful, coughing against her fist on the exhale.

DoDo appraised her thoughtfully, but refrained from comment, thank goodness. After a moment, she regarded Madeira. "I'll get to work on that list bright and early tomorrow, and I insist on paying for all the parts, at least. In addition to feeding you, of course, which is my pleasure."

"Whatever makes you happy, DoDo."

Panic rose in Grace's throat as she contemplated what exactly this fix-it arrangement would mean to her sanity. She pushed back from the table and began to carry dishes to the sink. Her heart pounded and her hands trembled as she filled the basin with water and added way too much soap. Tiny bubbles broke off from the steadily growing mound, rising in the air to pop in front of her like little unrealized dreams. How apt. Absently, she began to dump dishes and utensils into the water, grateful her back faced the rest of the room. If she was lucky, they wouldn't sense her trembling.

But seriously. Just what she needed—Madeira lurking about the house with sweat-sheened muscles and a low-slung tool belt. She was used to living with DoDo and Lola, totally uninhibited. What happened if Grace dashed down to the laundry room in her underwear to grab a shirt from the dryer, only to realize that Maddee was rehanging a squeaky door?

A sexy image that included Maddee in a skimpy tank top and tool belt, with Grace naked atop the washing machine during spin cycle, caught her by surprise. Her eyes fluttered closed. She reached out to scoop up more dishes and grabbed DoDo's very sharp Henckels chef knife by the blade instead of the handle, only realizing her mistake when the tempered steel bit into the soft flesh of her fingers. "Oh!"

Her yelp startled everyone to their feet.

She threw the knife into the empty side of the double sink with a clatter, gripping her sliced fingers with her other hand. A steady stream of bloody bubbles ran down the sink, and tears stung her eyes from the pain. "Damn." She bit her lip.

"*M'ijita*, what happened?"

"T-the knife." Grace blinked rapidly. "I wasn't paying attention."

DoDo tsk-tsked, dashing over to turn off the water. Her eyes widened when she saw the extent of the damage. "My goodness, you have to be careful," she chided, but not unkindly.

In a flash, Madeira stood beside her, steadying Grace with her warm, hard body. "Let me see." She tried to examine the cuts, but Grace held the injured hand in a shaky death grip. "Let go, Gracie. Don't squeeze so tightly."

"It h-hurts." Unshed tears raised her voice an octave.

"I know, baby. I know. I just need to see how deep the cuts are." Madeira managed to pry the injured hand loose from the other, and turned to Lola. She extracted keys from her pants pocket and lobbed them to her.

Lola palmed them easily, her eyes wide with worry. "What do you need?"

"My orange medical bag. Behind the driver's seat."

Lola lit off with a quick nod. "Hang on, Grace," she called over her shoulder.

"DoDo, do you have a towel or some muslin you don't mind ruining? The cuts are pretty deep. I'd like to wrap them before I take her to the hospital."

"Of course. I just bought some unbleached muslin for my quilting bee. Let me just…" DoDo bustled off, still talking.

"The hospital?" Gracie asked, or maybe whimpered, as the first tear trickled down her cheek. She felt dizzy just thinking about it. Hospitals didn't rank on her favorite places list after spending all those weeks in traction with her leg.

"'Fraid so. This is too deep, *rayito de luz,* I'm sure you'll need stitches." With sympathy in her eyes, Madeira wicked a tear from Grace's cheekbone with her rough-gentle finger, and Grace's breathing ceased. She remembered those fingers from the accident scene, from the year that followed when she'd only imagined them, and her, and dreamed she'd magically appear and touch her with them again. "Damn."

Madeira cast a quick glance over her shoulder. "You keep swearing and DoDo's going to make you write me a letter of apology," she whispered.

Grace knew Maddee was trying to cheer her up. Her chin trembled, and she stared at the sliced and diced fingers of her right hand, angry at her own carelessness. "I doubt I'll be writing anything anytime soon." Tears began to plink-plunk on her arm. "I'm such an idiot." And not just for the cuts.

"It's okay. Hey." They weren't so different in height, but Maddee still bent her knees until her face was level with Grace's. "Look at me, babe."

Grace did. How could she not when Maddee called her "babe" in that intoxicating voice?

"You'll be fine. And they'll give you some excellent pain drugs, too. I'll be with you. Okay?"

Grace wanted to be tough, to tell her she didn't need her. Didn't need anyone. But she couldn't. She hated hospitals after the semi crash. "Promise?"

"I promise." Madeira's smile lit up the room. "I won't leave that hospital without you, Gracie."

Another vague memory surfaced from the day of the crash. Grace gave a watery laugh, then shook her head, studying Maddee through her tears. "This rescue scenario is becoming way too big a part of our relationship, Maddee."

Madeira pulled her into a hug. "*Mira*. I'll rescue you as many times as it takes, *fierita*. Believe me. As many times as it takes."

Grace melted into the embrace wondering what exactly Madeira had meant by that.

❖

Grace shivered, cold on the uncomfortable gurney with only a sheet to ward off the chill. They'd made her remove her long-sleeved shirt, offering only a threadbare hospital gown in its place. The fact that she'd lost a bit of blood probably didn't help with the warmth factor, nor did the fact that Madeira sat next to her bed, as kind and caring and concerned as…a sister.

What did you expect?

With a sigh, Grace turned her head away and stared at the pastel-striped fabric divider. She didn't know what she'd expected, only what she felt. Right now she felt lonely and bleak and desperate. In the section next to hers, a mother crooned softly to her little boy, who'd come in with a broken leg that was waiting to be set and casted. The intimate, familial sounds of the woman's voice saddened Grace and made her yearn for things she'd lost…things she'd never really stopped wanting, no matter how much she'd tried to convince herself otherwise.

She knew her flip-flopping feelings about Madeira were flighty and unfair and that she needed to make up her damn mind what she wanted and then stick to it. Her good hand bunched the sheet. If only things were that simple.

If only she weren't so damn scared.

After the nurse pushed some sort of narcotic into her IV tube, several minutes passed while Grace lay stiffly on her back, jaw clenched against the dull, relentless throbbing in her hand. She remained silent, unable to bear the thought of carrying on a conversation until the pain dulled. She could pinpoint the exact moment the pain drugs kicked in. Her whole body loosened, including her traitorous tongue.

Turning to Madeira without any provocation whatsoever, she blurted, "You know, I'm getting these tattoos removed next week. I wish I'd never gotten the stupid things." Her brain caught up with her mouth several seconds later, but the damage had been done. She tried not to cringe.

Madeira's face came up from the magazine she'd been perusing, and she immediately chucked it to the side. "Did you say tattoos, with an *s*? As in, plural?"

Whoops. Grace giggled like a cheap drunk. "No. I must have slurred or something." Her index finger shot up and wavered in the air between them. "One tattoo. Singular."

Madeira stood slowly and approached the gurney, leaning forward to rest her forearms on the metal side rails and smile at Grace with amusement in her eyes. "Let me guess, as if I need to. Drugs are on board."

"Yup. On board and riding first class. I think they're even ordering drinks." Maddee blurred before her eyes, so Grace squinted.

"Can I see it?"

"See what?"

Madeira nodded toward her chest. "The tattoo. Last time I only got a glimpse."

Oh, good. She'd believed Grace about the tattoos. So much for DoDo thinking she wasn't a good liar. Ha! And as for the *Easy Vixen*, what the hell? Maddee had already seen it once. Grace tugged down the top of the gown to expose the glaring yellow beast, staring up at the wavering white ceiling tiles while Madeira scrutinized it. "You remember the little yammerhound from the day of the assembly?"

No answer.

She peered over and found Madeira just a little too entranced with the tattoo, so she hid it again.

Maddee looked at her, swallowing thickly. "What?"

"The talkative boy in my class. Remember?"

"Oh. Yes, of course." Madeira shook her head a couple times as though to clear it. "What about him?"

Grace took a deep breath. "His older brother, Steven, was in my first short-lived class, pre-semi. The night of the accident was parent/teacher conference night. My very first, which is why Ms. Right was in the car with me. Moral bear support."

"Ah, I didn't know that."

She nodded. "Anyway, in Steven's enthusiasm to tell me a story—"

"Hard to believe."

"Yeah." She laughed, and a little too boisterously. "Runs in the family. Anyway, he tugged on my sweater to get my attention and flashed the tattoo to his parents." She rolled her head from side to side on the crisp, waterproof pillow, listening to it crunch beneath her ears. She forced a swallow past a throat tightened by the ugly memory. "I remember the exact moment I realized they'd seen it. Their faces just… changed, Maddee." She closed her eyes, reliving the humiliation anew and hating it just as much.

"He didn't mean to do it."

"I know."

Madeira's hand smoothed her hair, her cheek, and Grace nestled into the caress. It felt so good to be touched by her, even simply as a gesture of platonic comfort. At this point in a very crappy day, she'd take what she could get. She drifted into an undulating sea of calmness, losing track of the story, of everything except the feel of Maddee's hand on her skin.

"So, what happened?"

"Oh, um…" She shrugged, sluggish. "Nothing, really. I finished the conference and moved on to the next parents. But I knew. Know what I mean? I had a sinking feeling in my stomach for the rest of the night, and it was all I could think of on the drive home. I wondered if maybe it was a sign that I wasn't fit to be a teacher. That I should go back behind the bar where I belonged."

Madeira gave her a sly look. "I thought you said you didn't believe in signs."

Whoops. She dodged the question. "Would you quit changing the subject?"

Chuckling, Madeira rolled her hand as if to say "go on," but a thought struck Grace's brain launching her off onto a previously unexplored tangent. "You know, maybe if I'd been paying better attention—"

"Shh." Madeira placed two fingers over Grace's lips to silence her, removing them when she settled back. "I saw the accident happen, Gracie, start to finish. No way you could have avoided that semi."

"You're probably right." Grace touched the spot on her chest marred by the so-called art. "The point is these tattoos give people the wrong impression about me."

"I thought you said you only had one?"

Damn drugs. What did they give her, a truth serum/morphine hybrid? She sighed, flopping her healthy hand on the sheet. "Okay, fine. I have two. But, no, you can't see the other one, so don't even bother asking."

Madeira arched a brow, one corner of her mouth quivering with a hidden smile. "Is that a 'for right now' rule or a forever rule? I'm just askin'." She grinned, and her curious gaze traced the form of Grace's body beneath the sheet, no doubt wondering which part the second tattoo adorned.

Grace tingled under the perusal, despite the drug haze and the fact Madeira wasn't even touching her. She ignored her question. "I'm trying to say…I've changed. I'm not the same jaded bartender who'd let some biker—named Burn, mind you—talk her into a couple of sleezy tattoos just for grins."

"Of course you're not, Gracie. We all grow and change."

She pulled her bottom lip between her teeth carefully, afraid her wicked buzz might make her bite down too hard and draw blood. "Even you?"

"I seem to change every day." Madeira smiled. "But back to you. Not that you asked my opinion, but I don't think you should get the tattoos removed."

Shock riddled through Grace. "Why not? They're ugly."

The roughened tip of Maddee's index finger touched Grace's nose lightly, and her whole face felt it. "They're you, *fierita*. As much as the sweet, innocent third-grade teacher is you. Everything in your life up to this point has made you who you are, so everything is valuable and nothing's a mistake."

"Oh, trust me. Some things are mistakes. Ex-things, for example, named Lurch, Rat, and…what was that other biker chick's name? Ah, yes. Mongrel. Arf, arf."

Madeira's eyes widened. "You went through a biker phase?"

"Yup."

She inclined her head toward Grace, conceding the point. "Okay, perhaps Lurch, Mongrel, and Rat were…errors in judgment. But, mistakes or not, we learn from all our experiences. They still shape us."

Maddee had a point. Grace would give her that. She'd never let another woman fix a Harley on her carpeting, thanks to Rat and her cronies, that was for damn sure. She blinked up at Madeira. "But don't you think if I want to show the world I've changed—"

"No." Madeira clasped Grace's uninjured hand between both of hers. "Listen to me. You don't have to run from your past just to have a better future. All you have to do is make the decision to live differently. Whether that happens slowly or because of some kind of life-changing epiphany doesn't matter."

Grace repositioned her head on the pillow and studied her. "How do you know all this?"

A mischievous grin lit on Maddee's face. "Show me the other tattoo and I'll tell you."

"No deal."

She sucked one cheek back in playful regret. "Ah, well. Can't blame a woman for trying."

Grace rolled her eyes, regretting it immediately when the wave of dizziness hit. If she thought she could reach, she'd hang her good leg off the gurney so her foot touched the floor. It had always worked for bed spins, if she remembered correctly.

"And to answer your question, I know because despite what you may think, there is more to me than meets the eye." Madeira looked mildly reproachful. "I have my share of deep thoughts, too."

"More than your fair share tonight, apparently."

They both laughed, drifted off, then the air between them stilled again. Grace's gaze fell on Maddee's strong, solid-looking hands. She reached out tentatively and touched the back of one lightly, making the gesture appear almost accidental. It felt hot and deceptively soft.

God, she wanted Madeira.

But Grace knew, if she had her once, she'd want her forever, and Madeira wasn't a forever kind of woman. She'd said so herself and, if anything, Madeira seemed like an honest person. Regret stabbed at Grace.

She could never have Madeira temporarily.

Not if she planned on being happy once it ended.

A woman couldn't be expected to survive with just a little bit of Madeira.

Mama, what should I do?

"Gracie?"

She jumped, startled to hear the nickname spoken immediately after she'd cast up a plea to Mama. Remembering that *two* people called her that, she swallowed. "Yeah?"

"Don't get the tattoos removed."

She sighed.

"They make you who you are. You don't have anything to prove to the world. Plus, removing them doesn't mean they were never there."

"I know."

Madeira shrugged. "I like them."

"You like them," she repeated, in a skeptical tone.

"Yes."

"Can I just ask…do you also like velvet Elvis paintings?"

Madeira laughed in that rich full way of hers that reached right down inside Grace and scrambled her sanity. She listened to her and drifted into a languid kind of ultra-cared-for warmth. Madeira's words made Grace feel special, tattoos and all. "Okay, I'll think about it."

"Really?"

Now, why had she gone and promised that? She sighed. Because Madeira was Madeira, and Gracie was all kinds of too-far-gone on her. "Yeah, really."

Both of Madeira's brows rose. "You know, these drugs make you really easy to get along with." She maintained a serious expression, but her eyes glittered with mirth. "I wonder if we can buy them in bulk."

Grace feigned offense and took a halfhearted, drunken swing at her, but all she could focus on was the one little word Madeira had used so casually.

We.

Grace experienced that wonderful team feeling again, the "Madeira and Grace against the world" sensation, and it emboldened her. She garnered her nerve to ask the question that had nagged at her for almost twenty-four hours. "Hey. Last night…"

Something in Grace's tone seemed to alert Madeira to the conversational shift. She tensed. "Yes?"

Grace sniffed, as if it were just a meaningless question. "When you were leaving…why did you blow me a kiss and tell me to sleep with the angels?"

"Oh, that." Madeira's body relaxed, but she cast a bashful gaze down at the gurney, thick, black lashes shadowing her eyes. "It was silly. Forget it."

"No, I—" Grace touched Maddee's hand again, letting her fingers rest against the warm, brown skin this time. "I liked it. I just wondered… what made you say it?"

Madeira studied her curiously then shrugged. "It's what my mother used to say to us before bed every night from the doorway of our room after she'd tucked us in. In Spanish, of course."

Shock rattled through Grace's insides before she stilled. "Are you serious?"

"Ah…yes. Why?"

"My mom said the same thing," she whispered, her voice shaky. "In English."

Their eyes met, and Grace could see from Madeira's stunned expression that she'd caught the implication, too.

One of DoDo's signs.

But the insight came much too soon, she feared, when Madeira straightened, backed up a step, and sank into the chair.

Gracie's heart began to thud with regret and she wanted to snatch back the question, pretend she'd never paid attention to the words. Madeira was shutting down for reasons Grace couldn't pinpoint, but she imagined it had something to do with pressure she didn't want to feel.

Signs.

Fate.

Connection.

Before Grace could ask what was wrong, before she had a chance to try to regain some of the tenuous intimacy they'd so carefully built, the curtain swept aside and the nurse bustled in with her tetanus shot and suture tray.

Just that quickly, the fragile new bond between Grace and Madeira snapped.

CHAPTER THIRTEEN

El mundo es de los audaces.
Faint heart never won fair lady.

There were different kinds of silences, Grace realized, during the ride home from the hospital. Not all of them golden. The comfortable silence of family or old friends, where nothing is said because no words are needed—that was golden. The silence of exhaustion, where words are too much trouble and you don't much care? She'd rank that a bronze. The very worst silence, however, had to be the tense, uncomfortable sort, stuffed to bursting with all that is left unsaid.

No gold whatsoever there. Not even tarnished tin.

Grace glowered at herself in the darkness of the car. What idiocy had compelled her to bring up last night, just when things seemed to be going so well? Drugs? They'd almost worn off now, but honestly the thumping of her heart troubled her more than the throbbing in her stitched and bandaged hand. Madeira drove in silence—good or bad, Grace couldn't tell. But Maddee didn't look at her, she didn't joke around, and she didn't flirt. As far as *signs* were concerned, considering this was Madeira Pacias, none of those were good ones. So they both continued ignoring each other, because if Grace glanced over now, Maddee would read the neediness on her face in a red-hot minute. Frankly, Grace would rather Maddee think she was angry.

Grace counted the seconds through two songs, using the "one, one-thousand, two, one-thousand" method just to pass the time, but when a third song aired, she had to bite her lip to keep from screaming.

Madeira simply drove, but Grace could sense the silence was getting to her, too.

"Gracie, I—" Madeira started, just as Grace said, "Look, about what I asked you—"

They both stopped. Damn. If only she'd waited. Grace took a measured breath, then pasted a brave smile on her face and turned to her. "You first."

"No. Go ahead."

Grace steeled herself, wishing like hell she had a beverage with which to wash down another painkiller. Her buzz had worn off at precisely the wrong moment, judging by her tongue's reluctance to cooperate. "I just want to make sure you know that I realize"—she shrugged—"well, just because our mothers used the same sappy phrase to tuck us in at night…I know it doesn't mean anything."

Despite the fact their mothers spoke different languages and came from different cultures in different countries.

Despite the fact that the tuck-in phrase was unusual.

Despite the fact that Grace's life kept intersecting with Madeira's in mysterious ways.

Totally beside the point.

Yeah, right. She wouldn't contradict herself by mentioning how implausible that "coincidence" sounded. Right then, she simply wanted to get back to the place where they felt comfortable with each other, whatever that took.

For a moment, Madeira said nothing. When she did speak, her tone was low and strangely calm. "You don't think so?"

"Of course not," Grace said in a soothing tone, managing to sound like she actually believed it. "Don't worry. It was a coincidence."

Madeira did a double take. "Pretty strange one, though. Don't you think?"

Grace managed a half-shrug, half-nod. "Well, sure. Strange coincidences happen all the time, though, don't they?"

"This strange?"

She cleared regret from her throat and tried to make her subtext clear. "It doesn't have to mean anything…if we don't want it to. Okay?"

"Oh," Madeira said, as if Grace had finally said something she could understand. "I see where you're coming from. Okay." She remained silent for a moment longer, than stole a quick glance at her. "But, to be clear, you're saying you don't think it's one of DoDo's signs?"

Grace shook her head. Firmly. Decisively. Trying to convince herself as much as Madeira, it seemed. "I don't believe in signs, remember?"

"So you keep telling me."

Not going there. She clenched her jaw. "Anyway, that's all I had. What were you going to say?"

Madeira didn't answer quickly, but when she finally got around to it, that familiar mask of untouchable charm had slipped over her face, which made Grace inexplicably sad. "Nothing, Gracie. Pretty much what you said, I guess."

"Oh." *Damn.* "About it…not mattering?"

"Yeah. Sure."

Grace gulped, feeling as if she'd missed something important. "So, everything's okay?"

Madeira smiled, her lips in a flat line, words in a strange monotone. "Fine. Everything except your hand, that is."

Grace bit down on her lip. Good, then. Everything was back to normal, whether it felt like it or not. Grace faced forward, not feeling much relief for having unburdened herself, not really liking this "normal" state they'd gotten back to. Not much she could do about it, though. Deep inside, she harbored the sneaking suspicion that they'd let something great slip away far too easily, but Madeira was running the show at this point. The distance between them made her sad, sure, but it also protected her heart, and anything was better than getting hurt.

Especially by Maddee.

❖

Madeira realized that Gracie's hand would likely heal faster than the frozen river of polite distance that had yawned between the two of them would thaw. She still couldn't get over the fact that their mothers used the exact same good night phrase. She hated to admit it, but when Gracie had told her that her mother said it, too, Madeira suddenly believed in DoDo's signs. Because of that, after some internal struggle, she'd decided the time had come to risk her heart. She'd just drummed up the nerve to reveal how she felt about Gracie, once and for all, when fortuitously, they'd interrupted each other.

Thank God she'd let Gracie speak her mind first.

In the very next breath, she'd learned that expressing her feelings would've been a colossal mistake. The "sign" that had been an epiphany to her hadn't meant anything to Gracie, which meant Madeira didn't dare come clean about her feelings—not yet. No sense confessing her love when Gracie still had no use for it.

So, she'd stick with her original plan no matter how difficult. She would steel her heart and bide her time as nothing more than a friend until Gracie woke the hell up and realized she couldn't live without Madeira. However long that took. Then, and only then, would Madeira hand over her heart. Patience had just become her middle name, like it or not, because Gracie was running the show at this point. The distance between them made her sad, sure, but it also protected her heart, and anything was better than getting hurt.

Especially by Gracie.

❖

The weeks passed quickly, and soon the evening they spent at the hospital faded into memory. Grace's hand healed nicely, with no remaining problems from the deep cut. By unspoken agreement, neither she nor Madeira ever mentioned their uncomfortable discussion from the ride home again. She took that as solid evidence she'd ventured too close to her danger zone, a mistake she wouldn't make more than once. She didn't want to push, so she did the only thing she could think of to banish Madeira from her mind. She launched into her search for the perfect girlfriend with a renewed vigor based more in desperation than any kind of hopeful excitement. Any woman with the basic requirements was fair game, except Layton. In addition to being perfect, Layton was really sweet and Grace considered her a friend. She didn't want to hurt her. Though Layton asked her out on several occasions, Grace had managed to walk the line between avoiding date two and actually snubbing her. Thank God.

Instead, she dated the frustrated poet who mixed espresso drinks behind the counter at Jolt and lived in a charmingly hideous garret in Capitol Hill. She went out with a mild-mannered teacher she met in a training class who ended up being conceited to the extreme. (Boring, too.) She'd even lunched with the young plastic surgeon she'd consulted about having her tattoos removed after she'd called to cancel the procedure, thanks to Madeira's influence.

While the dates ranged from mildly enjoyable to mercy-date miserable, none of these women even came close to being Grace's perfect match. All of them were improvements over the Lurch and Rat days, but none of them were…Madeira.

Luckily, she still saw Maddee frequently. Those initial odd jobs at DoDo's evolved into some fairly complicated remodeling projects and, as a result, Madeira seemed to be at the house all the time. DoDo had even given her a key and carte blanche to use the guest room any time she wanted. Every so often Grace awoke to find Madeira barefooted and barely dressed in the kitchen. The resulting lust generally distracted her for the full day.

Despite that, she grew so accustomed to having her around, it always struck her as odd and sort of…lonely when she came home and Maddee wasn't there. Her work schedule varied so much, Grace never could keep her days off straight. And of course, Maddee did still have a life—not that Grace wanted to contemplate *that.*

Tonight's impulse date with the cute but dim copy girl at Kinko's had been a complete bust. She'd been all hands and no courtesy, and Grace begged off early, calling a cab to bring her home when the woman argued one minute too long about her staying. It had been ugly, and she prayed Madeira would be home—at *Grace's* home—when she got there. She felt like talking to someone normal, which automatically excluded Lola and DoDo. Both of them thought her current dating frenzy was preposterous and neither had any desire to discuss what they referred to as her "denial of fate."

Madeira, on the other hand, gobbled up every detail, and tonight more than any other, she yearned to share, to simply spend time with her.

When the taxi rolled up to the curb, Grace didn't see Maddee's truck. But she'd taken to parking in back of the house so she could carry her tools in through the kitchen. She toyed with having the cabbie take a quick reconnaissance spin through the alley, but dismissed the notion almost immediately because it made her feel like a stalker. She could look for other signs inside—just had to be patient.

After paying the driver and letting herself in the house, her gaze immediately sought—and found—those signs. Steel-toed work boots stood neatly next to the hall tree, and the blaze orange medical bag sat in its usual spot beneath the console mirror. Grace smiled, relief flowing from her shoulders to her feet. She didn't hear any hammering or sawing, though. Only melodramatic dialogue in Spanish emanating from the television in the living room.

She peered around the corner and found Lola, Madeira, and DoDo huddled on the sofa beneath the brightly hued log cabin quilt Grandma had stitched by hand in record time while glued to the Oliver North trial coverage on TV back in the day.

Three sets of stockinged feet perched on the edge of the coffee table, which held evidence of munched popcorn and six empty pop cans. All eyes faced unblinkingly forward.

Grace glanced at the screen and found it filled with all the righteous indignation, passion, and intrigue only a *telenovela* could provide. How could she have forgotten? No talking allowed in this house when *Betty La Fea* was on.

She decided to risk it. "Hey, guys."

"Shhh!" in triplicate.

She rolled her eyes.

"Wait until a commercial, *m'ija*," DoDo stage-whispered. "We've been waiting for this part all month."

Conceding defeat, Grace folded herself into a side chair and picked up a magazine in which she had no interest. She flipped pages halfheartedly, but her amused gaze kept straying to the face of the woman she'd grown to care for, the woman her grandmother and sister cared for, too. How could a consummate player, a veritable rebel without a pause, become addicted to a damned soap opera?

A swell of affection filled her chest, and she bit back a chuckle. Madeira had no idea how much she'd transformed over the past month of hanging out with the Obregon women. She'd taken to critiquing Grace's outfits before she went out, and she seemed to be spending an inordinate amount of time with DoDo's quilting bee. Granted, Grace didn't believe Madeira had taken a single stitch, but she was getting damn adept at threading those needles. For a woman who wore a tool belt and wielded power tools as well as Madeira did, working thread through the eyes of those tiny quilting "betweens" was a pretty big departure from the norm. Quite an accomplishment.

Not to mention sexy, in a sweet sort of way.

God, Maddee was so…different than she'd assumed at the beginning.

If only Grace had realized…

She tried to hold out for a commercial, but *Betty* was in rare form and the exhaustion of a long work week along with tension from her bad date perched like an overweight vulture on her shoulders. She decided she could talk to Madeira another time. It would probably be better that way, considering how needy she felt. Grace had to remember she didn't have any kind of monopoly on Maddee's time.

Madeira had visited the bedrooms of many women in her day, but she'd never felt as anxious as she did right then, standing outside Gracie's. She'd glanced over when *Betty* ended, surprised to realize that Gracie had already gone up to bed. Madeira hadn't even noticed. Guilt twinged inside her. The whole reason she'd stayed late tonight was to speak with her after her date, but that darn *Betty La Fea* was a captivating show, something she could never admit in the presence of Torien. Madeira would never hear the end of it.

Outside Grace's door, Madeira paused, hoping Grace wasn't already asleep. They usually chatted after her dates, which kept Madeira sane, and she had no desire to abandon the ritual now. A small sliver of light showed beneath her door, so Madeira lifted her fist and knocked softly.

"What?" she barked.

Madeira smiled. Her Gracie, always the consummate lady. She cracked the door slightly, without looking in. "Forgive me, I speak Spanish and English, but I don't speak rude," Madeira teased. "Does that translate to 'come in'?"

She heard what sounded like a head hitting a headboard, a muffled swear word, and some rustling. "I'm sorry, come in."

"You decent?" She pushed the door open farther and made eye contact with her across the lamplit room.

Grace smiled, looking beautiful and nervous in one delectably feminine package. "Some would argue…never."

Madeira slipped into the room, closing the door behind her, then stood awkwardly on the opposite side, hands in her pockets. Now that she was here, she didn't know quite what to do. Imagine that, *la ladróna de corazones* not knowing what to do in a beautiful woman's bedroom. A groan escaped before she could squelch it. Torien could be right. Maybe Madeira was whipped. Maybe she *wanted* to be whipped. At least, by Gracie.

Madeira gulped. Maybe she'd lost it completely.

"What's wrong?"

"Nothing." Madeira's gaze bounced around the dusky purple walls of the room, taking in the soothing, simple decor softened by the light from a bedside single lamp. "DoDo's not going to call the cops if she finds me in here, is she?"

"Are you nuts?" Grace beckoned her over, leaning forward to pat the edge of the bed. The motion pulled the threadbare Denver Broncos T-shirt she wore more tightly over her breasts, and Madeira's mouth went dry. "You know DoDo and Lola have their own agendas when it comes to us. You're lucky she doesn't lock you in here with me."

Oh, Madeira should be so lucky.

"Would you come over here, for Christ's sake? You're making me nervous."

Far be it from Madeira to ignore a direct order to approach a woman's bed—especially the woman she loved. She closed the distance between them, and every step that brought her closer to Grace made her body throb. Not that anything would ever happen here, with DoDo and Lola just down the hall, but try telling that to her addled brain.

Madeira perched on the end of her bed, careful to keep her movements tentative and respectful. "How was the date? Who was it this time?"

"Kinko's copy girl. It sucked. I took a cab home."

Alarm surged in Madeira's throat. "What happened?" She searched Gracie's face for clues. "She didn't…try anything, did she?" Madeira's words sounded hoarse and dangerous, even to her own ears.

Grace's gaze dropped to the bright bed quilt almost in shame, and it made Madeira want to hunt this copy shop woman down and kick her ass.

"Gracie?"

Grace crinkled her nose. "Well, she was sort of…handsy. Nothing I couldn't handle, though."

Anger wavered through Madeira like heat off hot blacktop. Why would Gracie subject herself to these losers when Madeira sat right in front of her face, adoring her? She'd treat her like a queen, she'd protect her, she'd support every dream Gracie had. Hell, she'd—

Stick to the plan.

Madeira brushed adrenaline-shot fingers through her hair slowly, willing away the tension. "You shouldn't *have* to handle anything, Gracie. That's the whole point." Madeira paused to strip the growl out of her tone. "I'll go have a talk with her tomorrow."

"No, please." She sat forward and reached out to touch one of her clenched fists. "It's okay. She let me leave and I never have to see her again."

Madeira's ears exploded with heat. "She *let*—" She pressed her lips into a thin line. No. She hadn't come in here to nag Gracie. In a lightning swift movement, Madeira flipped her fist and captured Gracie's hand in between her own, caressing the smooth skin. It was hard enough to handle when Gracie went out with nice women. This was too much. "Why are you doing this? Why are you dating these creeps?"

"They're not all creeps." Her lashes brushed her cheeks as she absentmindedly traced one of the block patterns in the quilt that covered her. "Layton is really nice."

She's no good for you, Madeira yearned to say. She didn't. Because the truth was, Layton *was* a nice woman. Decent. And if that's what Gracie wanted, Madeira loved her enough to grit her teeth and support the stupid decision. "*Sí*, but you won't go out with her again."

Gracie bit her bottom lip, a motion Madeira had come to realize meant Gracie was holding something in. "Someday I might."

Madeira caressed her hand, absently staring at the framed art posters from the last three *Cinco de Mayo* festivals in Denver. This was insane. She'd never get anywhere with Gracie if she didn't start taking small risks. After a moment spent shoring up her courage, Madeira pinned Gracie with a gaze. "The Singles Auction is the weekend after next."

"I know. I remember."

"Still up for it?"

A small line bisected her brow line, and she blinked several times as though trying to catch up with her convoluted train of thought. "Of course. I wouldn't back out on you guys now."

"I didn't mean to imply that." Madeira was bungling this. Her fists clenched.

"Oh."

Now or never. "Gracie? Remember when we talked about you meeting my sister and her partner one of these days?"

"Yes."

"Come to a barbecue at their house next Saturday."

"Excuse me?"

Okay, so it hadn't been the best of segues. She frowned. "I didn't mean that to sound like an order. Let me try again. Would you like to come to a barbecue with me next Saturday afternoon?" She hiked one shoulder. "Toro and Iris always try to host one final outdoor party on the last gorgeous summer weekend of the year. Looks like next weekend, and I'd...like you to come. With me."

Gracie tucked her hair behind her ears with slow deliberate motions. "Oh. Well, I'd—"

"Come on, Gracie." Madeira couldn't bear to hear an automatic rejection, not after Grace had given every woman with a pulse in Denver *other than her* a chance. "I've met your family. Everyone wants to meet you, and things will be too hectic at the auction. Plus, Simon will be at the barbecue, so you'll know someone."

"I know you," Gracie reminded, a soft smile turning up the corners of her intensely kissable mouth.

"I meant besides me." Madeira flushed. "I was, you know, calling in reinforcements to try and convince you—"

"Maddee."

Her mouth closed, and she studied Grace for a moment, feeling as if she'd reached some sort of tipping point. "What?"

"I would love to come and meet your family."

A huge weight of dread tumbled off Madeira's shoulders, and she sat straighter. "Really?"

"Really."

"I should warn you, the whole gang's going to be there. My mother and sisters will be visiting from home."

Grace pulled a frightened face. “Uh-oh, I might embarrass you if that’s the case. My spoken Spanish is awful.”

Madeira grinned. “They all speak pretty good English.”

“Still.” She sat cross-legged beneath the quilt, pensive and intent. “I’d like to speak Spanish with your mother just out of respect.”

“Then I’ll help you.” Madeira leaned closer, close enough that she could smell Gracie’s skin, could see the pulse in her neck. She smoothed the backs of her fingers down Gracie’s unbearably soft cheek, then stood and backed away before she crossed boundaries she shouldn’t, broke agreements they’d made. At the doorway, she paused, schooled her tone. “And just so you know,” she said gently, “your desire to speak my mother’s language is one of many reasons why you could never, ever embarrass me.”

The next day, Madeira felt better than she had in months. Iris’s plan seemed to be working. She could feel Gracie warming up to her more each day. She would admit that her initial offer to play Ms. Fix-It in DoDo’s house had been laced with prurient intent. She’d wanted to be near Gracie without the pressure, and fixing creaky steps seemed as good a tactic as any. But over the weeks, things had changed in subtle ways.

She found she enjoyed working on the old brick home just for the sake of accomplishment and for the happiness it brought to the three Obregon women. Pleasing DoDo, the sweet but tough matriarch, had become paramount, and she’d also come to love listening to Grace and Lola banter so much that it ranked as her favorite new hobby. She thought she and Toro were bad—*hijole*. The Pacias sisters were rank amateurs when compared to Lola and Gracie. So far DoDo had ordered them to apologize for their “unladylike behavior” on twelve different occasions, which amused Madeira no end.

Madeira had grown so accustomed to the house and the unique people who made it a home, it had begun to feel a lot more like *home* than her own empty, lifeless apartment. The Obregon women, she’d concluded, brought something special, almost mystical, into a space. She couldn’t put her finger on it. All she knew was she actually enjoyed “living with” them. Who would’ve known?

Madeira had left their family home with Toro at nineteen, too young to have enjoyed the company of her little sisters and too ready for adventure to realize how her mother's presence had always transformed their house into a true haven. But in the past few weeks, she'd come to appreciate all she'd taken for granted growing up with her mother and sisters. She'd gotten a taste of comfort and acceptance that would be hard to relinquish when the time came—if it came. She hoped not.

Madeira's biggest remodeling goal was to chip away at the wall Gracie had built around her heart, but that would take time, patience, and caution. Possibly even a permit.

Lucky for Madeira, the old house needed lots of work and she'd managed to make herself useful in other areas as well. She'd built a free-standing quilting frame for DoDo's quilting bee and had begun to sit in with the ladies as they sewed, threading their needles and listening with a sort of horrified awe to their colorful gossip.

They accepted her—that was the best part. Those old women made Madeira feel like a keeper for the first time in her life. Gracie had ensnared her almost from the moment they met, but in her wildest dreams, Madeira hadn't imagined that the whole family—and their friends—would sneak into her heart and take up camp the way they had. It had gotten to the point where she couldn't bear the thought of losing them all if Gracie, God forbid, didn't come around.

Thankfully, Gracie's acceptance of the barbecue invitation renewed Madeira's hope. For all intents and purposes, it was a date.

Eager to share the news with her new favorite group of women, Madeira took the steps two at a time and pushed open the front door. "DoDo?"

"In here, *m'ija*," she called from the dining room.

Madeira found the quilting bee settled around the frame she'd built, plying their needles on a snowy white quilt covered in bright, multicolored, interlocking rings. The Bees, as they called themselves, might appear to be harmless little old ladies, but these afternoons were a hotbed of scandalous neighborhood gossip and racy innuendo Madeira hated to miss.

"We're so glad you could come by, Madeira. We were just talking about you." Murmurs rose up from the others.

Madeira grimaced. "No wonder my ears were ringing."

"How's work?" DoDo asked, beaming across the quilt. "Anyone we know kick the bucket recently? I'm behind on my obituary reading."

Madeira grinned. "No one you know. But work is good, *gracias*. I love it." Just as she loved DoDo's often frustrating granddaughter. "Don't let me interrupt you. I'll just sit quietly and thread some needles." She took a seat, earning appreciative smiles over several different pairs of powerful reading glasses.

The women resumed their conversation, speculating brashly on the torrid affair between a seventy-five-year-old gentleman neighbor of DoDo's and his fifty-year-old girlfriend. The way they spoke of the affair, the man might as well have robbed a cradle, layette and all.

Madeira settled in silently, enjoying the cadences of the women's warbled voices and the passion with which they exchanged gossip. She'd just finished threading the last of the idle needles when Marilyn Esquivel, an eightysomething grandmother of thirty, regarded her over purple half-glasses. "Enough about that tired-ass, Viagra-sucking *viejo*. What is Graciela up to these days, *m'ijita*?"

Madeira managed to remain nonchalant, wanting to dole out her news in tiny, delectable bits and pieces, the way the Bees tended to do with their scandalous dishes. "This and that. She's very busy with school. But—"

"Ach. Don't listen to Ms. Politically Correct over there. My granddaughter," DoDo informed them, "has been *dating*." She'd uttered the D-word with the same intonation she might use to announce that Gracie had become a mercenary killer.

"What?" Marilyn asked, the shock blatant in her tone.

DoDo nodded, disgust pinching her features. "You heard me right. It seems she's intent on finding *the perfect woman*."

All seven women shook their heads and laughed in that all-knowing way that made Madeira believe they were the wisest women in the world, the key holders to the mysterious workings of the female brain in a way she, unfortunately, hadn't absorbed as a young girl.

Ruby Carvajal, the baby of the group at a spritely seventy-three, rolled her eyes at Madeira over the quilt top. "Silly girl, no, our Grace? *Él que se fue a Sevilla, perdío su silla*. You leave your place, you lose it." She shrugged. "She'll learn."

"I hope." Madeira wasn't quite sure what Ruby had meant, but she always had the sense these women were on her side, and that was enough.

DoDo released a long sigh. “I don’t know. Our Graciela is a stubborn one, isn’t she, Madeira?”

“That’s for sure,” Madeira said, running the tails of thread through beeswax before handing the fresh needles to Mary Joachim and Isabel Fuentes, the two most experienced and hence the fastest quilters in the bunch, she’d quickly learned. “But—”

“Takes after her mamá that way, God rest her soul.” DoDo looked sharply at Madeira. “You don’t repeat that now. I love my daughter, but she wasn’t so savvy when it came to matters of love, *de verdad.* Graciela’s her mother’s daughter.”

“My lips are sealed.” She made a zipping motion with her fingers. “However—”

“So, she’s dating. What are you gonna do about it?” asked Magdalena Garcia-Romero-Martensen-O’Doul-Montoya, current record holder for collecting the most husbands. She was also an unrepentant whiskey nipper and the bluntest of the Bees by far.

Madeira shrugged. “Try to be that so-called perfect woman, I guess. Which is why—”

“HA!” Magdalena belted loudly, exposing her entire upper plate. Every white, blue, gray, auburn, and ash blond head lifted at once. Magdalena lifted her chin toward DoDo. “Someone needs to tell that Grace there is no such thing as a perfect woman. Or man. The quicker that absurd bubble bursts, the happier she’ll be.”

“Amen,” chimed the women together.

“Maybe a gingerbread man could be perfect,” Mary murmured, mostly to herself, it seemed. “If he was frosted.”

“You tell Graciela, Maggie,” Isabel said, a sly gleam in her eyes. “You’ve done more experimenting than the rest of us combined.”

Madeira stifled a smirk, not wanting to appear impertinent. Not that Magdalena felt one iota of shame for her husband collecting.

“Maggie’s right. The words ‘perfect’ and ‘woman’—or ‘man,’ for that matter—don’t belong in the same sentence. But as actual women go”—Mary waved her thimbled finger toward Madeira—“this one here is about as close as they come.” She tsk-tsked. “Why do we have to grow too old to catch them before we can start recognizing the good ones? Not that I ever dabbled in women, mind you. But if I were your age, little one…" Mary waggled her eyebrows suggestively.

"Why, Mary? Because life isn't fair, or God would've made women look more distinguished with age instead of men," Isabel said, nodding firmly.

"He would have given them the thighs, too, eh?" DoDo said, smacking a palm against her own.

"And the morning sickness."

"Cramps."

"He should've made them live with spouses more like themselves, too," Magdalena suggested. "That would've snapped a few knots in their stubborn asses. We women never get any breaks."

"Amen," the group chimed.

Madeira knew not to interrupt when the Bees were on a roll, especially when it involved their opinions about men. She'd be invited back into the conversation eventually, and then she'd share her news.

"But we're not talking about men right now. We're talking about women, and it appears, at least in my granddaughter's case, they're just as bad. Who would've ever imagined." DoDo released another sigh. "*Oy yoy yoy*." She waved a knuckle vaguely in Madeira's direction. "Not only is this one as perfect as can be expected, she's perfect for Grace. Cut from the same cloth, these two kids. Madeira's no smarter about women than Grace is—"

"Hey!" Madeira protested.

"But they could make each other happy if Graciela would open her damn fool eyes." DoDo tied a knot and snipped off the thread.

"It's her heart that needs opening, Dolores," Isabel said. "I don't think any woman could look at our Madeira and not see a woman she could love."

"She's sure got a hot tushie," whispered Anna Moreno, the smallest at four foot eight, with a personality to match her diminutive stature. Realizing that she'd spoken aloud, she covered her mouth with a gnarled hand, blanching until her rouge stood out in two mauve blotches on her papery cheeks.

When the rest of the women burst into gales of laughter, mortified Anna scuttled off to the powder room in search of her lost composure.

As though just now remembering Madeira was actually in the

room, Marilyn blinked. "Say, were you trying to tell us something, *querida*?"

"Actually, yes. I do have news."

All the women glanced up at once. Even Anna peered around the corner from the hallway. "Say it," she whispered.

"I've asked Gracie to meet my family."

After a communal inward gasp, DoDo prompted with, "And?"

Madeira smiled at each woman in turn. "Keep in mind, it's just a casual barbecue. Nothing major."

"And?" they asked in unison.

"And…" She drew it out, reveling in giving them a large dose of their own medicine "She said yes."

The women exclaimed their pleasure over this new development, but DoDo regarded her warmly and wisely without speaking. When the prattle died down, she told her, "I knew she'd come around eventually, my stubborn girl."

Magdalena snorted. "Not a moment too soon."

Madeira cocked her head to the side, unaware there'd been a time clock running. "Why's that?"

DoDo flicked her side of the gorgeous quilt, causing a ripple to ride its width toward her. "Because we're almost done with the commitment quilt for you two crazy kids, *m'ija*. Why else?"

CHAPTER FOURTEEN

Algo es algo; menos es nada.
Half a loaf is better than no bread at all.

Madeira had to admit, the quilt had thrown her.

She wanted Gracie with an intensity that awed her, and she loved her—no doubts there. But commitment? And a quilt to go with it, no less? Hell, she'd just gotten Gracie to agree to a casual "date" and hadn't even dared to use the D-word in relation to it.

DoDo and the Bees were getting *way* ahead of themselves. The last thing Madeira wanted to do was make Gracie think she was in cahoots with them. She needed to tread lightly. One casual date was all she asked, and the implications of a commitment quilt—an item she was sure the Bees had just made up to serve their purposes—at this juncture could very well ruin everything Madeira had worked so hard to cultivate.

Her jaw clenched, despite valiant efforts to remain calm. If the unexpected pressure of that quilt had spooked *her*, she could only imagine what it would do to Gracie, who still considered Madeira nothing more than friend material, and definitely not someone with whom she'd snuggle beneath a commitment quilt.

Jumbled thoughts and uncertainties had put Madeira on guard since that day with the Bees, and as a result, she'd dragged her feet about telling her family that Gracie would be accompanying her to the barbecue. The last thing she and Gracie needed was coercion from both families. The only problem was, she hadn't mentioned any of this to Gracie, and the time on her luck-o-meter had just run out.

In five minutes, they'd be at the barbecue—their first non-date, no expectations…date. But thanks to Madeira, Gracie had no idea she would be the surprise of the day, the center of attention, the object of bald curiosity and speculation.

Not to mention pressure.

Madeira's throat constricted. Should she warn Gracie before they arrived? Part of her thought yes, the other part no. Why bring on a certain end before they'd even had a chance for a beginning? If Gracie had any idea how pivotal this non-date was, she'd scurry back to the safety of square one before the first burger was flipped.

Whatever possessed Madeira to plan their first non-date with family?

If it were just the two of them, Madeira could maintain the no-expectations friend act as long as Gracie needed to hear it. But Madeira had been so damned eager to bring Gracie into her life, her family, that she hadn't stopped to consider the implications. Just because Gracie would officially become the first woman Madeira had ever brought home, and just because no one actually knew she was coming, just because her entire family would realize immediately that Gracie was vitally important to her and would likely bring it to Gracie's attention…well, those minor, unmentioned details shouldn't ruin their day.

Right?

Guilt set free a colony of bats in her empty cave of a stomach, but she pressed her lips together to keep from blurting a confession. She hoped to slip Gracie casually into the family setting as if she'd always belonged, and prayed that no one would blow her cover. Perhaps the whole thing would end up being no big deal.

Uh-huh. Sure.

If Madeira knew her family, a big deal was both inevitable and an understatement—precisely why she hadn't warned them in advance. That, and well…Gracie threw her off balance. She wanted to do exactly the right thing where Gracie was concerned, but damn it all, she had no idea what "the right thing" was.

Shit.

She might have really screwed up this time.

"Is something wrong?"

Gracie's voice from the passenger seat startled Madeira, and she took a silent moment to gather her thoughts.

Confess?

Lie?

She simply had no clue.

"Nothing," she lied through a forced smile. "Why do you ask?"

"Well…" Gracie drew out, as though the answer were obvious. "I asked you a question about the barbecue—twice—but you didn't seem to hear me." She regarded Madeira with objectivity in her expression. "Maybe we should talk about whatever worry has you so preoccupied before we get to your sister's."

Madeira glanced at her, chagrined, and realized the only way out of this dilemma was honesty. Gracie had given her an opening she couldn't ignore without destroying this non-date attempt even more than she already had. Now or never. She eased out a long breath. "We should talk, actually. I wasn't exactly honest when I said nothing was wrong. I'm sorry."

Gracie's expression clouded. "Don't be afraid of being truthful with me. If you'll recall, we've sort of been in this thing together from the beginning."

Madeira met Gracie's open gaze, pleading for her understanding. "Okay. You're right. I'll just say it." She blew out a breath. "My family doesn't know you're coming with me today."

Gracie's warm brandy eyes widened. "Why not?"

"I didn't tell them."

"Maddee, Jesus!" Gracie threaded her fingers into her hair. "I can't just show up uninvited. That would be rude."

"No, you misunderstand me." At the four-way stop, Madeira reached over and squeezed Gracie's shoulder. "The more the merrier at these events. That's not the problem."

She didn't look convinced. "What then?"

Madeira clenched her jaw and gazed unseeingly out the front window as they crossed through the intersection. How to put this? "My family is likely to make a big deal about this…this—"

"Date?"

She blinked in surprise. "I didn't know you thought of it as a date."

"Why wouldn't I? You asked me to go with you, I said yes. That's a date in my book, Maddee." Gracie's eyes narrowed. "I suppose that scares you?"

"Of course not." One corner of her mouth lifted. "I thought it would scare you."

Gracie laughed, relief replacing wariness in her expression. "We're idiots. You know that?"

Madeira shook her head. "If I'd known you'd react like this, I would've talked to you about it last week." She pulled to the curb in front of Toro's. "Gracie, it's just a barbecue. But be prepared for everyone to treat you like my…girlfriend. I didn't tell them because it would've given them a week to prepare their battle plans, but I can't promise an innuendo-free day."

"So, I'll feel right at home?"

Madeira chuckled. "Probably so."

Gracie patted her hand. "Look, I can handle the pressure. As long as you and I know where we stand on things."

Madeira studied her, wanting so much to kiss her, wanting so much for them to be a true team, wanting, wanting, wanting. "Where do we stand on things, Gracie?" she asked in a soft tone.

Gracie chewed the inside of her cheek for a moment, eyes downcast. Palpable uncertainty filled the car. They circled each other like wary boxers, neither wanting to lower her guard enough to throw the first punch.

"How about we simply enjoy the day? No expectations, no worries." She offered her hand. "Deal?"

Madeira slid their palms together, wishing Gracie had said she loved the idea of being referred to as Maddee's girlfriend. But, hell, she'd take what she could get. She'd become a very patient woman in the past month or so of loving Gracie. "Deal, as long as you promise not to hold my family's comments against me, whatever they may be."

"That's fair. You haven't held any of DoDo's or Lola's antics against me."

"Speaking of that…" Madeira swallowed, deciding to play the honesty card one more time "Did you know DoDo and the Bees are working on a…commitment quilt?"

Gracie groaned. "I should've figured. DoDo is bound and determined to pair us off, and since I'm older than Lola, I'm the first target. Listen, I'll talk to DoDo about it. I hope they didn't scare you too much."

"Why would you think they scared me?"

Gracie laughed. "Because you're way too much like me, Maddee. I know."

"DoDo told the Bees that I'm no better with women than you are." She brushed the backs of her fingers down Gracie's cheek. "I'm afraid we have bad reputations, *fierita*."

"You know, hon, that's not really a news flash." Gracie smiled sweetly, and Madeira's heart soared.

She turned off the engine and swung the keys around her index finger. "Well, unless you have anything else to add?"

"Nothing. We're cool." Gracie smoothed her hands together. "Let the games begin."

They headed up the walk, laughter, music, and the spicy rich aroma of grilling meat wafting over the fence to welcome them. The party was well under way, which was Madeira's standard arrival MO when it came to social events. She used to joke with her friends that the party never really started until she arrived anyway, so she might as well make a dramatic entrance. Today's tardiness was more a matter of calculated self-preservation. She needed to act as normal as possible. If she had showed up on time *and* brought a woman, Toro and the rest of them would start cracking "whipped" jokes immediately, shaming her in front of the only woman whose opinion of her truly mattered.

God, Madeira shook with the yearning to reach for Gracie's hand, but gut instincts warned her not to. Nevertheless, she guided Gracie onto the flagstone path that wound around the side of the house with a light touch at the small of her back. Palms moist, heart pounding, she scanned the crowd over the privacy fence.

Mamá and the twins sat on the glider swing at the edge of the redwood deck. Iris and her best friends Paloma Vargas and Emie Jaramillo occupied the picnic table, heads pow-wow style, as usual. Toro stood with Paloma's partner, Deanne, nursing *cervezas* and grilling meat, and various children ran about the yard, screeching and laughing with Emie's partner, Gia. Simon and Lisa wouldn't arrive until after their daughter, Alex's, softball game a little later.

To the untrained eye, this gathering would appear as unthreatening as a church picnic, but all Madeira could see was a lion's den. She turned to Gracie, her little lamb to the slaughter, feeling cruel for pushing her into this. "Last chance for escape. We can take the coward's way out and go to a movie."

"Don't be silly. I can't wait to meet everyone. Everything will be just fine."

"I'm going to remind you of those words when the pressure gets heavy. Here goes, then." She took a deep breath and reached for the latch. The hinge groaned inordinately loud and long as she pushed open the gate. Staving off the urge to hide her behind her back, to delay the inevitable, Madeira stepped aside and allowed Gracie to enter ahead of her. She wouldn't make the mistake of acting ashamed of Gracie when inside she felt the exact opposite.

"We're here," she called out, more tentatively than usual. "Let the party begin."

"Eh, Mosq—" Toro's astonished gaze jerked from her sister to the woman at her side. Torien's mouth snapped shut and she froze. In fact, everything froze.

Talk stopped.

Laughter silenced.

Movement ceased. Just for a moment.

Gracie took a small, faltering step, then stopped, her shoulders lifting with a deep, steadying breath. The smile she flashed at Madeira had reassurance at the corners, and when she winked, Madeira knew everything would be just fine. Still, Madeira stood there with a dry throat, unsure of the next step.

Not Gracie, though.

Spine erect, head held high, she moved forward and introduced herself to Madeira's mother in beautifully accented, perfectly executed, and obviously practiced Spanish.

God almighty, Madeira loved this woman.

Grace had more fun with Madeira and her family that day than she'd ever had on a date. She especially liked the fact that she didn't feel compelled to hover nervously by Madeira's side the whole time. Everyone made her feel so welcomed, every bit of her "meet the family" nervousness had faded within minutes of their arrival. She spent time with Maddee's mother and little sisters, joked with Torien, and had a long tattoo conversation with Iris and her engaging friends.

Every so often her eyes would meet Madeira's across the yard and the result was nothing short of electric.

Her attraction to Madeira grew with every subtle exchange, each moment together and those spent apart. As the afternoon passed, she grew more aware of Maddee on a visceral level until she felt almost overstimulated. She took a seat on the empty glider, partially to rest her tired leg but mostly to gather her wits. She was dangerously close to exposing her true feelings about Maddee. That scared her.

"Hey. You look pensive." Iris flashed that oft-photographed, world-class smile as she approached, a longneck beer in each hand. She offered one to Grace.

"Oh. Thanks." Grace tucked her hair behind her ears, then reached for the bottle. "I'm not exactly pensive." She considered it, and something inside her knew that she could be honest with Iris. "Well, maybe a little pensive."

Iris tilted her chin toward the glider. "Is there room for another person there?"

"Of course." Grace slid to one side as Iris settled next to her. "My leg aches when I'm on my feet too long. I try to take frequent breaks."

Iris's forehead crinkled with concern. "Do you need an ice pack or painkillers? Something?"

Grace shook her head and saluted with the bottle. "This is more than enough. Thanks."

"So." Iris rested her own bottle along the arm of the glider. "Any desire to discuss what has you so lost in thought?"

Grace sighed. "What else?" She stared off toward Madeira, who sat on the picnic table with her little sisters flanking her, joking with Torien. A pang of envy struck her as she watched her take Reina in a headlock and give her a noogie while the teen shrieked—at least until their mother rapped Madeira on the head with her knuckles in playful reprimand. Maddee seemed so different in this milieu. Then again...she didn't. If Grace replayed the tapes in her mind, she could see that Maddee had always been playful, kind, and full of life. "I'm... envious."

Iris tracked her line of observation. "Envious, huh? I'm sure Mad would give you a noogie if you asked nicely."

Laughing, Grace turned toward Iris in surprise.

"I'm just kidding. I know what you're saying." Iris regarded her, one long arm extended across the back of the glider. "She cares about you, too, you know." It wasn't as though Iris was trying to play matchmaker. Her statement came off as matter-of-fact, informational.

Still, Grace shrugged off the reassurance, far too melancholy considering how perfect the day had been. Iris might think Maddee cared, but Grace had an inside scoop on the mind of a player. "I'm a challenge to her, Iris. That's different than being cared about."

"You might very well be a challenge, but if so, it's exactly what she needed." Iris took a long swig from her bottle that still managed to look ladylike and graceful. "I've seen her come alive since you've been around."

"That's not my doing. It's her job. She loves her job."

"Do you really believe that, Grace?"

Grace's throat closed; she couldn't answer. "Do you know what happens once a challenge is met? It ceases to be interesting, and the person moves on to the next exciting challenge."

Iris nodded. "In some cases, sure." A beat passed. "I don't believe that would happen with you two."

"Maybe. Maybe not. To be honest, I'm not up for taking the risk." *Not with her*, Grace added silently.

"Look, Mad trusts me," Iris said. "I think I'm the first woman she's related to on a non-flirt basis, so we've developed a sort of rapport. A big sister, little sister thing. She confides in me."

Grace's heart revved. Was Iris offering to help her get inside Madeira's head? That's exactly what she needed to figure out her motives. "What has she said?"

Iris pressed her lips together in apology. "That's the thing about sharing something in confidence. You have to know it will go no further. I want to respect Mad's privacy. She deserves that from me."

Grace's face heated thinking she might have sounded like she'd been pumping Iris for info—which, of course, she had been. One hand fluttered to her neckline before reaching out to touch Iris's forearm. "I didn't mean to—"

"Don't apologize." Iris grinned. "Trust me, I would've paid hard, cold cash for the inside scoop on Toro when we were stumbling blindly toward love."

The implication brought stars to Grace's vision. Could the entire world see she was falling in love with Madeira? Before dismay could swamp her at the thought of being so vulnerable and transparent, Iris went on.

"I will tell you this."

She paused, and Grace found herself holding her breath.

"You should give her a chance."

Her air whooshed out. Not exactly a revelation. "Oh, well, sure you'd suggest that. She's your family. You're not the one who might end up hurt, though."

"Granted. But I know her." Iris's eyes sparkled with amusement. "Not Ms. Thief of Hearts, mind you, but little Mad Pacias—Mosquito. The woman she rarely lets out." She glanced toward Madeira, and Grace read the true affection on the woman's face. "But she lets her out with you, and that's…quite something. She wouldn't intentionally hurt you, Grace. She's one person who shouldn't be judged by her track record. And I'm not making excuses—I know she's got a long one."

"There's no need to defend her. I haven't exactly been an angel myself." Grace twisted her mouth to the side. Odd how she no longer felt quite so ashamed about her checkered past. She didn't exactly know what had changed her perspective. "But I've also been hurt one time too many by women like her. Much as I wish things could be different for us, I think Maddee and I should settle for friendship."

"I understand, believe me. Friendship is safe and tidy." Iris tossed her long hair over one shoulder. "Madeira mentioned you've been dating. Any luck there?"

The question had been innocently posed, yet its impact nearly doubled Grace over emotionally. "Not really. I've had some good dates, but none of the women are—" She bit her lip.

"None of them are Madeira?"

Grace sighed. "Damnit, yes. I don't know why I insist on using her as my standard of comparison. I mean, seriously, how will anyone ever measure up?"

"Grace, *listen* to yourself. To the words you're saying from the heart. I know you're scared, but let down your guard a bit. I've given the same advice to Mad, because both of you need to. What's life without risk?" Iris paused. "Do you know I turned down a multimillion-dollar modeling contract to stay in the U.S. with Torien?"

Grace gaped. "I'm on a teacher's salary. I can't even imagine."

"She was worth it. *Love* is worth it." Iris leaned in and raised her brows. Her tone lowered to a conspiratorial level. "Take a risk on my little sis. I wouldn't give that advice to any woman except you, Grace. Then again…I've never had the opportunity, considering you're the only woman Mad has ever brought home to meet the family. *Ever*," she added, her tone firm, "in case you missed that word the first time."

Before Grace could grasp the impact of the statement, Iris had patted her leg, stood, and walked away. Grace still hadn't digested the magnitude of being Maddee's first take-home date, or the implication of it, when a new shadow fell across her lap. She glanced up, and her stomach contracted with a combination of nerves and lust. "Hey."

Madeira held both palms up to face her. "Whatever stories my sis Iris told you, I assure you none of them were my fault. I was framed." She grinned.

Grace hiked her chin. "Those sound like the words of a woman with a guilty conscience." She patted the glider next to her, and Maddee sat.

"No comment." With a sigh, Maddee spread her arms along the back of the swing, one hand resting loosely on Grace's shoulder. For a moment, they simply swayed in the balmy air, watching the activity around them.

"Penny for your thoughts," Madeira said.

"I love Iris."

"Everyone loves Iris. But yes, she's awesome. My sister is a lucky woman."

Grace pondered what Iris had told her and decided she had nothing to lose by asking for details. "Tell me something."

"Anything you want to hear, *fierita*."

Grace turned to regard her with a level gaze. "Why have you never brought any of your girlfriends home?"

Madeira cringed. "I knew Iris was spilling my secrets."

"Why haven't you?" Grace wouldn't let her weasel out of answering this question. She needed to know.

Madeira sobered and studied Grace for a moment, then tilted the corners of her mouth down and tipped her head to the side at the same time. Her tone came out unabashed, straightforward. "How many players do you know who would bring their women home to the family, Gracie?"

"Not many," Grace admitted. Madeira's explanation made sense. But why the change now? Because Maddee considered her a surrogate sister of sorts?

Madeira twirled her fingers in Grace's hair, which she pretended not to notice. "When you were living *la vida loca*, did you bring all your dates home to meet DoDo?"

She splayed a palm on her chest, horrified. Images of Rat and Lurch drifted into her mind. "God, no. But then again, I'm not so proud of my behavior back then."

"And you think I am proud of mine?"

Grace hiked one shoulder. "*My* wild days were a long time ago."

"You're evading the question."

"I don't know, Maddee. Your, ah, lifestyle didn't seem to bother you so much when we first met."

"Based on what? The articles in the newspaper? The same newspaper whose articles convinced me that you wanted to stand on the beach with me in Provincetown, exchange rainbow-colored rings, and pledge your undying love? That you'd stop at nothing to reach that goal?" She raised one brow pointedly.

Realizing how shallow her judgment made her sound, Grace glanced away. Her chest flamed and she bit her lip. She had based their entire relationship thus far on hearsay. How would she feel if Maddee had done the same with her? She had never considered herself the kind of person who relied on stereotypes and preconceived notions to judge other people. These months around Madeira had taught her some lessons about herself that were hard to accept. She sighed. "I guess this is your way of implying I owe you an apology for all the assumptions I've made about you?"

"An apology?" Madeira considered it, pulling closer to the warmth of her body, stroking the side of her hair with her fingers.

Grace didn't resist. Maddee felt too good, too right. Grace didn't want to be anywhere else.

"Actually," Madeira said, her tone warm and rumbly, "I'd be more than happy to settle for a second chance."

Grace's stomach flopped.

She wanted to believe.

She did.

God, why was this so hard?

"S-second chance at what?"

Maddee eased Gracie gently over to rest on her shoulder, a sigh lifting her chest. "Stick with me, babe. If fate's on our side, we'll muddle through and find that answer together."

CHAPTER FIFTEEN

Gato escaldado del agua fría huye.
The scalded cat flees even from cold water.

Madeira had a busy work week after the barbecue, so Grace didn't see her again until the night of the auction, and then only in quick flashes as she appeared on stage or passed through the crowded event hall. By then, Grace was feeling quite proprietary—dangerous considering Madeira would be auctioned to the highest bidder pretty soon while Grace stood by and watched. The thought stuffed her with dismay. She could only hope some philanthropic dowager would win her as opposed to one of the many well-dressed young women with greedy eyes and fat purses wandering through the event hall, leeringly examining the available singles—male and female.

Dixie's of Denver, a local company that rented event space all over the city and up in the mountains, had donated their largest facility for the auction. Blossoms, a local florist chain, had provided the centerpieces for all the tables, and Coasters, a large liquor retailer near the foothills, had supplied the hooch. The place was packed.

Grace had to admit, piggybacking the auction's advertising on the "Samaritan Soul Mate" media coverage had been divinely inspired. The event had received so much press, the expected donations of auction items had more than doubled, and attendance at the event was standing room only. The EMS Benefit Society thought they might be able to afford two additional ambulances, including a costly mobile trauma unit, thanks to the extra money.

Unfortunately, Madeira was the hot commodity.

Grace had caught glimpses of her interviewing with various media representatives throughout the evening. No doubt she'd bring in top dollar. Grace clenched her jaw and jabbed the button down on a blender full of piña coladas, annoyed for this misplaced jealousy. It was for charity, for Christ's sake. Grace had entertained a fantasy of bidding on her herself until she read an article about how much Madeira was expected to collect. Once again, the Thief of Hearts was out of her reach. *C'est la vie.*

As she poured the coladas into their bulbous glasses, she scanned the schedule for the evening, printed on the back of a merchandise list she'd picked up earlier. Forty-five minutes of each hour was dedicated to displaying auction merchandise, items that ranged from ski lift tickets and bed & breakfast weekends to quilts, artwork, and even a new car. The singles themselves presented the items, thereby acting as walking advertisements for the main event and grand finale—the singles auction.

During the remaining fifteen minutes of each hour, EMS officials showed slideshows and provided statistics about emergency medical service in the city.

Volunteer waiters circulated through the crowd with trays of hors d'oeuvres donated by Grab-a-Bite Catering, and Grace mixed drinks as fast as the paramedic and EMT wait staff could deliver them. DoDo's table was setting records for knocking back booze, Grace mused, as she placed the last one on the tray. All of the dolled-up Bees drank fruity frozen concoctions except for Magdalena, who preferred whiskey straight up. Grace quickly jabbed paper umbrellas in each of the glasses, scanning the crowd for an idle waiter. "Simon," she called, spying him taking a break near the back of the room.

He turned toward the bar, then shoved off the wall immediately to approach her. "You rang?"

She indicated the drink-laden tray, wiping perspiration off her forehead with the crook of her elbow. "Can you deliver this to my grandmother and the ladies?"

"Again? Gladly." He squatted and deftly shouldered the heavy tray, his smooth, confident actions telling Grace he'd worked in food service sometime in his life. "DoDo's table is tipping bigger with every round. I'm going to win that week off if it kills me."

Grace laughed. Though all tips went into the ambulance fund, the "waiters" were in competition with each other to see who collected the most. The winner received a week of paid vacation, with each of the five workdays donated, one half-day from each of the remaining waiters.

Taking a momentary break to catch her breath, Grace watched with pleasure as a fierce bidding war ensued over one of the three quilts DoDo and the Bees had donated to the cause. The king-sized scrap masterpiece included original feedsack cloth from the 1930s as well as reproduction fabrics to make up the difference. The fact that it had been hand-pieced and quilted drove the price up to three thousand dollars, and the enthusiastic bidding continued.

Grace glanced at her grandmother's table. The ladies stared with rapt attention at the stage, flushed with pride that their creation was so in demand.

"Ladies and gentlemen, a quick break in the bidding. We'd like to reintroduce you to one of our available singles for the evening," announced the Master of Ceremonies, Bill Fulton, a seasoned, well-spoken paramedic who served as the media contact for the department.

Grace watched Madeira strut on stage. Excitement and envy warred inside her, and she pressed a palm to her abdomen. Madeira looked so incredibly hot in low-slung black tuxedo pants, white cuffs gleaming with rhinestone cuffl inks, and a white tank. Her bare arms and shoulders gleamed with honed, oiled muscles. Not an ounce of fat marred the picture of pure decadence Maddee presented. Whoo-boy. Madeira made the so-called "hot" Hollywood lesbians look like a motley Girl Scout troop.

The audience whooped and whistled, applauding their approval as Madeira sauntered from one end of the stage to the other, blowing kisses and bending to touch the hands of the women up front who reached out to her as if she were some kind of a rock star. In spite of herself, Grace's stomach soured as she struggled to maintain a pleasant expression. She had to be the world's biggest idiot for putting herself in the position of watching this.

"EMT Madeira Pacias purportedly helped with this quilt, created by the Peacemakers Quilting Bee." A spotlight shone down on DoDo's table, where all the ladies beamed, tittered behind white-gloved hands, or waved.

"Dolores Obregon tells us Madeira, the infamous Thief of Hearts, spent many an afternoon threading needles for them so they could finish this work of art in time for the auction. Isn't that just sweet," Bill joked.

Madeira flashed a playfully threatening look, and the audience ate it up.

"Let's show Madeira and the Bees some respect by bidding often and bidding high for this one-of-a-kind quilt." Instantly, the bidding rose to forty-five hundred.

Grace turned away to wash some glasses, smiling when one of the volunteer bar backs brought her two cases of Cab Franc from the storage room. She needed to keep her focus on tending bar, not on Ms. Unattainable. To do so, she silently reminded herself this was all for a good cause.

"What's a guy got to do for service around here, cupcake?"

Grace spun, recognizing the endearment as well as the voice. Pleasure spread through her like the sun's warmth on a winter afternoon. "Harold!" She ducked around the edge of the bar and embraced the stout reporter like a long-lost friend. He clapped her back.

Funny. When the Samaritan fiasco happened, Harold had been her nemesis. Now she felt nothing but fondness for the wizened old wordsmith.

Grace held him at arm's length, smiling. "I didn't know you were coming."

"Are you nuts?" He patted Grace's cheek with a hand that smelled of Old Spice and cigarette smoke. "This is news, dollface. You know Harold and news. I wouldn't miss it."

The crowd roared when the Bees quilt went for $7,500. Both she and Harold glanced at the stage, but Grace's gaze immediately sought and found Madeira. She squatted at the edge of the stage, deep in conversation with a shapely blonde whose gym-toned bod had been poured into a low-backed black cocktail dress.

She looked gorgeous.

She looked enthralled.

She looked…familiar.

Grace swallowed, but it wasn't easy.

"You going to bid on her?"

Harold's question jerked Grace's attention back. She raised her chin and sniffed. "Who? Madeira?"

"Who else?"

Grace tossed her hair. "She's too rich for my blood, Harold. I'm an elementary school teacher, remember?" She moved to the business side of the bar and braced her hands on the formica top, doing her best to look placid and unaffected. "What's your poison, mister?"

"A 7-Up."

She smirked. "And here I imagined you'd be the beer and chaser kind of a guy."

"I was." He fished his wallet out of his back pocket. "Ten years and twelve steps ago. Now I stick to soda."

"Good for you," Grace said, meaning it sincerely.

"I have to say," Harold eyed her closely, "I was a bit surprised to find Madeira still on the roster of *eligible* singles tonight."

Grace filled a tumbler with ice and snatched up the spray hose of 7-Up, pegging Harold with a droll stare. "Exactly what info are you trying to wheedle out of me, bucko?"

Harold laughed. "Kid, you're a tough cookie."

A grudging smile lifted one side of her mouth as she handed over the fizzing soda and took the two crisp dollar bills Harold offered, stuffing them into the till. "I could say the same to you."

"One of the many reasons I like you so much. You remind me of me, and I like me." Harold beamed. "Seriously, what's up with you two? I haven't seen hide nor hair of either of you since the press conference."

"Nothing's up, I guess. Hard to say." She sighed. There really was no simple way to describe her relationship with Madeira. "But I can guarantee you one thing. I won't be bidding on her tonight. Do you know they expect her to go for ten grand?"

Harold whistled low. "That ought to bolster her ego a bit."

"As if she needs it." Grace shrugged. "But, hey. It's for a good cause." *Who are you trying to convince?*

"Of course." Harold bent his head forward and sipped from the straw. Colored lights from behind the bar shone through his thinning pate to the gleaming pink skin beneath. He reached out and plucked a maraschino cherry from the dispenser box on the bar, dropping it into his drink. The bubbles cradled it like diamonds around a ruby. "That's precisely why the paper put up some good bucks. We're hoping to win her." Harold grinned. "What a human interest scoop that'll be, eh, sugarplum?"

Grace frowned, confused. "The paper's bidding on Madeira?"

"Not the paper. Just the reporter who pitched the angle. With the paper's money, of course." Harold scanned the crowd, finally pointing toward the back of the room. "There she is. Britt Mullaney." He turned back, innocent question in his eyes. "Do you remember her from the press conference?"

Grace's gaze homed in on the woman Harold had indicated and her stomach dropped to the floor like a cinder block off the Empire State Building. Britt Fucking Mullaney—the upscale blond reporter who'd practically thrown herself at Madeira during the press conference, a.k.a. the dressed-for-sex blonde Madeira had been talking to at the edge of the stage.

The hair on Grace's neck bristled. She offered Harold a hard slash of a smile—all she could manage with this much jealousy tightening her jaw. "Oh, yes. I remember her. Gosh, what a clever idea she had, bidding on Madeira so she could get a scoop."

Duplicitous, self-serving cow.

Harold didn't pick up on her snide tone. That, or he chose to ignore it. "Well, do your old pal, Harold, a favor and cross your fingers that Britt wins the date. Nothing would please our managing editor more."

"Of course," Grace managed to say through gritted teeth.

"I'm out, buttercup." Harold grinned, tipping a nonexistent hat as he backed away from the bar.

"Tell Britt I said good luck." Grace gave a "toodles" wave with her fingers, unsure what had compelled her to offer the phony wish.

She glanced from Britt to Madeira, an angry throb in her temples, cold resolve in her heart. *Good luck is right, you ice bitch.* She'd assured Harold she wouldn't bid on Madeira, but the tables had just turned. No, Grace couldn't afford her, but she'd let that Barbie doll bimbette win this date with Maddee just as soon as hell froze solid, and not a moment sooner.

❖

Naturally, the auction coordinators left Madeira as the very last "item" up for bidding. The crowd hadn't thinned at all. Bright white television camera lights illuminated various sections of the event hall as the crowd perched on the edges of their chairs to watch the bidding.

In an effort to keep the actual bachelor auction tasteful, the singles themselves weren't on stage at the time of the bidding. Instead, the audiovisual folks ran a slide show of each person, showing shots of him or her on the job, at home, and posed in true calender cheese format.

A couple of elderly widows jumped in on the early bidding for Madeira but gracefully bowed out when the price edged over five thousand dollars.

"I have seventy-five hundred, do I hear eight thousand? Eight thousand, can someone give me eight thousand?"

Grace nodded toward the caller. The crowd roared.

Britt cast a glare both venomous and exasperated, but Grace didn't falter. Call her jaded, but she knew damn well the reporter had more than a *scoop* on her mind.

"Eight thousand, do I have eighty-five hundred?"

"Gracie," Madeira rasped, half hiding behind the doorway to the service area behind the bar.

She spun, and her mouth dropped open slightly. "What are you doing? We're still bidding on you."

She frowned, eyes concerned. "What in the hell are you doing? Stop bidding, for God's sake."

The crowd roared, and Grace glanced over her shoulder in time to catch the expression of catlike superiority in Britt's calculating eyes. She turned back to Madeira. "Why should I? It's for a good cause."

"Gracie—"

"Eighty-five hundred, going once, going twice—"

Grace spun. "Nine thousand," she called out.

Madeira spread her arms. "Nine thousand dollars. You're bidding *nine thousand dollars* for a date with me, Gracie. Jesus, do you have any idea how absurd—"

"Twelve thousand!" Britt yelled, cool and confident.

Pandemonium broke out in the event hall, and Grace gasped. Holy fuck. Twelve thousand dollars? Reality punched her in the gut. She simply didn't have the kind of money it would take to go up against a powerhouse like the *Post*, she realized. She reached up and clenched the neck of her white shirt, heart pounding. The entire crowd stared toward her, waiting, smiling.

"Damnit, just let Britt win me," she heard Madeira whisper behind her, her voice an angry rasp that cut like a knife blade straight down to Grace's soul. "This is craziness. Don't offer another dime."

She ignored her.

"Gracie, did you hear me? Let Britt win. I want her to win."

And there it was.

The truth.

An ache in her heart nearly doubled Grace over. "Just go, Madeira. You're not supposed to be up here."

She heard the door jerk shut as Maddee left. The room swayed before her and she closed her eyes a moment, pain clogging her throat. Her hands gripped the bar, knuckles white.

Maddee didn't want Grace to win the date.

She wanted Britt.

God, how could Grace have been so stupid?

Madeira wanted that phony bitch? Fine. She could have her. Grace shook her head with regret, shrugging at the nearest caller. "I'm out," she whispered.

"She's out," the caller relayed to Bill.

"Twelve thousand dollars, going once, going twice..."

Grace glanced toward DoDo's table to find all the Bees and her sister staring at her with sympathy she couldn't bear and didn't want. They should have been looking at her with scorn. With shaking hands and a never-ending supply of humiliation, she untied her apron and chucked it on the countertop. She made it through the back door, but not before hearing the crack of the gavel and—

"Sold! To the lovely blonde up front."

Madeira stood by Britt Mullaney's side but her gaze never stopped scanning the crushing crowd for Gracie. She couldn't believe Gracie had considered dropping that kind of money on her. Didn't she realize Madeira was hers for the asking? Free and clear? Britt, on the other hand, was operating off an expense account. Madeira had no qualms about taking twelve thousand bucks of the paper's money, but she couldn't stomach the thought of Gracie unnecessarily spending the lion's share of her yearly salary on her.

Where was she?

Britt's hand snaked around her arm. Madeira's instinct was to jerk away, but she realized it was her obligation to be cordial. She tucked Britt's cold hand in the crook of her elbow and fake-smiled down at her.

"Let's lose this crowd for a few minutes," Britt said, in a tone Madeira recognized.

Red flag.

"Sure."

Britt's hand slipped down Madeira's forearm to entwine hands and she led her through the crowd toward an empty back hallway. From her caboose position, Madeira continued to look for Gracie. No sign of her. Lola and some of the guys were behind the bar cleaning up. She met Lola's gaze questioningly.

Lola shrugged as if to say she had no idea where Gracie had gone. Before Madeira could signal for Lola to call her later, Britt gave her a sharp tug and Madeira stumbled forward until their bodies pressed together. Britt undulated her hips in a way that left no question as to what she offered.

"What do you say we get out of here, hmm?" Britt purred. "We can go to my place or"—she pressed her lips to Madeira's throat—"yours. Wherever."

Disgusted and, to be honest, offended, Madeira wrapped her hands around Britt's bony upper arms and set her away as gently but firmly as possible without making her angry. "Look, Britt. You've got this all wrong. This was a charity event. What you paid for is a dinner date. Tomorrow night. That's all."

"We can let them think that if it's important to you." She reached out and grazed a fingernail over Madeira's nipple.

Stunned, Madeira's hand snapped up and clamped around Britt's wrist. She shoved it away. "I'm not interested in what you have to offer."

Britt smirked, but her blue eyes flashed with barely banked anger. "Sure you aren't. I've heard all about you."

"If you'd heard *all* about me, sweetheart, then you'd know that I'm in love with Gracie."

"What's love got to do with it?" Britt flicked her hand. "I'm not asking you to marry me, I just want my money's worth. I want to be fucked senseless by the so-called Thief of Hearts."

Madeira's anger crested like a tsunami. She'd never been treated quite so much like a piece of meat, and the blatant disrespect blinded her with rage. "We can go to dinner tomorrow night and do the interview for your article—period—or we can forget the whole thing."

Britt lurched forward, arms rigid at her sides, fists clenched. "Listen up, Madeira. I paid a hell of a lot of money for you and I demand—"

"Demand what? Your *employer* donated the money. To EMS, need I remind you. What they expect is an exclusive article, and that's all you're getting."

"Says who?"

Madeira shrugged, feigning a nonchalance she didn't feel. "If you'd like me to let them know how you manipulated me with their money for your own purposes, how you used their money to try and get…how did you put it? Fucked senseless? I'd be glad to give them that particular scoop. How long have you been with the paper?"

Fear and disbelief gleamed in Britt's eyes. After a moment, they dulled to resignation. She brushed her hair back with slow, shaky fingers and swallowed, visibly subdued. "Shit. No need. Listen, I guess I misunderstood."

"I'll say."

Embarrassment mottled her pale skin. "It's just…I thought I sensed something between you and me at the press conference."

"You did. That something between us is called Graciela Obregon. The woman I love."

Britt's palms raised in surrender. "Fair enough. I get the picture. I didn't buy the two of you at the press conference, but I guess I was wrong."

Madeira stepped back. "And you know, at this point, I think we should conduct our interview over the phone instead of over dinner."

"Th-that's fine. Look, I'm sorry."

Madeira couldn't see holding a grudge. It wasn't her style. She blew out a breath, feeling her muscles relax in slow increments. "Britt, no hard feelings. We appreciate the publicity the paper gave the auction and the money you brought into the EMS program. I'm just…not in the market for anything more than that."

Britt studied Madeira for a moment, then crossed her arms and shook her head slowly with a small huff.

"What?"

"I thought you were supposed to be the one who stole hearts, Madeira."

"So they say."

"But instead, Grace stole yours. You're an imposter. Grace Obregon is the real thief in this story. And it is one hell of a story."

Madeira warmed just thinking of Gracie. Her crazy *fierita*, willing to shell out thousands of dollars she couldn't afford just to keep Madeira from a woman she wouldn't want in a million years. Madeira had never felt more special, had never felt more like…a keeper.

"That's another thing you don't understand." She stared sadly at the aggressive reporter. "Gracie didn't steal my heart. I gave it to her willingly."

CHAPTER SIXTEEN

Quien quiera saber, que compre un viejo.
If you wish good advice, consult an old man.

Grace had almost made her escape from the event hall unheeded when Simon intercepted her.

"Hey, Grace," he called, just as Grace had reached for the door handle.

Damn. She could run, but she didn't want to tip her emotional hand. Instead, she turned slowly toward the tall paramedic with what she hoped was a placid smile on her face. "Hey, Simon. What's up?"

He cocked his head. "Are you okay?"

She managed a quizzical pause, ignoring the enthusiastic chatter of the auction attendees who were leaving in steady droves around her. It had been a fun, successful evening for just about everyone. "Sure. Why wouldn't I be?"

"Uh…because you lost the bidding?" He spread his lanky arms. "Because you're running out without saying good-bye to anyone? I'm not sure. That's why I'm asking."

"Ohhh, all that." Grace rolled her eyes. "Look, I only bid to drive the price up so you guys could make more money. I never intended to win."

Simon looked unconvinced. "Oh."

"And I'm leaving because I have a date." She tapped the crystal of her wristwatch. "I didn't realize how late it was getting. I hope you guys don't mind closing up bar."

Lo and behold, the worry fled from the man's expression. Simon actually believed her—more evidence she was a better actress than DoDo gave her credit for.

A slow, chagrined smile lit on Simon's face. "For a second I thought you and Madeira—never mind." He crossed his arms and rocked on his long feet. "Anyway, we don't mind breaking down at all. That was the plan, actually. The least we can do to thank you for all your help is do the dirty work." He grinned.

"It was my pleasure. I'm glad you guys brought in so much money." Unshed tears ached in her throat almost to the breaking point. She glanced at her watch again. "I have to run, Simon."

"Okay, you go on." He raised his hand in good-bye and began to back away. "Hey, I did win that week off, thanks to your grandmother and her friends."

"Good for you." Grace swallowed, heart pounding with the lie she was about to tell, the lie she felt she had to tell in order to guarantee Madeira didn't come after her. If Grace saw her now, she'd humiliate herself for sure. "If Madeira asks where I am, can you do me a favor?"

"Sure thing."

"Tell her I was sorry I couldn't say good-bye, but that I had a date. With Layton."

❖

The only problem with the lie, Grace realized later, as she glumly nursed a cappuccino at the farthest back table in Muddy's Java Hut, was that she *didn't* have a date with Layton. She didn't even want a date with Layton, not like that, but the fact that she'd used her as an excuse made her feel like a total asshole. Her karma was shot to hell. Layton Fair didn't deserve to be a pawn in Grace's emotional chess game with Madeira. She was a great woman, a friend, and a respected colleague. Grace didn't want to be the kind of a person who would use a friend.

She had to come clean or the guilt would eat her alive.

Fishing her cell phone out of her purse, she punched in Layton's number before she lost her nerve, hoping it was okay to call this late. She chewed on a wooden coffee stirrer and listened to the phone ring once, then again.

"Hello?"

The coffee stirrer snapped, and she turned her head to spit out splinters of wood. "Layton?"

"Yes?"

She swallowed past the lump in her throat that could very well be her heart. "It's Grace Obregon."

The pause was short, surprise-laced, but her tone when she recovered was warm and welcoming. "Hi, Grace. Gosh. It's great to hear from you."

Guilt stung her like a scorpion. Layton had pursued her plenty after their first date, despite Grace's repeated refusals and excuses. Finally, Layton had stopped asking, and Grace didn't blame her one bit. She bit her lip and held it for a moment. Layton had every right to dislike her, but Layton Fair was a much better person than she was. "I hope I'm not calling too late," she said, aware of the double meaning of her words.

"Not at all. I'm a night owl."

"Good. Then how about you let me buy you a coffee at Muddy's?" she asked, tucking her hair behind her ear.

A pause. "Now?"

"Yes."

"Is everything okay, Grace?"

"Yes." Wait a minute. The time for lies had ended. Grace needed to be straight with Layton. "Actually…no." She sighed. "I need to get something off my chest."

"Don't move. I'll be right there."

Forty-five minutes and two cappuccinos later, Layton reached across the back table at Muddy's and covered Grace's hands with her own. Her warm expression softened with sympathy. "Grace. Do you really think it's a news flash to me that you're in love with Madeira?"

Grace sniffed, wicking away a tear that had escaped her eye. "It's a news flash to me. I swore I would fall in love with a great woman like you this time. Not someone like her. I'm sorry you got mixed up in all of it."

"Whatever gave you the impression Madeira isn't a great woman?"

Grace shrugged. "I don't know. I'm an idiot?"

"You just need to relax and let things happen." Layton tucked her chin. "As for you and me, there are absolutely no hard feelings."

Now she knew Layton was too good for her. "You sure?"

"One hundred percent." She released her hands and sat back, looking vaguely sheepish. "Which brings me to my own difficult question."

Grace cocked her head, feeling so much better for having confessed. "What's that?"

Layton twisted her mouth to the side in apology, then grinned. "What are the chances your sister, Lola, will go out with me?" She smoothed her palm over her wavy hair. "She gave me a trim the other day and well...no offense, but I haven't been able to get her out of my head since. She's so...darn effervescent."

Grace's mouth dropped open for a moment, then she laughed with glee. "Layton, it would be my utter pleasure to play matchmaker with you and Lola."

❖

As she and the others combed their way through the event hall, stacking chairs and tables and bussing trash, Madeira reeled from the knowledge that Gracie had left the auction for a date with Layton. Layton! The allegedly perfect woman. How had she managed to miss that?

"Hey, Pacias," a gravelly voice bellowed.

Madeira glanced up to see her old pal Harold LePoulet winding his way through the crowd. Nostalgia hit her, that and pleasure. Harold was a connection to Gracie, and she'd welcome any connection to Gracie at this point.

Madeira straightened. "Harold, my man." She grinned, genuinely pleased to see the reporter. They clapped palms together, hooking thumbs, then pulled each other into a warm, back-pounding hug. "Long time, no see, old man."

"I'll say."

"How'd you enjoy the auction?"

"Definitely newsworthy." Harold hoisted his slacks higher up on his hips, lifting his chin toward the stage. "You brought in a pretty penny up there."

"Yeah," Madeira said, without much enthusiasm. "Thanks to the *Post*." This small talk seemed a deliberate effort on both their parts to skirt the real issue—Gracie. Madeira knew she should be thrilled that they'd raised so much money for EMS, but all she could think of was the rigid set to Gracie's spine when Madeira had asked her to stop bidding. She'd meant to save her from making a huge, unnecessary donation to the event. Had she insulted her instead? God knew, they'd both been given more than their fair share of pride. "Listen, did you get a chance to talk to Gracie before she left?"

"I did." Harold pursed his lips, his gaze both intelligent and assessing. "She mixes a mean 7-Up."

Madeira tried to laugh but the sound that emerged rang more like a morose choke. She covered it by bending over to collect some trash from beneath one of the tables, stuffing it into the trash bag she'd hung on the back of a nearby chair.

"What's up with you and Grace, anyway?" Harold asked. "I asked her earlier and she didn't have much to say."

More evidence of her ambivalence? Madeira's heart sank, and she shrugged nonchalantly. She didn't want to come off like a lovesick pup. "Nothing's up. We're friends. Gracie is dating other women. I'm busy with work." She raked a hand through her hair and gave her best player smirk. "You didn't expect some stupid newspaper set-up to lead to lasting love, did you?"

To Madeira's surprise, Harold looked crestfallen. "Well, to be honest, I'd hoped."

Madeira narrowed her gaze. "You're serious."

"Sure. Forty years behind the reporter's desk has jaded me, Madeira." Harold flipped a hand. "That story about you and Grace… well, I won't lie. At first, I bitched incessantly about having to write fluff. But meeting the two of you…seeing you together? It lifted my tired, old spirits, which are usually a bunch of surly curmudgeons." He uttered a regretful sound out of the side of one cheek. "I really thought you two had something special."

Yup, that one hurt. "Yeah, okay. I did, too. But we were both wrong." Madeira's defenses pulled up like drawbridges. "This is one fairy tale that was doomed from the beginning. I'm just not Gracie's type, bro. Never will be."

"Well, you gave it the old college try," Harold said, after a moment of studying her face.

"I did."

"Nothing wrong with accepting the truth and moving on."

"My thoughts exactly," Madeira lied.

The old reporter gave a mock salute. "Good luck, Madeira. If you ever need anything, you know where I am, okay? I mean that."

"Yeah." They shook hands once more, then Madeira watched him go, the words replaying in her head. Harold was right. Difficult decision or not, Madeira knew the time had come to abandon the chase once and for all. Sadness draped her like a coffin blanket. She'd made the mistake of falling for a woman who didn't want to be caught, at least not by her. That was her cross to bear. But if Gracie wanted a future with Layton, or some other woman...well, Madeira loved her enough to respect her wishes.

It might kill her, but she had to let Gracie go.

❖

The week dragged on like a bout of influenza: achy, weak, and hopeless. She and Gracie hadn't talked.

Madeira said a prayer of thanks that she and Simon had agreed to work the early day shift that week, if only for the distraction of traffic and the excuse of not being a morning person to explain her sullen behavior. The sun shone brightly in the east Colorado sky on Friday. Madeira hid behind her dark sunglasses and brooding silence. The radio had been dead for several hours. Simon, who wasn't much of a morning person himself, didn't seem to mind the lack of conversation.

The auction had been an overwhelming success, bringing in double what they'd expected. Madeira's coworkers were touting her as some kind of a hero, but what the fuck had she done? The Samaritan Soul Mate publicity hadn't been her doing. Britt Mullaney only bid on her because she thought she'd get some hot sex from it. Madeira didn't deserve the kudos she'd received, and she didn't want them. All she wanted was Gracie.

Too bad, sucker.

The EMS community might have scored big, but she still felt like loser of the year. Even this job she'd come to love so much didn't seem to mean quite as much without Gracie and the rest of the Obregon extended family in her life.

Jesus, Madeira had never even kissed Gracie, she realized, with a stab of pure pain. *Cállate! Let it go.*

She braced her boot-covered foot on the dashboard and leaned her head back, trying to pinpoint exactly how she felt on this Friday, day six of the post-Gracie portion of her miserable life.

Sad?

Lonely?

Bereft?

She pondered it. Actually, Madeira didn't feel any of those emotions. She didn't feel anything, and that's what scared her. It was as if Gracie had been her conduit to the world of deep feelings, and now that she was gone, Madeira had been cast adrift.

Gracie had tilted her whole world on its axis, sent her reeling. But time healed, no? She still had her friends, though she'd been more out of touch with them in the past two months than she'd been in years. With a little work and distance, though, she might be able to get back into her pre-Gracie groove. It had worked for her before. No reason why it couldn't work for her again.

After work, she'd call Kita or Carmen and find out when they planned to go out next. She had to get back in the saddle if she ever expected to gallop freely again.

The radio crackled, pulling her attention from her ruminations. "Rescue eight-seven-three, copy a call."

Simon accelerated automatically as Madeira reached for the mic hooked on the dashboard. "Eight-seven-three, by." She pulled a pen out of her shirt pocket, quickly scribbling down the address and info on the legal pad fastened to the front of their run clipboard. Three minutes later they arrived on the scene of a core zero in a small home. A double EMT unit had already arrived and begun resuscitation efforts, but they'd called for paramedic assistance. Based on the details provided by dispatch, she and Simon didn't have much more of a chance of saving this patient than Madeira had of reviving her relationship with Gracie.

Laden with life-saving equipment, Madeira and Simon trotted into the open house, and Simon immediately took charge of the scene. Madeira hung back, monitoring the equipment and supplies, since she was the junior EMT on scene. Their patient was an elderly woman, older than DoDo, her body wasted by cancer.

Madeira squatted beside one of the original EMTs on scene, Becky Braden.

"She was gone when we got here," Becky whispered, so only Madeira and Simon could hear. She lifted her chin toward the patient's distraught husband, who hovered on the other side of the room between two police officers who had responded to the call—standard procedure. "We're working her for the husband, period. I've never seen a guy quite so broken up. He just doesn't want to believe she's gone."

Madeira glanced up at the gaunt old man who had to be staring ninety in the face. He shifted unsteadily foot to foot, every few seconds emitting out a grief-stricken groan. His thin skin gleamed pale and diaphoretic. Most of all he looked broken. Madeira got to her feet. "I'm going to check the husband's vitals. Maybe get him out of the room."

"Good idea," Simon said.

"What's his name," Madeira asked Becky.

"Mr. Harris," she said.

Madeira crossed the room, touching Mr. Harris on the forearm. The man barely took notice of her, his focus centered on the body of his dead wife. "Is she going to be okay?"

Madeira's heart sank, and she met the police officers' sympathetic gazes for a moment before giving her full attention to the old man. "They're working on her, sir. How about you let me take your pulse and blood pressure? We're worried about you."

"Not me, hon. Not me. *Her.*" The old man continued to half moan, half cry, but he didn't resist when Madeira guided him gently into the kitchen.

"She's been ill, you know," Mr. Harris said, his tone hollowed with grief. "Cancer, that damned disease. I take care of her. I've always taken care of her."

"Of course you have."

"She was fine when I checked her earlier. Fine. I told her I loved her, and she said she loved me, too."

Madeira guided Mr. Harris to a chair, a well of sadness springing inside her at the utter emptiness in the man's tone. She wrapped the blood pressure cuff around Mr. Harris's thin, drapey arm, trying not to notice the man's vacant, shell-shocked stare through the doorway into the living room. In an effort to distract him as she inflated the cuff, Madeira asked, "How long have you folks been married, Mr. Harris?"

A beat passed.

The man's watery brown gaze came up to meet Madeira's, his chin quivering with pain and loss. In those eyes, Madeira saw a love so deep it was bottomless.

"Forever," Mr. Harris whispered, in a shaky, bereft tone that left no doubt in Madeira's mind that losing Mrs. Harris was well and truly the end of this old man's world. "We've been married forever."

A zing of recognition moved through Madeira and her extremities went ice cold. The depth of love in this house stunned her utterly silent, and she realized one thing: crossing paths with Mr. and Mrs. Harris on the day death separated them was one sign she didn't intend to ignore. Love this pure, this meant-to-be, didn't come along too often, and only a fool would ignore it.

Madeira didn't want to be a fool anymore. Not where Gracie was concerned.

She continued to work with and talk to Mr. Harris, but inside Madeira's brain, something shifted. Despite the risks to her heart and pride, she had to lay out her feelings to Gracie once and for all. Perhaps they had a chance at a forever like the Harrises.

Perhaps not.

But Madeira had to get Gracie's attention, had to let her know how much she loved her, had to *try*...before simply walking away.

❖

Catching her attention would be the difficult part, Madeira realized. Gracie was so damn gun-shy, she couldn't see past her protective walls to what stood right before her. So Madeira had to do something flashy, something that would stop Gracie short, make her think.

Madeira racked her brain all day until inspiration hit, and it wasn't until lunchtime that she found a spare moment to pull it all together. When they arrived in the ambulance bay, Simon went in ahead of her. With shaking fingers, Madeira dialed. The phone didn't even make it through one ring.

"LePoulet."

"Harold? Madeira."

"Hey, dumpling. What's up?"

Madeira didn't waste any time. "You remember telling me to call you if I needed anything?"

"Yep."

"Well, I need you now."

"Yeah?"

"Yeah. I may not be the woman for Gracie, but she's the only woman for me."

Harold laughed, the sound tired. "I could've told you that months ago."

Damn. Everyone seemed to have realized how perfect she and Gracie were for each other except the two of them. She smoothed a palm down her face. No time for regrets. The time wouldn't have been wasted if it all worked out. "I wouldn't have listened. I needed to find out for myself. I needed...some kind of a sign."

"At least you've come to your senses."

"Yes. Now I just need you to help me bring Gracie to hers."

"Never let it be said that Harold LePoulet chickens out of a tough challenge. Lay it on me."

Madeira smiled.

This would work.

It had to.

"What's the deadline for Sunday's paper?"

A meteor hit her bed, jostling her bones and rattling her brain in its cage. Grace groaned.

"Get up." The meteor poked her. "Read this."

Wow. The meteor had a voice, and the fucking thing sounded like Lola. What an unfortunate and yet apt metaphor for the pathetic state of her passionless life. Grace covered her head with a pillow, praying she could sink back into oblivion for another several hours. At least when she was asleep, her dreams allowed her to be *with* Madeira instead of away from her. Consciousness served no purpose to the seriously depressed.

"Get out of my room, Lola."

Instead, she bounced. "Not until you read this, Sister Mary Sunshine, so you might as well get it over with."

Grace lifted the corner of her pillow and slit one eye barely open. "What in God's name possessed you to wake me up this early on a Sunday?"

"The newspaper." Lola grinned.

Covering her face again, Grace marveled at her sister's chipper audacity. "The paper will still be out there waiting for me at noon. Get out."

"It might be," Lola said, in a sly tone, "but by then Ms. Right will have missed her chance."

Off came the pillow. Grace squinted into the brash sunlight, orienting herself to the room. Lola, smiling from the end of the bed. DoDo, beaming from the doorway. Something was definitely up. Her heart began to thud and she scrambled up to prop against the headboard, knees pulled up to her chest. "What are you talking about?"

Lola smiled, flipping the personals page of the paper around to face her sister. She'd drawn a large red circle around an ad with the bold header, **IN SEARCH OF MS. RIGHT**. Curiosity seized Grace. "Give it to me."

Lola did as she asked, and Grace read.

IN SEARCH OF MS. RIGHT

Plush, single brown stuffed female in search of her Ms. Right. Must be a teddy bear of a gal, color unimportant—in fact I'd prefer you rather faded with time, life, and experience. Mismatched button eyes a must, and I'm a sucker for a purple neck ribbon. If you're a bear who has seen heartache and disaster, but you're ready to take a chance on true love, then meet me today at noon, at The Fool's Last Chance Cafe, downtown.

Grace crumpled the paper in her lap, stomach in knots. She wanted to believe...wanted to hope, but almost didn't dare. She quickly reread the ad, then speared her sister with a narrowed, distrustful gaze. "Did you do this, Lola?"

Her sister spread her arms and gave her an incredulous look. "Why in the hell would I place a personal in the 'teddy bear seeking teddy bear' section of the paper? Which, by the way, didn't exist until today."

Indeed. Why would anyone…except Madeira?

She picked up Ms. Right, clutching the little bear to her chest. And why would Madeira place such a preposterous ad, unless she—?

Grace's heart soared. It wasn't a sign, it was an invitation.

One last chance for a fool like her, one she didn't intend to turn down.

Laughing, her sister and DoDo cheering her on, Grace tore out of bed to get ready.

❖

It was four minutes past noon when Grace entered the small, dark café in central Denver, Ms. Right peeking out of the top of her backpack. She paused in the entrance to let her eyes adjust, then scanned the very Irish decor of the virtually empty pub. Dark walnut tables and banquettes filled the room, smoke from the kitchen hanging on the sunbeams angling weakly through the leaded glass front windows. Two women shared the window table, and an old man sat reading Tom Wolfe in a side booth.

In a far back corner sat Madeira, a furry brown teddy bear at her side.

Grace melted.

She shook her head, a smile on her face. What kind of woman would place a personal ad for a bear? A perfect woman, she realized. A heart stealer.

Madeira stood as Grace approached, warmth in her eyes despite the wariness. When, at last, Grace stood before her, neither one of them seemed ready to speak.

"Hi," Madeira said finally, brushing the backs of her fingers down Grace's cheek.

"Hi."

"I miss you."

Grace's chin quivered. "Me, too, you."

"I'm glad you came."

"Yeah, well"—she slid into the booth and pulled Ms. Right from her backpack—"Ms. Right hasn't quite mastered her driving test since she lost her original button eyes. Plus, there's that no opposable thumbs issue. So I had to chauffeur her." Grace propped Ms. Right against the condiment caddy.

To her surprise and pleasure, Madeira slid into the booth next to her, caging her between the wall and her own chest. Grace blinked as a wave of emotion rocked her. "Maddee, what is this about?"

"A sign."

"What?"

"I had a sign. One of DoDo's." She waved her hand. "It's a long story, time for that later. First—" She swallowed, then reached for the bear she'd brought along, setting it on the table to face Gracie's Ms. Right. "I figured I needed to marry the old girl off if I ever wanted to take her place. Ms. Old-school Right? Meet Ms. New-school Right."

Grace laughed. "That's sweet, but you're not making a whole lot of sense," she whispered.

Madeira sighed, hanging her head forward for a moment. When her face lifted again, her expression was ravaged, pleading. "Aw, hell, Gracie. We both know I'm nobody's Princess Charming. I'm the furthest thing from perfect, and God knows, I'm probably not even close to being your Ms. Right." Madeira's jaw ticked, and she splayed one hand on her chest. "I'm just a woman, faults and all. A woman with a past, sure, but—"

Grace ached for her. "Maddee, you don't have to—"

"No." Madeira held up a palm to stop her. "Let me finish. I've held this in too long to stop now."

Grace nodded, tears welling in her eyes, love filling her heart fuller than she'd ever imagined it could be.

"As I was saying, I'm a woman with a past. I don't deny that. But I'm also a woman who wants to give you a future, the one you've always wanted, *fierita*, whatever that may be. Because I love you, heart and soul, battle scars and tattoos." She ran a finger over the *Easy Vixen* tattoo. "You make me new, Gracie." She paused, the love so evident in her ravaged tone, Grace didn't know how she ever missed it. "Please let me do the same for you."

Through a jumble of laughter and tears, Grace threw her arms around Madeira's neck. For a moment they simply clung to one another. When they finally pulled away, Grace's face wasn't the only one wet with tears.

"How can you know for sure?" Grace asked. "You've never even kissed me." She reached up to smooth tears from Madeira's cheeks, accidentally jostling the table with her elbow. Madeira's bear teetered, then fell forward and landed lips to furry lips with Gracie's Ms. Right.

Madeira flipped her palms up. "How many more signs do you need before you believe, *querida*?"

They laughed, then Madeira reached out and traced her lips with a gentle finger. "I haven't kissed you, Gracie. This is true. But I know my heart, and my heart is your possession. I love you."

Gracie pressed her palm against Madeira's heartbeat, to assure herself this was truly happening. "I love you, too."

They embraced again, and her lips moved against Grace's ear. "As far as the kissing is concerned," Madeira drawled. "Some things are worth waiting for."

Madeira's warm, whiskey voice resonated in Grace's chest, as intoxicating and reassuring as it had been the first time she'd heard it, underneath that crushed car when fate and tragedy had brought them together. Grace suddenly knew with utter certainty that meeting Maddee had been no accident. She didn't plan to waste one more second of her life being scared.

She laughed, low and seductive, leaning her head back to allow Madeira's insistent lips access to her neck. "Well, worth the wait or not, I'm running out of patience. I suggest you take me home and prove it."

Never one to deny the wishes of a beautiful woman, especially the one with whom she planned to spend the rest of her life, Madeira did just that.

About the Author

Lea Santos has been concocting tall tales since she was a child, according to her mother. Usually these had to do with where she was, who she was with, and whether or not she'd finished her math homework (which she hadn't). When it came time to pick a career, Lea waffled, then dabbled in everything from guiding tours in Europe, to police work, to bookkeeping for an exotic bird and reptile company—probably not the best choice, since (1) she never did finish that math, and (2) the Komodo dragons freaked her out. (A lot.) She eventually decided to go with her strengths and continue spinning wild stories, except this time, she'd turn them into whole books and call it a career. She rarely lies anymore about where she's been or who she was with…

By the Author

Amigas y Amor Series

Little White Lie

Under Her Skin

Picture Imperfect

Playing the Player